NICHOLAS ROYLE HAS published three collections of short fiction: *Mortality* (Serpent's Tail), shortlisted for the inaugural Edge Hill Short Story Prize in 2007, *Ornithology* (Confingo Publishing), longlisted for the same prize in 2018, and *The Dummy & Other Uncanny Stories* (The Swan River Press). He is also the author of seven novels, most recently *First Novel* (Vintage), and a collaboration with artist David Gledhill, *In Camera* (Negative Press London). He has edited more than twenty anthologies, including seven earlier volumes of *Best British Short Stories*. Reader in Creative Writing at the Manchester Writing School at Manchester Metropolitan University and head judge of the Manchester Fiction Prize, he also runs Nightjar Press, which publishes original short stories as signed, limited-edition chapbooks.

Also by Nicholas Royle:

NOVELS

Counterparts
Saxophone Dreams
The Matter of the Heart
The Director's Cut
Antwerp
Regicide
First Novel

NOVELLAS

The Appetite
The Enigma of Departure

SHORT STORIES

Mortality
In Camera (with David Gledhill)
Ornithology
The Dummy & Other Uncanny Stories

ANTHOLOGIES (as editor)

Darklands
Darklands 2
A Book of Two Halves
The Tiger Garden: A Book of Writers' Dreams
The Time Out Book of New York Short Stories
The Ex Files: New Stories About Old Flames
The Agony & the Ecstasy: New Writing for the World Cup
Neonlit: Time Out Book of New Writing
The Time Out Book of Paris Short Stories
Neonlit: Time Out Book of New Writing Volume 2
The Time Out Book of London Short Stories Volume 2
Dreams Never End
'68: New Stories From Children of the Revolution
The Best British Short Stories 2011
Murmurations: An Anthology of Uncanny Stories About Birds
The Best British Short Stories 2012
The Best British Short Stories 2013
The Best British Short Stories 2014
Best British Short Stories 2015
Best British Short Stories 2016
Best British Short Stories 2017

Best {BRITISH} *Short Stories* 2018

SERIES EDITOR **NICHOLAS ROYLE**

CROMER

PUBLISHED BY SALT PUBLISHING 2018

2 4 6 8 10 9 7 5 3 1

First published in Great Britain in 2018 by
Salt Publishing Ltd
12 Norwich Road, Cromer, Norfolk NR27 0AX United Kingdom

www.saltpublishing.com

Salt Publishing Limited Reg. No. 5293401

A CIP catalogue record for this book is available from the British Library

ISBN 978 1 78463 136 9 (Paperback edition)
ISBN 978 1 78463 137 6 (Electronic edition)

Typeset in Neacademia by Salt Publishing

Printed and bound in Great Britain by Clays Ltd, Elcograf S.p.A

Salt Publishing Limited is committed to responsible forest management. This book is made from Forest Stewardship Council™ certified paper.

To the memory of Colette de Curzon 1927–2018

CONTENTS

NICHOLAS ROYLE
Introduction ix

COLETTE DE CURZON
Paymon's Trio 1

ADAM O'RIORDAN
A Thunderstorm in Santa Monica 16

JANE MCLAUGHLIN
Trio For Four Voices 33

WILLIAM THIRSK-GASKILL
How to Be an Alcoholic 41

ALISON MACLEOD
We Are Methodists 49

ADRIAN SLATCHER
Life Grabs 69

M JOHN HARRISON
Dog People 80

JO MAZELIS
Skin 94

CONRAD WILLIAMS
Cwtch 104

KELLY CREIGHTON
And Three Things Bumped 116

WYL MENMUIR
In Dark Places 132

OWEN BOOTH
The War 146

TANIA HERSHMAN
And What If All Your Blood Ran Cold 152

MIKE FOX
The Homing Instinct 163

BRIAN HOWELL
Mask 171

CD ROSE
Sister 189

CHLOE TURNER
Waiting For the Runners 197

ELEY WILLIAMS
Swatch 207

LISA TUTTLE
The Last Dare 214

IAIN ROBINSON
Dazzle 233

Contributors' Biographies 241
Acknowledgements 248

NICHOLAS ROYLE

INTRODUCTION

A VERY SHORT introduction this year, because there was, as you no doubt remember, only one short story published during 2017 and that was 'Cat Person' by Kristen Roupenian, which went viral on social media after its appearance in the *New Yorker*. A unique alignment of popular opinion, media frenzy and hashtag bingo made it virtually impossible to express any opinion of 'Cat Person' other than unreserved, drooling approval.

Oh, all right then, there were some other stories published last year, but you wouldn't think so from *Prospect* magazine's 'Winter Fiction' supplement, dated January 2017, which devoted seven of its twelve pages to extracting Peter Hobbs's story, 'In the Reactor', from the Faber anthology he had edited with Sarah Hall, *Sex & Death*, in 2016.

There were, however, lots of notable anthologies published during 2017, including, among many others: *New Fears*, a major new horror anthology edited by Mark Morris for Titan Books, the first of a new series; *She Said He Said I Said: New Writing Scotland 35* (Association For Scottish Literary Studies) edited by Diana Hendry and Susie Maguire; *Tales From the Shadow Booth Volume 1* (no publisher given; I especially enjoyed Timothy J Jarvis's 'What the Bones Told

Hecate Shrike') edited by Dan Coxon; *Ruins & Other Stories* (Cinnamon Press) edited by Adam Craig; *Bristol Short Story Prize Anthology Volume 10* (Tangent Books); *The Mechanics' Institute Review* edited by an extensive team at Birkbeck, with excellent stories by Alan Beard and Sarah Evans; *Unthology 9* (Unthank Books) edited by Ashley Stokes and Robin Jones (I loved Roelof Bakker's 'Yellow'); *New Ghost Stories III* (The Fiction Desk) edited by Rob Redman; *The Bridport Prize Anthology 2017* (Redcliffe Press) with an outstanding second-place winning story, 'Ends', by Chris Neilan; and three issues of *The Lonely Crowd*, described on its web site as a 'literary journal' although each issue is an 'anthology of new short fiction, poetry and photography' – but who cares about minor details of nomenclature when the editor (John Lavin in this case) has such great taste and publishes so much good work?

The highlights of last year's *Lonely Crowd* issues may – or may not, according to taste – be the stories reprinted in this book (by Kelly Creighton, Iain Robinson, Jo Mazelis and CD Rose), but number six included stories by Neil Campbell and John Saul, who are always interesting, while in number seven I liked Durre Shahwar's 'Nowadays' and Eley Williams's 'Channel Light Vessel Automatic', and number eight in particular was packed with good stories by Jenn Ashworth, Thomas Morris, Jane Fraser, Angela Readman, Giselle Leeb, Jaki McCarrick, David Rose, Toby Litt and others. *Gorse* continues to publish probably the most attractive journal-anthology in these islands, each issue bursting with envelope-pushing fiction, poetry and essays. Issue eight contained an excellent story by David Rose, 'Translation', riffing and punning on the problems facing any literary translator, and an interesting piece by Hugh Smith, 'John 1.1'.

The good magazines keep on publishing good stories. For this we must be thankful to *Ambit*, *Anglo Files*, *Bare Fiction*, *Black Static*, *Brittle Star*, *Confingo*, *Lighthouse*, *Structo* and others. Two stories in *Ambit* 230 stood out for me: Tom Heaton's 'The Writer Didn't Know the Pen Was Still Writing' and Paul Brownsey's 'Time and the Heart' (Brownsey's 'Peace and Goodwill' in issue 22 of Scottish literary journal *Southlight* was notable, too). *Ghostland* was new to me; it feels net-based, with the editorship credited to Twitter handle @havishambler, but exists only as a print zine. *Painted, spoken* edited by Richard Price had reached issue 29 before I came across it (thanks to David Rose's recommendation); it appears 'occasionally'. I enjoyed Bill Broady's story 'The Man Who Broke the Bank'. For more information go to hydrohotel.net. Speaking of hotels, I think I'd like to live in *Hotel* edited by Jon Auman, Holly Brown, Thomas Chadwick, John Dunn, Dominic Jaeckle and Niall Reynolds. They seem to add a name or two to that list with every issue, so I hope I'm more or less up to date. The first issue came out in 2016 and I'm really quite cross with myself for missing it, but I've got issues two and three, which came out in 2017. It feels like a cousin of *Ambit*, and *Ambit* had better watch out, because *Hotel* is *very* good.

It was a strong year for short story collections, with new titles from Alison MacLeod, Martyn Bedford, Tania Hershman, Eley Williams, Leone Ross, Conrad Williams, M John Harrison, Adam O'Riordan, Joanna Walsh, Lucy Durneen, Mike O'Driscoll, Erinna Mettler, Michael Stewart and others. Stories from some of these are included in the present volume. The story that spoke most clearly and poignantly to me in Gregory Norminton's collection, *The Ghost*

Who Bled (Comma Press), was the title story, which I remember reading for the first time in *Prospect* magazine in 2004. Joanna Walsh's new collection, *Worlds From the Word's End* (And Other Stories), reprints stories first published between 2013 and 2016, but, unless I'm misreading the acknowledgements, did not include any new work.

Stonewood Press published *When You Lived Inside the Walls*, a lovely little mini-collection of three stories by Krishan Coupland, including his Manchester Fiction Prize-winning story from 2011. Among the British writers shortlisted for the same prize last year were Jane Fraser, Hannah Vincent and Dave Wakely. Their stories were published online.

Also online I came across a fine story by Jaki McCarrick, 'The Collectors', on the *Irish Times* web site and, on – or should one say at? – *Music & Literature*, I read, with mounting excitement, a piece called 'I Went to the House But Did Not Enter' by Paul Griffiths. Mounting excitement because it was the best thing I'd read for some time and had been created as a piece of experimental writing under a set of constraints. It's always rather wonderful when constraints appear to have a liberating effect. Sadly, I discovered it had been first published, elsewhere, some years earlier, making it ineligible for inclusion in this book.

The Galley Beggar Press Short Story Prize 2017/18 longlist included 'Cluster' by Naomi Booth, in which a sleep-deprived mother observes and tries to connect with her surroundings. There's something moving about the realisation that she's not the only person who called the police over an incident of domestic abuse she witnesses. 'Other people have called too,' the call handler tells her. Robert Mason, previously shortlisted for the Manchester prize, made the Galley Beggar shortlist with 'Curtilage', a disturbing story about a man who preys on vulnerable targets. What makes those two stories stand out is their attention to detail. Detail is not always necessary and quite possibly it often needs to be cut, but in these stories it's what elevates them.

There's something especially pleasing about short stories - especially good short stories - turning up in unusual places. Issue 102 of *Pipeline: The Journal of Surfers Against Sewage*, a handsome, full-colour 60pp A5-size magazine, contained an original environmental ghost story, 'The Gyre', by Man Booker Prize-longlisted author Wyl Menmuir, who also features in the current volume with a story published in chapbook format by the National Trust, the launch title for a series of such publications.

TSS Publishing, run by Rupert Dastur, started publishing short story chapbooks in 2017, with three titles by Sean Lusk, Chloe Turner (reprinted herein) and Matthew G Rees. They are attractive, small-format booklets, uniformly designed and numbered. Nightjar Press (founded in 2009 by the editor of the book you may be holding in your hands if you are reading these words) entered its tenth year of publishing with new chapbooks by Claire Dean, David Wheldon and Colette de Curzon. 'Paymon's Trio' by Colette de Curzon was written in 1949 when its author was 22. She put it away in a folder of her work where it stayed for 67 years until one of her daughters, the novelist Gabrielle Kimm, found it and was advised by Alison MacLeod to send it to Nightjar Press. Thanks partly to the enthusiasm of poet and artist David Tibet, who championed and recommended the story to his many followers, it became one of Nightjar Press's fastest-selling titles. It is reprinted in the current volume, which is dedicated to the memory of Colette de Curzon, who sadly passed away in March 2018.

Chapbooks are not a new phenomenon. Indeed, an article about them by Ruth Richardson on the British Library web site is written entirely in the past tense. Just lately I have been reading (and rereading) a lot of Giles Gordon's fiction, including his alarming short story 'Couple', published exclusively as a chapbook by Sceptre Press of Bedford in 1978. I have written about Gordon before in one of these introductions. People sometimes say to me, 'Giles Gordon, he used to edit that series you're editing now,' or some variation on that, because he co-edited a series called *Best Short Stories*, which ceased publishing in 1994, while this series started in 2011, under the very obviously different title *Best British Short Stories*. That was years before anyone ever uttered the hideous word 'Brexit', but every year I work my way through magazines and anthologies reading only stories by British authors and ruthlessly ignoring work by Americans and Australians and writers of other nationalities even if they are writing in English. I feel as if I'm locked into some awful rotten marriage of bitter inconvenience with Nigel Farage or Jacob Rees-Mogg, or Theresa May, for that matter, or even David bloody Cameron, whose responsibility it all surely is. As if I were, like some of the above, motivated by isolationism and xenophobia and misplaced patriotism. Four previously unpublished stories by Raymond Carver's editor Gordon Lish in the third issue of *Hotel?* Any sensible person would be all over them. But pressure of time means I generally limit myself to the British contributors in any publication of this type.

When we started *Best British Short Stories* there was already a *Best British Poetry*, so it made sense to stick to the British-only rule. Since then the Man Booker Prize has, regrettably, been opened up to American writers, which in a way makes one happy to remain British-only with this series, but then there is Brexit. There is always Brexit. Unless, of course, it doesn't happen. I live in hope.

NICHOLAS ROYLE
Manchester
May 2018

Best {BRITISH} Short Stories 2018

COLETTE DE CURZON

PAYMON'S TRIO

I HAD ALWAYS been fond of music: it was a kind of passion in me, around which I centred my whole existence, and in the beauty of which I derived all the pleasures I required from life. I was well up in anything and everything connected with music, from the earliest and most primitive of rondos to the latest symphonies and concertos. I played the violin passing well, though my ability of execution fell far short of my desires. I had played second violin in various concerts, provincial ones, of course, for a natural shyness prevented me from daring to launch my meagre talent into higher spheres. Besides which, the violin for me was not a profession: it was merely a friend in whom I confided all the thoughts and emotions of my soul, which I could not have expressed in any other way. For even the most retired of men needs to express himself in one way or another.

I had always connected music with the beautiful side of life. In this, for my fifty-odd years, I was strangely naïve. The experience I went through shook the rock-solid foundation of my innocent belief. It will, no doubt, be hard for anyone reading this story to believe it all, or even any part of it; but I am here to testify that every word of it is true, I and my two very dearest and noblest of friends, for we all three went through the same experience, and all three unanimously declare that every word of it is solid fact. A few years have elapsed since the evil day that brought a passing shadow on my life's passion, but the memory of it is still fresh in my mind.

I will start at the beginning and try to impart all its vividness up to you.

It was on a raw November's evening, with dusk swiftly descending on windswept London, as I was returning from Hyde Park, where I had taken my dog, Angus, for his afternoon exercise, that I suddenly remembered I had gone out for a double purpose: the first already mentioned, the second a half-hearted quest for a second-hand copy of Burton's Anatomy of Melancholy. To say that I was interested in that work would be a great exaggeration. I had heard various reports about it that did not rouse my enthusiasm, but as it had got a new vogue and was much talked of, I wished to acquaint myself of its content, so as to know, roughly, at any rate, what it was about.

I prided myself on being erudite – such puny accomplishments are very satisfactory – and my ignorance concerning Burton's work was a serious lapse in my literary learning. So, *Melancholy* bound, I made my way down some narrow side streets, ill-lit by bleary lampposts, where I knew I would find a number of barrows of second-hand books, and where I hoped to find the work in question. The first two barrows revealed a great deal in the nature of melancholy, but not Burton's. At the third, which was overshadowed by the towering bulk of a surly woman vendor, who eyed me as suspiciously as though I were a notorious nihilist, I found the book I was looking for. Or books – for it was in three volumes. But they were wedged behind a tall black volume which I found necessary to remove in order to reach them.

I daresay I was clumsy, or perhaps Angus chose that particular moment to tug on his leash and jerk my arm. At any rate, Angus or no Angus, my hand slipped from the black book which, having been dislodged, fell with a thud on to the muddy pavement, its binding being badly stained in the process. I remember thinking, in spite of my vexation, that the fat woman was no doubt proud of having suspected me of evil intentions from the start, for I was certainly proving myself to be no ordinary customer.

I picked up the book, and seeing how badly damaged it was, I thought it only civil of me to buy it off her, though many of her books were in more distressing conditions. She accepted my offer grudgingly, and had the impudence to charge me an extra 6d on the original two shillings. Being hardly in a position to argue, I allowed her to engulf my half crown and departed with my new acquisition under my arm . . . and the *Anatomy* still skulking dismally in its barrow.

When I got home to my flat - which I shared with my most faithful and congenial of friends, Arnold Barker, with whom I had seen two wars and a prison camp in Germany - I inspected the book I had just purchased. Arnold was out at the time, so I had the flat all to myself. I dreaded so the fearful trash which would have disgraced my library - some cheap romance that would make me shudder. But the binding calmed my fears: no romantic author would have chosen thick black leather to garb his story. The title in gold print was hardly discernible.

I opened the book and felt a little shiver of pleasant

anticipation run down my spine. In bold black lettering, ornamented with fantastic arabesques à la Cruikshank, the title displayed itself to my eyes: *Le Dictionnaire Infernal* by J Collin de Plancy, 1864. It was in French, which pleased me all the more, as my knowledge of that language was more than fair, and it was full of weird, humoristic and infinitely varied engravings by some artist of the middle of the last century.

I perused it avidly and rapidly acquainted myself of its contents. An Infernal Dictionary it was, written in a semi-serious, semi-comical style, giving full details concerning the nether regions, rites, inhabitants, spiritualism, stars reading, fortune telling etc, which, as the author informed us, all had to be taken *cum granu salis*. I hasten to say that I in no way dabbled in demonology, but this book, though certainly dealing with the black arts, was harmless to so experienced a reader as myself. And I looked forward to several days of pleasant entertainment with my unusual discovery. I pictured Arnold's face as I would show him my find, for the occult had always fascinated him.

I skimmed the pages once more, smoothing out those which had been crushed in the fall – or perhaps before – when my fingers encountered a bulky irregular thickness in the top cover of the book. The fly leaf had been stuck back over this irregularity, and gummed down with exceedingly dirty fingers.

To say that I was puzzled would of course be true. But I was more than puzzled: I was very intrigued. Without a moment's hesitation, I slipped my penknife along the gummed fly leaf and cut it right out; a thin piece of folded paper slipped out and fell onto the carpet at my feet. What made me hesitate just then to pick it up? Nothing apparently, and yet fully ten seconds elapsed before I took it in my hand and unfolded it. And then my enthusiasm was fired, for the folded sheets - there were three of them - were covered with music: music written in a neat, precise hand, in very small characters, and which to my experienced eyes appeared very difficult to decipher.

Each sheet contained the three different parts of a trio - piano, violin and cello. That was as far as I was able to see - for the characters being very small and my eyes not so good as they had been, I could not read very much of it. I was, however, thrilled; childishly, I must confess, I hoped - even grown men can be foolish - that this might be some unknown work from a great composer's hand. But on second perusal, I was quickly disillusioned. The author of this music had signed his name: P Everard, 1865, which told me exactly nothing, for P Everard was quite unknown to me.

The only thing that intrigued me considerably was the title of the trio. Still in the same neat hand, I saw the skilfully drawn figure of a naked man seated on the back of a dromedary, and read, '*In worship of Paymon*' underlining the picture.

It may have been a trick of the light, or my imagination, but the face of the man was incredibly evil, and I hastily looked away.

Well, this was a find! However obscure the composer, it was interesting to find a document dating back to the nineteenth century, so well preserved and under such unusual circumstances. Perhaps its very age would make it valuable? I would have to interview some authorities on old manuscripts and ascertain the fact. In the meanwhile, the temptation being very great, I set about playing the violin part on my fiddle.

My fingers literally ached to feel the polished wood of my instrument between them and I was keenly interested at having something entirely new to decipher.

Propping up the violin part on my stand – the paper, though thin, was very stiff and needed no support – I attacked the opening bars. They were incredibly difficult and at first I thought I would not be able to play them, although I can say without boasting that I am more than a mere amateur in that respect. But gradually I got used to the peculiar rhythm of the piece and made my way through it. Strangely enough, however, I felt intense displeasure at the sounds that were springing from my bow. The melody was beautiful, worthy of Handel's *Messiah*, or Berlioz's *L'Enfance du Christ*, for it was religious. Yes, religious: and at the same time it seemed only to be a parody of religion, with an underlying current of something infinitely evil.

How could music express that, you may wonder. I do not know, but I felt in every fibre of my body that what I was playing was 'impure' and I hated as much as I admired the music I was rendering.

As I attacked the last bar, Arnold Barker's startled voice broke in my ear. 'Good God, Greville, what on earth is that you're playing? It's terrible!'

Arnold, in all his six-foot-three of ageing manhood, brought me out of my trance with his very material and down-to-earth remark. I was grateful to him. I lowered my fiddle.

'Well, I daresay it could be better played,' said I, 'but it is amazingly difficult.'

'I don't mean you played it badly,' Arnold hastily interposed. 'Not by a long chalk. But . . . but . . . it's the music. It's wonderful, but extraordinarily unpleasant. Who on earth wrote it?' He took off his mist-sodden coat and hat, and picked up one of the two remaining sheets of music.

As he scanned it, I explained my little adventure, and how I had come into possession of the unusual manuscript.

The book did not appear to rouse much interest in him: his whole attention was centred on the sheet of paper he was holding. As I was finishing speaking, he said, 'This appears to be the piano part: I could try my hand at it, and accompany you. Though, as you say, it appears to be extraordinarily difficult . . . the rhythm is unusual.'

He was puzzled as I had been, and I watched him as he seated himself at the piano and played the first opening bars. He was a born pianist: these short competent hands, as they stretched nimbly over the keys, were sufficient proof of that. The only defect in his talent that had prevented him from making a career of it was his deplorable memory and total incapacity to play anything without the music under his eyes. Now, he did not appear to find his part difficult – not as I had done. Of course, the piano, in this trio, merely featured as an accompaniment, a subdued monotone which now and then picked up the main theme of the piece and exercised variations upon it.

Arnold played the piece half-way through, then stopped abruptly. 'Of course my part is rather dull,' said he. 'It needs the violin and the cello to bring it out. But, well . . . I don't mind admitting that I don't like it. It's . . . uncanny . . .'

I nodded in agreement.

'What do you make of the man's name?'

'Nothing.'

'As far as I can tell, the name Everard has never become famous in the music world, and yet the man was gifted, for this piece has rare qualities. It reminds one of some strains of *The Messiah*, and yet . . . well, there's just that something in it that makes it all wrong.'

'It's peculiar,' I admitted. 'Extraordinary luck my finding it. I suppose it has been in the binding of that book since the date when it was written. But why was it . . . well . . . I should say "concealed"? I can't think. And what about that dedication? Who is Paymon?'

Arnold bent closer to the picture, and I noticed him suck in his breath as in some surprise. He straightened himself up and cast me rather a furtive look. 'I don't know,' he mused. 'Paymon . . . and "in worship" too. Somebody this fellow Everard must have been frightfully fond of. But have you noticed the expression on the man's face? It's rather unpleasant.'

'*Evil* is more like it – the man was an artist as well as a musician. It's very odd. I will have to take this manuscript to old Mason's tomorrow and see what he can make of it. It may have worldwide interest for all we know.'

But, the following day being a Sunday, I did not care to trouble my old friend with my mysterious manuscript, and I spent my time, much to my reluctance, practising my part of the trio. It fascinated me, and yet repelled me in every note I drew across the strings. When I looked at that small, hideous picture, I felt as though a cunning little devil had got inside my fingers and compelled me to play against my will, with the notes dancing and jumbling before my eyes, and the weird strains of the music filling my head and making me loathe myself for yielding to that strange force.

Late in the afternoon, Arnold, who had been strangely moody

as he listened to me from the depths of his favourite armchair, rose to his feet and came over to where I was playing. 'Look here, Greville,' said he. 'There is something definitely wrong with that music. I feel it, and I know you do too. I can't analyse it, but it is there all the same. We ought to get rid of it somehow. Take it to Mason's and tell him to do what he likes with it, or burn it, but don't keep it.'

I was stubborn. 'It may have its value, you know,' I remonstrated. 'And, after all . . . it's really beautiful.' And I wondered at myself for praising something which I loathed with all my heart.

'Yes, it's beautiful. But it's bad. Don't lie to yourself – you think so too. I have been watching you all the time you were playing, and by Heaven, if anyone seemed to be in absolute terror of something, that person was you. That thing's infernal – I've a good mind to destroy it here and now!'

He seized the three sheets that were lying on the violin stand and made as though to throw them into the fire. But I stayed his hand and murmured quite feverishly (and quite, it seemed, against my will), 'No! Not just yet. After all, it's a trio, and we have only played two parts of it. If we could get Ian McDonald to come round this evening with his cello, we could play the whole thing together – just once, to hear it as it should be played. And then . . . well . . . we can destroy it.'

'Ian? That boy will be scared stiff!'

'Scared? Of what? Of a few notes on a sheet of paper eighty-five years old? You're being foolish, Arnold. We both are. There's nothing wrong with the music at all. It's weird, uncanny perhaps, but that's all that's to be said against it. So is *Peer Gynt* for that matter, and yet no-one would dream of being scared by it, as we are by this trio . . .'

Arnold still looked very doubtful, so I pressed my point.

Why, I wonder now . . . why was I so eagerly enthusiastic about my find, when deep down in my mind I felt a lurking fear of it, as of an evil thing that polluted whatever it touched? I detested it, and yet that little naked figure on the dromedary's back held my senses in a kind of spell and made me talk as I was now doing: without my being able to control my thoughts and voice as I wished.

'After all,' I argued, 'this is *my* discovery, and it's only natural that I should wish to know what the whole effect of the trio is like. As we've played it – you and I – it was, well, lop-sided. It needs the cello to complete it. And, you said yourself when you first heard it that it was beautiful!'

'And ghastly,' Arnold added sulkily, but he was clearly mollified. He perused his part of the trio once more.

On the three sheets was repeated the detestable little figure, and I noticed that Arnold kept his hand carefully over the wicked face, and on replacing the sheet on the music stand, he averted his eyes. So, that drawing held that strange influence over him, too? Perhaps . . . perhaps . . . there was something after all.

But Arnold prevented any further speculation.

'All right,' he said, in a resigned voice. 'I'll go round and collect young Ian. But remember, I take no responsibility.'

'Responsibility? What responsibility?' I asked.

Arnold looked embarrassed. 'Oh, I don't know. But if . . . well . . . if this blasted trio upsets the lot of us, I want you to know that I wash my hands of the whole thing from this very minute.'

'Don't be a damned idiot, Arnold,' I said with some heat. 'I never knew you to be so ridiculously impressed by a piece of music. You're as silly as a five-year-old child!'

I felt my inner thoughts battling against the words I uttered.

The little man on the paper seemed to grin at me, and I suddenly felt physically sick. I turned to stop Arnold, but he had already left the room, even as I opened my mouth to speak to him. I heard the clang of the front door as he slammed it. I regretted my insistence. I hated myself for having persuaded Arnold to fetch Ian, and, obeying a sudden impulse, I seized the papers and prepared to throw them into the smouldering fire. The little man's eyes on the paper followed mine as I moved, as though daring me to carry out my intention. I stopped and stared at the grinning face . . . and I replaced the sheets on the music stand, with a thrill of unpleasant fear running down my spine.

Arnold was away some time. When he came back, he had brought Ian with him and between them they carried the latter's cello – a very beautiful instrument in a fine leather case. Ian, compared to both of us, was a mere child: he was barely twenty-eight, with a gentle, effeminate face and a weak body that was greatly at a disadvantage beside Arnold's towering strength and healthy vitality. But he was a fine fellow for all his physical deficiencies, and in spite of the difference in our ages, we were all three the best of friends, brought together by our common interest in music. Ian played in various concerts and was an excellent cellist.

I greeted him warmly, for I was very fond of him, and before showing him the music, made him feel quite at home. But Arnold had probably put him on his mettle, for almost at once, he asked me *what this blessed trio was about*, and why we were so eager to play it, and why we made such mysteries about it?

'Arnold told me it was beautiful and awful all at the same time, and quite a difficult piece even from my point of view, which I presume must be taken as a compliment. I don't mind admitting I'm keen to play it.'

Arnold grunted his disapproval from behind the thick clay pipe he always smoked, and I felt a guilty qualm in my mind that for some reason made me hesitate. As Ian looked a little surprised, I overcame my reluctance and, taking up the old manuscript, handed it to him. He looked at it carefully for several minutes without uttering a word, then he handed back the piano and violin parts, keeping the cello part, and remarked, 'It ought to be deuced good, you know. Yes, that is quite a find you've made there, Greville, quite a find. But what an unpleasant little picture that is at the top. It is quite out of keeping with the music, I've a feeling.'

'I don't know about that,' Arnold murmured. 'I can't say I agree.'

Ian looked up in some surprise, and I, sensing some embarrassing question concerning the music, rose to my feet and said, 'Well, since we are all ready, there's no sense in wasting time talking. Let's get to work.'

There was little time wasted in preparing our instruments. Ian was eager and in some excitement; I was, for some strange reason, peculiarly nervous; Arnold, I noticed with a little irritation, was moody, and placed himself at the piano with a good deal of ill grace. Why did he accept to play his part so grudgingly, I wondered as I tuned my fiddle. After all, this was just a piece of music like any other. In fact, it was more beautiful than many I had heard and played. Surely his musician's enthusiasm would be fired at being given such scope to express itself! For this trio, in its way, was a masterpiece.

I ran a scale and looked at the little man; the name Paymon in that neat, precise hand danced before my eyes and made me blink. I would have to stop my eyes wandering to the picture if I wanted to play my part properly. But wherever I looked, the man on his dromedary seemed to follow me and leer at my futile efforts to evade him. I glanced at Ian and noticed that he was looking a little annoyed.

'This damn little picture is blurring my eyes,' he complained rather crossly. 'It seems to be everywhere!'

'I noticed that myself,' I admitted.

'I can't get it out of the way: the best thing to do is to cover it up.'

I gave them a small sheet of paper each and we all three pinned the sheets down upon our respective pictures. I felt a certain amount of relief at not seeing that ugly face and, tapping my stand with my fiddle bow, said, 'Are you fellows ready?'

Two silent nods, and we began.

And now, how can I describe what happened, or how it happened? It is fixed in my mind and yet I cannot find words suitable to impart to you the horror of our experience. I think the music was the worst part of it all. As we played, I could hardly believe that this . . . this hellish sound was really being created by our own fingers. Hellish. Demonic. Those are the only words for it, and yet in itself, it was none of those things. But there was something about it that conveyed that ghastly impression, as though the author had composed it with the wish to convey profane emotions to its executants. I confess that I was frightened – really and truly afraid – possessed of such fear as I have never experienced before or since: fear of something awful and all-powerful which I did not understand. I played on, struggling to drop my fiddle and stop, but compelled by some force to continue.

And then, when we were half-way through, a strangled cry from Ian broke the horrible spell. 'Oh God, stop it, stop it! This is awful!'

I seemed to wake as from a dream. I lowered my violin and looked at the young man. He was white and trembling, with dilated eyes staring at the music before him. He looked, with his thin face and yellow hair, like a corpse.

I murmured hoarsely, 'Ian, what is the matter?'

He did not answer me. With one hand, he still held his cello; with the other – the right one – he made a sign of the cross and murmured, 'Christ – oh, Christ, have mercy on us!' and sank in a dead faint onto the carpet.

In two seconds, galvanised into action, we were beside him and, Arnold supporting his head and shoulders, I administered what aid I could to him, though my intense excitement made me of little use. He was very far gone, and it took us nearly twenty minutes to revive him. When he opened his eyes, he looked at us both, a prey to abject terror, then, clutching at my coat in fear, he murmured, 'The music . . . the music . . . it's possessed. You must destroy it at once!'

We exchanged glances, Arnold and I. Arnold seemed to say 'I told you so' and I accepted the rebuke. But I obeyed. This music was evil and had to be destroyed. I rose to my feet and went to the music stand. Then I suddenly felt the blood draining from my face and leaving my lips dry. For the music lay on the carpet – clawed to pieces. Only the grinning man on his dromedary was intact . . .

It was some weeks later, when we had somewhat recovered from our experience, that I ventured to open the book I had recently bought and which had been the cause of so much trouble. I had the name Paymon on the brain, and quite by chance, I opened the Infernal Dictionary at the letter P. I had no intention of looking for the name Paymon. I did not, of course, think it existed in any dictionary. I merely turned the pages over and looked at the illustrations. At the sixth or seventh page of that letter, my attention was attracted by the only picture in the column – that of a hideous little man, seated on the back of a dromedary. The name Paymon was written beneath it, along with a small article, concerning the illustration.

I read avidly. '*Paymon: one of the gods of Hell. Appears to exorcists in the shape of a man seated on the back of a dromedary. May be summoned by libations or human sacrifices. Is very partial to music.*'

ADAM O'RIORDAN

A THUNDERSTORM IN SANTA MONICA

HARVEY WAS SITTING with Teresa in the courtyard of Aguilo, a fashionable restaurant on Abbott Kinney. They had come straight from the airport. Teresa would drop him at the house after lunch before returning to the office, but promised they would do something special that evening. This was Harvey's third trip to Los Angeles in the past eighteen months. He had met Teresa at a private view in London. She had been at Vassar with Eric Harkness, a friend who owned the advertising agency where he occasionally worked freelance as a copywriter. She was in the city looking to finance a film. At the private view she had mocked the untidy blocks of colour on the massive canvases, each named after a Station of the Cross, and he had liked her for that. That night they had made love in her hotel suite overlooking Hyde Park. As Teresa slept, the sheets tangled around her legs, Harvey sat smoking in an armchair by the window, looking out at the chain of orange lamps winding through the deserted park.

At ten to six, after an hour dozing beside her, Harvey kissed Teresa on the ear and left. He heard her murmur as he clicked the door shut and had been surprised to find himself hesitating in the corridor, his corduroy jacket draped across his arm. The jacket smelled of fried food and damp, of his cramped studio apartment, with its three exterior walls and bad light after midday, where he had moved after his marriage had broken down.

A fortnight later her note arrived, alongside an envelope bearing his accountants' insignia and stamped 'URGENT'. Eric must have given her the address. Teresa's letter asked him to come to Los Angeles. No strings, no promises. Why not? Harvey asked himself, as he rinsed a handful of cutlery in the sink, rubbing the cold tines of a fork with his thumb as he waited for the tap to run hot. It might be what he needed. Shake things up. Harvey borrowed the money for that first flight to LA from Eric, who watched from behind his desk, making a steeple of his stubby fingers as Harvey explained what the money was for. Harvey, in a tubular steel chair, tobacco tin on his knee, rolled a cigarette as he waited for Eric's response to his petition. 'Go. Soak it in,' Eric said in his terse, semi-Anglicised way as he tore the cheque from its book and slid it across the desk. He beckoned Harvey in for a hug – beaming, gregarious, like a small-town mayor, his arms spread wide before his chest. Harvey wondered if Eric and Teresa had once been lovers.

What had been a whim had now become an expensive and, Harvey knew, unsustainable habit. It wasn't the sex, the tide of Teresa's desire hard to navigate or predict; sometimes animalistic, his torso raised with welts and scratches as they lay together in the afterglow. Other times, as tentative as teenagers as Teresa's hands slowly mapped the geometry of Harvey's face. It wasn't the play at coupledom they made on strolls along Venice boardwalk past the street performers and panhandlers with their brassy handwritten signs. And it wasn't their in-jokes at the industry parties Teresa was obliged to attend, where they met and mocked with a look or squeeze of the hand the people, restless in their spheres, who came to court Teresa's influence. Other-worldly models teetering unsteady as foals in their high heels, their big, underwater eyes expressing a desire to act; downtrodden actors locked into five-year deals with prime-time shows, confessing a compulsion to direct; directors sick of being pushed around by studio heads, who now wanted to exec-produce for themselves. 'I can confirm it: the earth is tipped towards Los Angeles, all the prettiest girls roll this way,' Harvey told Eric one evening during that first trip, feeling alien and unfettered for the first time in years. He had Teresa pinned to an island table of a sports bar as he talked. They had retreated inside after walking by the ocean to see if they could catch a glimpse of the famous green flash said to appear on the horizon at sundown. 'Here, Teresa wants to speak to you,' Harvey said passing the phone, looking up at the massive glistening athletes, sweat-drenched on the big screens around the bar.

No, it wasn't any of these things, Harvey told himself. What he was hooked on, he was sure, was the eleven-hour lacuna of the flight and all it entailed. It began at take-off. The cabin hushed. The cutlery rattling in the galley as the plane gained speed, the plastic cabin beginning to creak. The engines roaring like beasts heard from the bowels of an amphitheatre. The focused quiet of an examination hall as passengers concentrated on keeping calm and pretending what was happening was perfectly normal. The plane would continue to ascend, the patchwork of fields dropping away below as London's suburbs petered out into countryside. As the plane gained height Harvey would feel his body respond, increasing the pressure on his heels, righting itself as it tried to adjust to the altitude. Until the nose of the plane dropped a few degrees and the plangent note of the electronic gong told passengers take-off was over and they were free to undo their seat belts. After the thrill of take-off came the endurance test of the hours mid-air. He would start and then abandon films, leaving their protagonists frozen on the small screen. Harvey relished this restlessness, the boredom of a quality last known in childhood. Then would come a few hours of fitful sleep. Slack-mouthed, snapping awake as his neck gave under the weight of his head.

Then, just when the tedium seemed interminable, the limbo of the flight never ending, the captain would come over the intercom and announce the final hour in the air and the beginning of the descent. Then came the prospect of landing and the dissipating tension as time re-engaged and found its thrust. Now the plane would pass for miles over Los Angeles, the low-rise city: its dense acreage of parking lots and freeways punctuated by the oasis of a baseball ground or a football field: the light charged with a biblical intensity. Looking out to the brown mountains that hemmed in the city and seemed to drive its seething mass towards the ocean. Then the sound of the landing gear like a winch hauling the world below towards the belly of the plane and a final thrill: that burst of speed towards the runway. Then the judder as the plane touched down, past the tower and the terminals until he could make out the faces of the baggage handlers and engineers in their coveralls. Then the spell was broken. He would adjust his watch. He was certain it was this – not

Teresa, not the distance from his life in London – that he had come to crave.

In the courtyard of Aguilo, a bank of railway sleepers and an ivy-covered wall provided shade from the swimming-pool-size section of sky. Teresa was busy at her BlackBerry straining to hear over the noise of the lunchtime crowd, as she pushed the glossy black tear of the headset into her ear. She looked over to Harvey who had paused his meal, anxious not to finish before Teresa had started hers. She flashed two fingers at him, grimacing theatrically. Harvey set down his fork and watched a Mexican busboy in his fifties deliver a baked egg floating in a pool of green lentils to a pregnant woman at the table opposite. A skinny compatriot refilled her water glass. A blond waiter with a clover tattooed behind his ear hovered nearby with his notepad, as if scoring their performance.

Harvey inspected himself in the back of his spoon. His eyes were puffy from the flight. He was still a little tanned from his last trip out. The lines on his brow had grown deeper over the past few years. He tilted the spoon to inspect the few silver strands that had recently appeared at his temples. As Teresa continued her conversation Harvey noticed a girl in a floral-print dress, looking up at him from her dessert. She could be no more than nineteen, wore no make-up or had been made-up to appear as if she wasn't wearing any. Harvey couldn't decide. She had a soft, cherubic face and wore two slides in her short hair in an attempt to suppress the natural curl or disguise a recent change in length. He caught her eye and she looked away.

Harvey glanced over to Teresa, still on the phone, the food on her plate untouched. She had been there to meet him at the airport. He had spotted her checking her watch by the Arrivals board. Teresa would be forty-eight next month. Compared to the girl she had an unshowy beauty, but she carried herself with a lightness that was itself girlish. When Teresa had spotted Harvey at Arrivals, she had run to hug him. She had brought him flowers: huge sunflowers, their long stems wrapped in brown paper. Harvey imagined her picking them out, double-parked outside the florist on Washington Boulevard, shaking her head at the alternatives before holding out a crisp twenty when the right bunch was proffered. All this without breaking from her conversation on her BlackBerry.

'You made it!' Teresa had said. Then pulling him close into her, 'So good to have you back, baby.'

The plane had been empty when Harvey boarded. At check-in he had gambled on a seat in a central section between the bulkheads. In front of his seat there was a fold-down platform for a bassinet. Harvey had reasoned that a mid-week midday flight to Los Angeles would not be full of families. As a tinny aria was pumped through the cabin, he wondered if he might have the whole row to himself. He changed into his complimentary flight socks, pushed his shoes out of sight below his seat and buckled himself in. Contemplating the flight ahead he closed his eyes.

'Nick Antonopoulos,' said a voice.

The words pulled him from a maze of memories, a fervid series of unconnected images, summoned before take-off in his semi-dreaming doze. The voice repeated:

'Nick Antonopoulos.'

Harvey opened his eyes this time and looked at the hand

held out to him. Standing above him was a man in his thirties. He was dressed in khaki slacks, the crease ironed sharp down the front of each leg, and a black long-sleeved polo shirt, the shining nylon like something a professional golfer might wear. His dark hair was clipped militarily short around his ears and at his neck. He seemed generically clean-cut, politely forthright, indistinguishable from many other Americans you might meet in airport lounges travelling on business across the western world. He was smiling softly, a large and sensual mouth, a smile that suggested he was amused by the archetype he found himself inhabiting. Nick Antonopoulos gave off the impression that the two men shared a long-standing arrangement to meet and that he was now finally making himself known. Harvey offered his own hand and attempted to stand, before realising this was impractical.

'Second flight of the day for me,' Nick said, smiling more broadly now as he unpacked his briefcase. He pulled out a magazine. On the cover were arrayed pyramids of unnaturally bright apples and oranges. As he sat down Nick gestured to the cover and explained that he worked in the fruit industry. He had spent the previous night in Versailles, in what he described as a *heinously* small hotel room, where he had been attending his firm's annual European sales conference. He was now flying to Los Angeles, deputising for his manager at the International Conference where he would be delivering a paper on the drivers and barriers behind consumers' fresh fruit choices. He would be flying back to England after two nights at the Four Seasons on Doheny. At first the men exchanged a few platitudes: the clichés and curiosities of international travel; stories from Nick's life on the road, told with great exuberance where little actually happened. A mention of his wife and two daughters at home in Windsor where they had moved recently, and where, walking through the Great Park one day with his daughter, he was sure he had seen Queen Elizabeth drive past.

As the plane taxied towards the foot of the runway, Nick took a mobile phone from his briefcase. He scrolled through the names, then pressed his thumb on the touchpad.

'Samantha?'

Something in the sureness of Nick's responses gave Harvey an unexpected comfort.

'OK. About to take off now. Love to the kids. Talk later. I know. I know,' and then with a lingering smile, 'OK.'

Nick finished his call and turned off the phone, gesturing with a raised palm to the air-hostess who had been approaching with a frown. He turned and flashed a smile at Harvey.

When they hit the turbulence Harvey was sleeping. The map on the headrest screen was the first thing he saw when he opened his eyes. They were somewhere over northern Canada. The jolt was so hard it lifted him from his seat, his lap belt biting into the top of his pelvis. He glanced to his right and saw Nick gripping his armrests, bracing himself against the movements of the plane. The plane was rattling harder now, throwing passengers from side to side. Harvey heard a sharp intake of breath from an air-hostess as she pulled herself along the aisle to the jump seat. He watched as she exchanged a brief and unmistakably fearful glance with her colleague in the aisle opposite. Now the noise of the engines increased as if struggling to keep the plane airborne. Harvey knew something was terribly wrong. An elderly woman in the row to their right had begun to sob and was being comforted by her husband, who was patting her bony shoulder ineffectually with one hand, while gripping his armrest with the other. Her husband's single-serving wine bottle had fallen from his tray and was cannoning along the aisle as the plane was buffeted roughly. Harvey thought of the footage he had once seen of an office during an earthquake in the Philippines. Then he thought about the flight deck, as he knew from the reconstructions he had watched on TV, the pilots wrestling at their dual controls trying desperately to keep the plane aloft, some series of fatal mistakes already placing them beyond safety. Harvey was sure this was the end. In a moment the plane would be lost in vast white tracts below. It would be days before the rescue parties reached them, or what parts of them were left. Their luggage, the bright clothes picked out for beach holidays in California, would be strewn for miles across the snow. It was then that Nick placed his hand on top of Harvey's. He gripped it strongly with a force that left Harvey in no doubt it was deliberate, before returning it to his own armrest. Neither man looked at the other but it was understood by Harvey that he had been reached out to in his last moments. That humanity had prevailed and that men had faced their fate together. They endured several minutes more of extreme turbulence before the plane's movements became at first less frequent and then less severe. The first officer came over the intercom to announce they had hit several big pockets of air as they passed around a storm front and that as they were expecting a little more chop up ahead, he would be leaving the seat-belt sign on for now. The first officer sounded relieved to be delivering this news.

As the flight wore on, both men retreated into themselves but Nick continued to offer the same amused, ironic smile whenever Harvey got up to stretch his legs or use the toilet. Harvey watched Nick scrolling through spreadsheets on a laptop, biting the thumbnail on one hand while running the forefinger of the other down the columns of numbers. As they waited to disembark, standing in the aisle of the business class section, the empty seats littered with newspapers and magazines, Nick turned to Harvey and offered him his card. 'This is me. Keep in touch,' he smiled, and patted Harvey on the back. Harvey placed the card in his pocket. He wanted to thank Nick Antonopoulos, if not for his company – for a few minutes of conversation over the eleven hours in the air could hardly be called company – then for his proximity. To tell him of the unexpected comfort his fleeting companionship had given him. He felt he was taking leave of an old friend. But instead he nodded and smiled and said, 'Yes, thanks, well, good luck with everything.'

Harvey stood in the empty living room of Teresa's house, more drunk than he would have expected to be from the bottle of Gavi at Aguilo. When Teresa had dropped him off she had pointed out an elderly neighbour in front of one of the smaller houses across the street, staring at them from below a Stars and Stripes the size of a double bedspread that flew above his lawn. 'Poor Republicans. Worst kind,' Teresa said as Harvey got out of the car. 'I'll see you later.' She had waved an arm from the window as she drove off. The house was between owners – Teresa had taken up a series of sublets since selling her own place in the Palisades. She was waiting for the market to even out before buying somewhere new, probably farther up the coast towards Malibu. Where, in her fantasy life, she would hike and paddleboard every weekend and buy two Weimaraners and walk the ghost-grey gundogs out along the shining sands each evening. But as she had to travel so often for work this place was fine for now. The living room of Teresa's house was bare except for a few sticks of furniture: an oversize easy chair that sat on top of two thick wooden rockers, some wilted roses in a narrow-necked vase, a pair of shot-silk curtains in translucent green that only partially covered the doors leading on to the brick terrace with its hip-height wall and the small lawn slanting upwards above it. Harvey walked through the rooms of the house, absent-mindedly opening and closing the closets and drawers. This was the third rental Harvey had visited Teresa in. No matter how earnestly she talked about the life she planned in Malibu, she seemed drawn to these temporary, transitory, anonymous spaces, the residue of someone else's life hanging about them still.

He walked into the bedroom and stood under a lacquered wooden fan on to which four flower-shaped light-fittings were fixed. As he looked at the made-up bed Harvey remembered his last trip. The afternoon he arrived Teresa had been lying reading a script with the cover across her as Harvey dressed after showering. She had drawn back the duvet to reveal her naked lower half, instructing him to 'kiss it'. She had smelled of fresh laundry and as he kissed her, as asked, he had tasted that unmistakable sweet, dry alkaline. He sat for a moment on the corner of the bed looking at a pile of jewellery on Teresa's bedside table, the rings and fine chain-link bracelets tangled up inside one another, remembering that summer afternoon when the tang of eucalyptus came through the open window.

The rooks were loud in the garden outside, their raw cawing and flapping audible. Harvey went into the en suite bathroom. The surfaces were crammed with conditioners and beauty creams with French names: Beurre de Karité and Crème Vital. Harvey took a towel from the rail and, walking back through the bedroom and out of the sliding doors, arranged it for sunbathing on the lawn. He lay back and felt his face warming in the sun. He closed his eyes and tried to reconstruct the face of the girl from Aguilo. He tried to imagine what she might look like naked. Her high breasts, the silvery down in the small of her back, her long, tan, slightly bowed legs. How her skin might smell up close in the well of her collarbone or might feel as he ran his fingertips across it. If she would taste like Teresa or if she would have some different tang or musk. Unthinking, he tucked his erection under the belt of his jeans, rolled over on to his front and took a cigarette from the box. There was a single match left hanging from the book he had picked up at a bar back in London. He bent the head back against the strike-strip and clicked his fingers. He lit the cigarette and let the burning match fall on to the grass. He took a long drag, then watched the blue ribbons of smoke from his cigarette dissolve into the clear sky. Above him he heard a single-propeller plane heading towards Catalina. He looked up at the acacia in the far corner of the garden, the fringe of late afternoon light around its outer edge. He thought back to the last view of London from the cab on the way to the airport. How the trees were nearly bare. He remembered the wet leaves on the pavements and the gardens of the Victorian houses as he waited in traffic.

As the afternoon wore on Harvey worked his way through a pile of old magazines, Italian and French *Vogues*, that Teresa had stacked in the corner of the living room. Picking up a new magazine every time he went inside to light another cigarette from the stove the previous owner had painstakingly restored, that Teresa had told him about in the car on the way over, the makers' names, O'Keefe and Merritt, how the previous owner couldn't afford to have it shipped to his new place. Harvey's cigarette butts littered the terrace like the droppings of a caged bird. He thought he should collect them before Teresa got back, which would be any time now. As he lay out in the garden, the light softening, the late sun sluicing over his closed eyes, he felt a heaviness fall over him. He told himself he must not sleep.

He was woken a few moments later by the telephone. By the time he reached it the answer-machine had kicked in. He listened to Teresa's voice:

'Harvey, baby, I have some bad news.' There was a pause. 'I have to fly to New York . . . tonight. Don't be mad,' then as if angered by her display of weakness, 'I told you when you booked your ticket this was always a possibility.'

Then she added in a staccato burst, 'The car's at the studio. Won't be more than a couple of days. I'll call you from the airport.'

Harvey thought he should be angry but registered that anger was not forthcoming. He walked out into the garden and stood on the brick terrace. The light was fading now and a sliver of crescent moon was clear in the blue sky. Teresa's neighbours were home. He had heard their car pull up as he listened to her message. Now he was back in the garden he heard them bickering behind the flannel bush separating the two properties. Then their back door slamming, followed by the sound of a man pedalling hard on an exercise bike in the garden. Harvey's drowsiness had lifted. Maybe some exercise would do him good. He would take a stroll. Closing the doors to the garden, he pulled a woollen sweater from his hand luggage and picked up the spare set of keys from the counter.

It was a short walk from the house to Lincoln Boulevard, where the freshly mown lawns suddenly gave on to four lanes of loud traffic and neon signs. Harvey walked along Lincoln past the strip malls offering manicures and discount household goods, the ten-dollar tyre balancing, the car lots and charity shops with rotating signs on their roofs, past the taco shack where he had eaten hog maws with Teresa on his first trip out. The only other pedestrians were off to work night shifts or, having served their purpose for the day, were waiting at the bus stops to be ferried out of the city. Harvey had ridden on one on his first visit when Teresa had been delayed and unable to meet him at the airport. It had seemed to him a kind of mobile psychiatric ward, where the ill and the underpaid were condemned to spend their days. He stopped a few blocks before Pico outside a bar that advertised itself as a 'British Pub and Restaurant'. The exterior was painted to resemble the whitewashed wattle-and-daub of an English country cottage. He peered in through the tinted and unwashed windows. The bar was hung with photographs of soccer players from the 1970s, some of whom he recognised, and faded reproduction advertisements for ale. He decided to go in. He took a seat at the bar and ordered a glass of lager, looking up at the three antique horse brasses set in the ceiling beams, a collection someone had begun and then clearly abandoned. The barmaid who served him had looked younger in the gloom as he had entered the bar, but up close Harvey saw the skin on her face was heavily lined and creased from what could only be decades of overexposure to the sun. She set the drink down on a paper napkin in front of him, strings of bubbles rising up inside the amber glass. 'What's that?' a grizzled man with a muzzle of pure white stubble, wearing a foam baseball cap with the name of a local haulage company on it, called out to the barmaid as she flicked through the channels on the TV above the bar. 'Storm. Blowing in from Alaska. Time to go home, old man,' she said, patting his arm. Harvey waved his glass at the barmaid, who promptly set another beer down in front him. Perched on his stool, Harvey watched the bar fill up. The after-work crowd of middle managers and studio assistants, here to shoot a few frames of pool or watch a soccer game on the big screen. Harvey watched a pockmarked, mustachioed man flirting with a fat Latina. It seemed almost everyone in the bar was talking about the storm, questioning the barmaid, who was now the self-appointed authority on the subject, as they came to order more drinks. There was an atmosphere of growing excitement and anticipation in the crowded room as if a foreign dignitary were visiting the city. The bar filled up and then thinned out again but Harvey kept to his stool drinking steadily, unnoticed among the regulars. Before he left he changed three dollar bills into quarters. The barmaid was reluctant to spare the change until Harvey waved a thumb in the direction of the pool table in its tent of fluorescent light. Looking at his watch, in the second it took the numbers to swim into focus, Harvey saw that it was getting on for midnight now and he was drunk. He staggered on to Pico, the electric power lines on their wooden masts buzzing above him. He wanted to see the Pacific Ocean, to be near that massive expanse of water. To hear the waves breaking on the sand of Santa Monica State Beach, the fierce hiss as each one sank into the shore.

It was raining as the pier came into view but Harvey could

make out the lights of the fairground that occupied part of it. As if the big wheel was reeling in the weather from out at sea. Mountainous inky clouds formed on the horizon. His sweater was soaking, the wet wool releasing an acrid, peroxide smell. As he scrambled up the terrace of planting to the mouth of the pier, Harvey spotted a phone booth and stumbled towards it. He fed a handful of quarters into the slot and punched in a number. The phone rang several times before someone picked up.

'Nick, Nicky?'

The person on the other end of the line swallowed. Harvey heard the whistle and sigh of heavy nasal breathing, then the sound of someone rolling over heavily and faintly behind that the springs of the mattress.

'Nick, it's Harvey . . . from the plane.'

'Mmmm.' Then nothing but the crackle of the line.

'I wondered if . . . if you wanted to meet? For a drink or something?'

'Mmmm,' lower this time. There was a pause and a soft click, then a recorded voice instructed Harvey to replace the receiver.

The rain was falling heavily now, bouncing high off the slats of the pier, blurring the lights of the houses farther up the coast. Harvey stepped over the guardrail and made his way down the deserted pier as if walking out on to a frozen lake, the boards slippery under his feet. The lights of the fairground rides were reflected in the pooling water. He looked out to the ocean as the first fork of lightning split the sky. He imagined Nick Antonopoulos rolling back to sleep, waking early to call his wife and run through his speech for the sales conference. Wondering what had disturbed him in the night, the memory of someone using his name and wondering if he had dreamt it. Teresa, mid-air, working through a list of red-flagged emails. He thought of the storm clouds forming earlier in the day over the Gulf of Alaska, the pressure driving them down the length of the country, over Point Conception with its white lighthouse where they had picnicked last trip, all the way down to Santa Monica, the rain taking shape then falling on the lanes of traffic on Lincoln Boulevard. He stood at the end of the pier at what seemed like the very tip of this city. He listened to the thunder out at sea. A white line of lightning cut sideways through the cloud bank. He would stay here a while longer, Harvey thought, and see the storm through.

JANE McLAUGHLIN

TRIO FOR FOUR VOICES

THE CHILD ALWAYS wears modish nostalgia – almost, but not quite tipping over into fancy dress: blue cotton with an organdie overall, black patent bar shoes, Alice band on her dark hair.

I can hear them speaking French, but I know they are not French. Americans, Bostonians probably.

From my balcony I can see the hotel gardens, terraced down in stages to the rim of the gorge. Each level lushly planted, meticulously mowed and trimmed. On the first level below me is the croquet lawn, surrounded by hibiscus in full flower and small palm trees.

The father and daughter are playing. Their voices rise and fall in the warm breeze wandering up the valley. In the daytime he always wears a pale linen suit, Visconti-style. He has dark hair slicked back and gold-rimmed spectacles.

Laughter, an intertwining of a man's voice and a girl's. A rhythm of moving in physical harmony. Click of mallet on ball.

He plays a terrible shot, hitching the ball into the air.

'*Espèce de con!*' she shouts at him.

He walks over to her and wags his finger at her, roguishly. She flounces her skirt and makes a gesture of two hands brushing her face that says 'So what?'

Later, in the lobby, I hear him call:

'Amelia! Come for dinner!'

She appears, wearing a red silk kaftan and trousers.

They walk past. She flashes a smile, he looks straight ahead.

They sit to the left of the tall windows overlooking the terrace. The mother is of a different period – Pre-Raphaelite features and mane of dark hair. A robe of grape and night sky, trimmed with expensive embroidery. The parents sit formally, straight in their chairs, making occasional low conversation.

The child roams the tables between courses, greeting the diners, chatting.

Then it is my turn. She seats herself opposite me, her red silk arms on the table. She asks me questions politely, with the total confidence of the child who talks mainly to adults.

I tell her how I have driven up the road from Malaga and will be going on to Arcos to meet my friend.

'Oh I so love the *pueblos blancos*. I've been coming here since I was three. Papa is writing a book about them.'

She pronounces the syllables of 'Papa' with even stress, not in the old-fashioned English way.

She is animated, charming, her dark eyes brilliant. I wonder at the privileges that have made her so accomplished.

Then she leans towards me.

'I'm going to tell you a really big secret!'

Again I am charmed, intrigued.

'It's so important, I want someone to know!'

I am silent during the pause.

'I hate my Mama. I am going to kill her.'

I lean back and stare at her.

'No. You can't say that. You mustn't make up such stories.'

'Oh it's not a story. I am really going to do it. My Papa

is going to help me. He hates her too. He wants to marry another lady, one who writes books like he does.'

'I have to speak to your parents.'

She gestures at their table. It is empty.

'It doesn't matter what you say to them. She will think you made it up. You'll see. Nobody will know. It will be suicide. She has tried to kill herself twice already.'

'You cannot say those things. It is not amusing. Maybe you don't have enough to do here but there is no reason to make up tales that upset people.'

'Oh I don't mean to upset you. But I am not making it up. My mama is a wicked witch and she deserves to die.'

I will not listen any longer. She must not be encouraged. She needs help. Or if she doesn't, I do. I get up and go to the window. Night has fallen over the mountains.

I cannot see the road any longer. The most beautiful road in Europe, they say. I drove it. How I wanted to do it. The hairpins, the precipitous drops, the steep ascents and descents, keeping my eyes on the road, trying not to be distracted by the soaring crests, the fantastic valleys.

Before I went, on the internet I read of fear. People who wanted to drive the road, but said they were afraid. Accidents, collisions, falling into the precipitous drop. But nothing blocked my dream of the road. So beautiful, everything I had hoped. And where does it lead me? Here, into the mind of a demented child.

When I turn, she is standing in the doorway of the dining room. She waves and runs down the corridor.

I sit down for a moment on one of the velvet chairs. Trying to make sense of the conversation, maybe even pretend it has not happened.

Ignore it? I cannot get it out of my head. Tell someone, and get involved? But who? Maybe the mother is indeed unstable and that is why the child is like this.

And what if it is true? Suppose the woman is found at the bottom of the gorge? Would I question the story that she had flung herself there?

I see the vertical walls of rock, the rippling waters of the swimming pool, failed brakes on one of the hairpins, the sound of the shotguns in the clay pigeon range at the end of the lower terrace.

These things are in my head now and I cannot get them out. Her words have taken control.

The next morning I open the shutters onto the balcony. Mist lies over the slopes of the mountains, the crests floating above it like islands.

After breakfast I sit reading there. The blue of the sky grows more intense as the mist dissolves and the sunlight grows strong.

I watch three people going down towards the gorge. First the woman, wearing a bright blue shirt and baggy linen trousers, striding out towards the crest of the hill. Behind her: father and daughter, side by side on the path, holding hands, skipping sometimes over roots or loose rocks.

Then they wind slowly down a path that leads to the rim of the precipice. The woman in the blue shirt climbs up onto a rock that juts out over the chasm. The other two remain below.

Then she disappears, I cannot see where.

The two figures hover, moving uncertainly. Then they turn and wind their way up the path again.

The woman is not at dinner that night.

I ask at the reception desk. 'The American lady - sorry, I don't know her name - she lent me a book and I would like to return it. Do you know where she is?'

'She has gone to Gaucín for two nights. She will be back on Thursday.'

I think of the hairpins on the road to Gaucín.

Amelia comes to my table again at dinner.

'I do not want to hear any more about that. What you told me the other night. You must stop telling those stories.'

She sighs.

'I know you don't believe me. But you will see. You will know when it happens.'

'Where is your mother right now?'

'She has gone to Gaucín for a painting workshop. She will be back on Thursday. Maybe.'

I do not reply. She pushes her chair back and walks away. As she goes she says:

'Papa and I know what to do. She won't come back. Maybe this time, maybe another time.'

Most of Thursday passes. I go walking along the gorge and return in the early evening.

As I go into dinner a taxi pulls up at the door and the woman gets out, carrying a holdall and a wooden paint box.

The child needs help.

I ask the woman if I can have a word with her. I walk into an alcove that is more private and she follows me.

She greets me pleasantly enough and listens.

I report the conversations.

Her reaction is extreme. I would say theatrical, except that she is clearly not acting.

She gasps, appears to be trying to catch her breath. Holding her hand over her mouth she makes a sound that sounds like a suppressed long sob.

She runs past me, up the stairs, still making the strange sound. If you heard it out of context you might not know whether it was laughter or sobbing.

There follows a scene of operatic extravagance.

Running feet, slamming doors, a woman shouting. The phlegmatic author comes charging down the stairs, roaring like a bull, his wife and child running after him.

I realise he is quite tall. He looms over me, his face lowered into mine, his eyes raging behind his gold-rimmed spectacles.

'How dare you! How dare you invent such terrible things about our daughter! Such disgusting, twisted, perverted ideas!

His wife keeps up a kind of counterpoint: 'Disgusting, warped, appalling!'

I literally have my back to the wall. I see Amelia standing on the stairs, watching the scene intently.

'*You will* withdraw everything you said to my wife. *You will* never repeat such things again. *You will* apologise to my daughter, who is likely to be permanently damaged by your accusations. Withdraw now, apologise now, or you will hear from my lawyers.'

He is breathing heavily, his shoulders shaking.

The man seems mad. I think more than ever: the child must be helped.

I look around for hotel staff for support, but none appear.

At home I would report threatening behaviour. There is not much point in calling the Spanish police, if only because my Spanish would not be good enough to explain, and he might turn the complaint against me if he speaks it better.

The child needs help. I am being threatened. But I have no choice.

'I apologise. I withdraw the statements.'

He exhales sharply and turns, shepherding the woman and child before him up the stairs.

That evening I get room service.

The next morning a clear day dawns, fresh flowery air blowing in from the balcony. But I have little pleasure in it now. I just want to get on the road to Arcos as soon as I can.

As I come down the stairs I see that they, the three of them, are standing in the entrance hall. They are talking in a close, intimate way, in a way that seems inexplicable to me having seen what went before: low voices, small laughter.

Amelia is wearing her blue dress again. She is holding a bouquet of pink roses. She comes forward and hands them to me.

Her mother steps up to me too.

'Thank you – thank you for being such a good sport.'

Her New England drawl is cool, soothing.

'Amelia gets bored to tears being hauled around Europe after us. She must have her little games. I hope you do not think us too extraordinary.'

I cannot say anything.

The mother has a cardboard folder in her hand; she puts it into mine.

'These are for you.'

They load their antique leather suitcases into a vintage dark green Bentley and drive away, laughing and waving.

As I watch them go I feel anger, but to my surprise a sense of loss washes over that.

I look inside the cardboard folder. Inside are four

watercolour sketches of the landscape around Gaucín – luminous, delicate, beautiful.

I walk down to the pool. It is empty, limpid blue with lights of the sun playing in it. On the way I throw the roses into a bush where they hang like foreign blossoms.

I take out the paintings one by one, tear each into tiny shreds, and drop them into the water.

WILLIAM THIRSK-GASKILL

HOW TO BE AN ALCOHOLIC

THE MOST IMPORTANT thing is to start gradually. Alcohol is wasted on the young. Get a decent education. Go to a respected university. Don't start until at least after you have taken your finals.

Do not, on any account, mix it with other drugs. In spite of the claims made by nicotine, heroin, cocaine, or cannabis, alcohol is the only drug you will ever need. It is legal, affordable, socially acceptable (mostly), and, if you want it to be, addictive.

Let us not get into an argument about whether absinthe counts as alcohol, or as something else. All we will say is that absinthe would not be nearly as fashionable at the moment if it weren't 55 per cent alcohol by volume.

As with most things, the secret is in preparation and dedication. You will need a reason to drink. Work is the most obvious one. Get a job. Any job. But preferably one in which your co-workers drink. Become a 'social' drinker. That is, a drinker who drinks in the same room as, and at the same time as, other people.

During your twenties, you will probably find that your

consumption is curtailed as much by financial constraints as by your own capacity. You will also find that you spend a certain amount of time throwing up into toilets, or gutters, or sinks. This is a terrible waste, but don't worry about it, because you will get over it, later. It's just a phase.

At about thirty, you will need another reason to drink. The most obvious is a bad relationship. It doesn't matter whether you are gay or straight: find a partner who is either deliberately or inadvertently trying to destroy you, and vow to stick with him or her, whatever happens.

If you have been careful, it is not until this point that you will be accused of having a drink problem. There are various ways of mitigating this. For a year or two, you should be able to manage only drinking a few days per week, or only drinking relatively low-alcohol drinks, such as beer. Once you have exhausted these techniques, you are ready to move onto the next stage, which is concealing alcohol. This is a graduation in your development, and probably the biggest since you started drinking.

The only limits to concealing alcohol are the dimensions of your house and the fertility of your imagination. It is tempting at first only to try to conceal spirits, because they are more concentrated, but that is missing the point.

That bottle of Ribena at the back of the cupboard that nobody has touched for three years could be emptied and refilled with port. That over-filled spice-cupboard could be augmented with a couple of bottles of Chinese cooking wine (13 per cent ABV) which are unlikely to be noticed and, even if they are, might legitimately be there as cooking wine. It helps if you altruistically promote the habit of going to the supermarket by yourself, and also if you keep the old, gunge-coated bottles, and refill them from the new ones. If you have got this far, you will already have established yourself as the partner who does all the cooking. The kitchen is your domain, in more than one way.

The kitchen is not only the place where much of your consumption takes place, but also where you carry out many of your concealment activities. For example, a partner who never cooks is unlikely ever – even after an incident – to be interested in oven gloves. An oven glove will easily accommodate a quarter bottle of vodka, and makes a much safer point of concealment than a shelf in a study or bedroom, or at the back of a clothes drawer.

Have no compunction about cleaning up your own vomit, or admitting to the therapist what you have drunk, when, and why.

Once the relationship which turned you into a serious drinker is over, you are ready for the next step.

You need to learn to drink just for the sake of drinking. How you do this is up to you. It is likely during this period that you may decide more than once that you want to stop drinking. Stay with it.

CASE STUDY

I moved into a house with Caroline and Jacob and the kitchen was too small and the bathroom had no shower and so we built an extension. The builders demolished the garage and built out across the drive and we got an extra bedroom and a bigger bathroom with a walk-in shower and a bidet and downstairs a utility room for the washing machine and vented tumble-drier and I was wondering where we were going to put the litter tray for Caroline's cats when she told me she and Jacob were moving out.

I sit on the new sofa in the extension. This area is too cold. This area doesn't have enough radiators. This area doesn't have enough plug-sockets. What do you want plug-sockets here for they said. I said mobile phone chargers, lap-tops, Kindle chargers, battery-chargers, and anything else that somebody might invent. I didn't bother to say portable electric heaters. They said no. I was angry because I have built an extension before and it didn't have enough plug-sockets. I know about plug-sockets and radiators. There aren't enough in this extension.

It is time for me to put my walking-boots on and walk to the filling-station. I could get to the filling-station much quicker if I drove there in my car, but that would not be a good idea. It only takes about nine minutes to walk to the filling-station. Of course, it takes about nine minutes to walk back again from the filling-station, but it only takes about nine minutes to get there.

There are two ways to get out of my house. I usually go out of the front door, but this time I decide to go out of the patio door at the back. I unlock the patio door. I turn the patio lights on. I open the door. I step through the door. I come back in again and turn the patio lights off. I leave the door ajar, because I can.

I walk to the filling-station.

I select a bottle of Argentinian Carmenère. I would prefer the Malbec, but the Carmenère is two pounds cheaper. I select a bottle of Sauvignon Blanc which is slightly above my usual price range. I select two bottles of Indian lager which are on special offer.

There is no queue. As I place my basket down, I ask for a half-bottle of Smirnoff. I pay with my debit card.

This is about the eleventh time I have gone out with the patio door open.

The first, second and third times, nothing happened.

The fourth, fifth and sixth times, I found a cat on my kitchen counter, looking for food. It was a ginger cat which sprayed piss. I had to clean the kitchen with bleach.

The seventh, eighth, ninth and tenth times, nothing happened. There might have been another time.

Having let myself out through the patio doors at the back, so that I could drop some bottles into the recycling bin, I return through the front. I don't remember having left the lights on.

'Hello, John,' someone says.

'Hello, Scott,' someone else says. That is me.

'What are you doing here?' says Scott.

'I live here. What are you doing here?'

'I was hoping I might be able to stay here for a while.' That question is typical of Scott. I hate Scott. He leaves toast crumbs in the margarine. He takes hours and hours in the bathroom, and he leaves damp towels everywhere. He insists on having the television on all day, whether he is watching it, or not. He uses food, soap, shampoo, shaving foam, deodorant, detergent, and every consumable you can think of, except salt. He brings his own salt, which he broadcasts widely over the sofa and the carpet, every time he sprinkles it.

I think it is the salt that does it. Somehow, I get him to move out. I can't remember how I do it, or how long it takes. All I can remember is that the neighbours complain.

I am drinking white wine from the off-licence, for the

fourth night in a row. Tomorrow starts in one hour and fifteen minutes, and is Tuesday, a work day, but this is only week 1 and so I don't have to do much other than sign in.

I have fleas. I have had fleas since the last of Caroline's cats moved out. I sit on the upstairs toilet and watch the fleas jump onto my legs. I spray a bit of eau de toilette onto the bidet, which is next to the toilet, and then I pinch the flea between my thumb and forefinger. If you press a flea onto a surface covered in eau de toilette, it can't jump away. I think it must be the alcohol. It goes into a stupor, and then dies. I'm killing them at an average of about six or seven a day. I think the record for one day is twelve. It is either twelve or twenty-two.

I go to bed.

I wake up. I don't bother to set an alarm. If I did, I would probably sleep through it. Eventually, I get up.

I sit on the sofa in the kitchen-dining area downstairs, either in my dressing gown, or with my trousers rolled up, and I watch fleas jump onto my legs. Because the eau de toilette is upstairs, I destroy them with my fingernails. You pinch it at first and get it between your thumb and forefinger. Then you get it under your thumbnail. And then you bring up a fingernail, so that it gets caught between the hammer and the anvil. You can see the legs fanning out as you flatten it. It is easy to tell the difference between a live flea and one that has been destroyed. They are piling up on the floor. I wonder what eats dead fleas. Some kind of spider, possibly. I am not afraid of spiders. I have stopped cutting my fingernails. I have two pairs of nail scissors, and I know exactly where both of them are. I still cut my toenails, sometimes. Toenails are no use for killing fleas.

The problem is while I am asleep. I tend to pass out, which means that the fleas get to drink warm Bloody Mary all night, on tap from me. When I wake up, I inspect my lower legs. What I am looking for is pale pink spots. That means recent flea bites. I released poison gas in my bedroom a few weeks ago, but it doesn't seem to have cured the problem. I check my phone and my emails to make sure nothing has exploded at work, and then I run the bath. At least I have a tiled bathroom with a walk-in shower, a bath that is big enough for two, basin, toilet, bidet and towel-dryer. I can't afford to pay for it, but it is still mine, for now. I have given up on Molton Brown bath bubbles, because I can't afford eighteen quid for a bottle. I buy Radox from the Co-op. It isn't as good, but I put up with it.

I wash my lower legs, especially the areas that have started to bleed or suppurate because I have scratched them. I don't want to go septic. That would not do at all. I make sure to put plenty of soap suds on those areas. The warm water makes the new bites itch unbearably, and so I scratch both legs alternately for a long time, from my heels to my knees. While I am in the bath, it doesn't matter if some of the bites start to bleed.

There is cricket on the radio: a test match. I kick myself for having slept in beyond 11 o'clock.

I look for my spectacles. If they are on the chest of drawers next to the bed, or the window ledge in the bathroom, that probably means that I knew what I was doing when I went to bed the previous night. If they are under a sofa or in the fridge, it probably means I did not.

I put the kettle on. I take 40 milligrams of fluoxetine, sometimes with water and sometimes with the remains of a glass of wine. Sometimes I have remembered to put the wine glass in the fridge before I go to bed. Sometimes I haven't. I make tea. I make two cups, including one in Caroline's old lady's cup, as if she were still here. I add sugar if I have a hangover. I drink the tea.

I log on again and I find that something has happened at work. I start to deal with it. I'm actually working. I know what I'm doing and I'm good at it. It is too complicated to explain what I do.

I have put LED bulbs in the bathroom. It is cheaper, because I never turn that light off. At least there is one light that never goes out. I've had a letter from work and another which looks like it is from the police. I don't know when I am going to open them. The police one might be something to do with the car.

When all the work stuff is over, I still have some white wine and some lager left, and two of my friends are online.

ALISON MACLEOD

WE ARE METHODISTS

TOBY – HE tells me he's called Toby – heaves his toolbox and himself up the spiral of my staircase. Toby is a plumber. A heating engineer. I am a client. A new homeowner.

We know our parts.

At the top of the staircase, he stands and stares. Above us, the old chapel window rises twenty-five feet to a vast pine arch. Once, this window was a Methodist view on Creation, on the hills of East Brighton and its glittering sea.

'That's something,' he says, and is slow to turn away. Through the clear panes, to the north-east, the green flanks of the Downs rear up with spring. To the south, the sea is silvered in the midday light. Above the chimney pots, the gulls are ecstatic.

I watch Toby measure the window's proportions with his eyes. From floor to ceiling, eight bright stems of glass rise up, pane by pane, until they burst, high overhead, into four golden arches. These arches, in turn, bloom into three circular windows that nestle beneath the main arch. What is it about circles? I don't know. I suspect Toby doesn't know. Heads back, chins up, we're moved to silence. At the top of my staircase, suspended in a moment we will soon disregard, we're strangers.

'Coffee?' I ask.

I move into the organ loft that is now my kitchen.

He blinks. 'Thank you. Yes. Milk, one sugar.'

I dig in the boxes marked 'Kitchen Cupboards, 3 of 6'. My things seem unfamiliar. I find cups but no saucers. Toby opens the boiler cupboard and prises off the casing. He is stocky with a low belly. Early forties, I estimate. An oversized tattoo runs up his forearm through the curling dark hair: 'MADISON', it reads in cursive lettering.

It's Day One of our four-day works schedule. Toby tells me, haltingly, that, this morning, he'll do the full boiler service. The boiler is old, so he'll check the controls and clear away dirt and debris; he'll do a gas analysis to monitor carbon monoxide; he'll confirm there are no weeping joints; he'll test the circuitry, the fan pressure and the inlet pressure. He'll inspect the heat exchanger and the burner. He'll clean out the condensate trap.

Toby's mouth has seen better days. His front teeth are missing, along with the cuspids and miscellaneous others. I hear the soft nasal sing-song of a Birmingham accent. I imagine backstreet punch-ups in his youth.

He speaks quickly, mistrustful of his mouth, but finally, he nods, relieved to have got through the speech. Later I'll be sent an electronic survey from his company; it will ask me to confirm that, prior to the given job, Toby explained the full nature of it.

'Thank you.' I pass him a steaming coffee. 'You've made everything clear.'

He nods. His head is small and neat, almost feral; his hair is shorn close to his scalp. The dark stubble along his jawline is flecked with grey, and his eyelashes are thick like a child's. He lowers them often.

When his phone starts to vibrate, he sighs. 'Hi, love. Can't. On a job. I'll call you later, right?' He slides the phone into a pocket. 'My girlfriend,' he explains. 'She's a lot younger.' He smiles apologetically. 'She does my head in.'

'That's wonderful,' I hear myself say. I make no sense.

Toby reaches, quickly, for a pair of pliers.

I blush and lift the vase of nearly dead tulips from the kitchen table. A new neighbour deposited the yellow bunch on my doorstep on the day of the move. At the sink, I turn away and let the water run and run. I cannot say what I actually meant: that I hope his broken mouth will kiss and be kissed. I cannot say it because what could it possibly matter to me?

In recent days, the tulips drooped, drowsy as narcoleptics. Now, their yellow heads are full-blown, too weighty for their slender stems and leaves. Since yesterday, they've been resting only millimetres above the tabletop, a lost cause. I fill the vase anyway. A distraction. An excuse.

Toby keeps his eyes, front and centre, on the boiler's innards. I switch on Radio 4, waiting for its calm to neutralise the atmosphere; to cover the odd sense of domesticity into which we've been cast. The proximity of strangers is a peculiar thing, and the open-plan design means there is nowhere to hide. I unpack dishes, pots, canisters, oven mitts, a stray pair of socks and a bra. I stuff the latter in a kitchen drawer.

Even so, when it happens, it seems wrong not to risk it, wrong not to say, 'Look. Toby, look at the tulips.' He turns, I point and, together, we watch the oversized heads rise, infinitesimally higher and higher, in an act of blind, magnificent will.

'You wouldn't think,' he murmurs.

'No,' I breathe.

I fold tea towels and behold the resurrection. He tinkers again in the boiler cupboard, glancing back to watch it over his shoulder. Before long, the tulips are half their natural height and still rising.

'Life,' he says. 'Bloody stubborn, isn't it.'

We find our equilibrium.

'Biscuit?' I venture.

He shakes his head and adjusts a pressure valve. 'Never eat in the day.'

'No breakfast?'

'Coffee only – till dinner time.'

There's something fight-or-flight-like in his bearing, a potential clenched in his shoulders. Yet his movements are slow, wary. 'See this dial?'

I walk to his side.

'The needle should hover around the *one* mark. When it's too low, just top it up, with this black knob.'

'Right.' I nod. 'Yes.'

He picks up his coffee. We look to the sea. Half a dozen sailboats navigate the dazzle, white sails tipping on the breeze.

'That's a view,' he says.

'Yes,' I say.

At home in Portslade, if he crooks his head a certain way in his toddler's room, he can just see a skinny 'V' of sea. He has a fishing boat which he hasn't had out since his youngest – Madison – was born. It's moored at Newhaven, waiting to be scraped and sanded. He says: 'I know I should say "she", like all the marina types do, but I always feel daft saying that.'

'I do too,' I say. I fold another tea towel. 'Maybe the "she" of me resists.'

'Feminist,' he says. 'That explains it.'

I look up. 'Explains what?'

'Being good looking and on your own.' He carries on tinkering in the cupboard. 'Me, I'm ugly and *surrounded*. Ex-wife always on the blower. Our son up in Stoke getting himself into trouble. My girlfriend. Plus her mates in our kitchen most nights of the week. I used to wonder why they behaved like teenagers till I realised they are teenagers, or not far off. Then there's her mother tutting and painting her toenails on the *Radio Times*. Not to mention our three kiddies. Each night when I get home, the two older boys are either on the PlayStation or torturing the cat. Forgot to mention the cat. One old, incontinent cat.' He looks up. 'It's a madhouse basically.'

These days, he says, the boat is like someone else's memory. So he makes do with an old reel near Hove Lagoon, at the edge of Fatboy Slim's private beachfront. As he speaks, he draws his arm back and casts an imaginary line in a long fluid gesture. Suddenly he is supple. His eyes shine.

But his fishing is interrupted by his phone. 'A perfect demonstration,' he tells me, 'of why I never take my phone when I'm off out with my reel.'

I turn off the radio.

'Like I said, love – can't.' He rolls his eyes for my benefit, then stabs the phone with his finger, and returns to the gauge hooked up to the boiler.

I hold out a packet of biscuits. 'Sure?'

He waves it politely away. 'I hear my kids say, "I'm starving! Dad, I'm *starving*." As if.' He starts to laugh, then draws in his upper lip.

I carry on unpacking boxes and smile. 'We have no idea, do

we?' Olive oil. Balsamic. Sea salt. Quinoa. Wild rice. Omega oil and green tea supplements.

The boiler fires up, so that, at first, I hardly hear him. 'It's an agony,' he says. 'Plain and simple.'

I straighten. I've missed some causal link.

'After the first week it gets a little easier. Because your body is giving up, and your head feels like it's floating away.' His words are a fast-moving stream. 'And that's what calms you down finally, what saves you, that floating feeling, as you start to die.' He turns and stares through the window at the twenty-five feet of consecrated sky.

In the direct light, lines and shadows appear on his face. I stand, clutching vitamin bottles.

He walks across the room to the nearest radiator and turns the bleed key. His hands are small and solid, but the joints on his fingers look overlarge, misshapen. A silence opens up between us, wide as a crevasse. His brow tightens, then in he lurches. 'There were four of us. All from the 42nd Commando Division. We were dropped into a port town near Basra. Iraq. March 2003. You know.' He glances up, smiling faintly. 'That malarkey.'

I nod. I fold my arms. To be steady.

'One minute, you're up in the Hercules, breathing in a hundred per cent oxygen so you don't get the bends, and the next minute you're in free fall for the longest fifteen seconds of your life. You have to pull the ripcord when you're crazy high up – twenty-five thousand feet – because otherwise, the sound of the chutes opening might be detected by the enemy lower down. The world is roaring around you and at the same time everything's deadly quiet, and the four of us form up in a stack, like quadruplets waiting to drop. All you want is to feel the ground beneath your feet. The chap at the bottom of the stack is the one with the compass. No GPS then. We're drifting cross-country, across a desert without landmarks, and just praying we don't freeze to death. It's minus twenty-nine degrees in the air, then forty-five degrees in the Drop Zone when we hit. Nothing prepares you for that.

'The truth is, nothing prepares you for any of it. When you do land, it's all rock and sand, so everything's always giving way underfoot. You can hardly run. Not even when you're twenty-three and fitter than you'll ever be again and your life depends on it' – his voice drops – 'which it did more or less.' He shrugs. 'Got ourselves captured on Day One, didn't we.' His eyes darken and the lashes dip.

'God,' I say. 'How awful.'

The radiator bangs and chokes, as if the dust of the desert is here too. 'Air lock,' he says.

He glances up, checking that I'm okay; checking that I'm not checking the clock. Then he looks away again. 'They left us tied to metal chairs in that heat. Four of us in a row in a concrete courtyard. By the second week, they didn't even need to tie us up because there was nowhere to go. No way out and no way back inside. We were dehydrated. Starving. We sat till we fell off. You only knew you'd fallen off when you came to on the ground. After a point, you were just glad of the chair. You're baking in the heat but you love your bloody chair.'

'I'm so sorry,' I say.

'I never had much religion but what I had left me out there.'

I pull out two kitchen chairs. Neither of us sits.

'Of course,' I say. 'No wonder.'

'No wonder. No feeling. No nothing after. Because all that

heat gets inside you and it flares sometimes. Like when my mates go on about their Sky being on the blink. Or when my ex-wife gets upset because I won't help pay for her European city break. Or when I see a busker in Brighton. Ever seen that chap in the zebra costume playing piano in East Street? I think, is he why we were tied to chairs? So he could dress like a zebra and play the piano? Did I join up so that, one day, my kids could feel deprived if they weren't given two-for-one Cadbury eggs? Not that I'm complaining. All that's *normal.* It's *not* normal to prefer fish to people. I know that. It's *not* normal to get worked up about a grown man who calls himself Fatboy Slim and owns the best of the flipping beachfront. Only trouble is, a couple years ago, I came off my motorbike, and the MoD claimed I tried to top myself. Now they're withholding my pension. I didn't try anything – a car came round the corner – but they're keeping it anyway.' He looks up. 'My girlfriend doesn't know.'

'About the pension.'

'No.' He turns the bleed key. 'About Iraq.'

In the morning, I'm woken by the buzzing of my phone beside the bed. It's ten past seven on the clock. 'Hello,' I say. I hear the sound of a child splashing in the bath. 'Hello?' Then the call is ended.

I check my log. Toby's number.

An accidental call. I go back to sleep.

But when I open my bedroom door, a hot breeze laps at my legs and a fine layer of yellow sand eddies across the floor.

At half past eight, Toby appears carrying six-foot lengths of copper piping over his shoulder and a long hose looped over one arm. He deposits it all, heads out to the company van and returns, manoeuvring a wet-dry vacuum.

I boil the kettle. I don't mention the call. I don't mention the desert sand.

Today, it's another speech. His boss is a sadist. 'I'll move the radiator as per. That means I'll have to drain the radiators first, on both levels. Don't worry. I'll run the extractor hose outside. I'll also need to remove the rad nearest the front door – because it doesn't have a drain-off valve. I'll cut and relocate the pipework, reposition the radiator you want moved and make tight the compressed joint-work. The soldering will stink – sorry about that – but it will clear quickly if you open a few windows. I'll plumb the rad back up, fill the new system and add inhibitor. Then I'll bleed off the air, and fix a drain-off valve to make jobs easier in the future.' He consults a mental checklist. 'I'll lay a water blanket and will hoover any spillages. I'll leave it like I found it. Three to four hours' work. We don't paint the new pipework but I recommend the use of a primer.' Spit dribbles down his chin, and he turns to wipe it with his sleeve.

'Thank you,' I say.

His gums are red and vulnerable when he smiles. I can see the uncertainty in his eyes, now that he's clear of the speech. He's wondering if he said too much yesterday. I'm wondering too.

Upstairs in my kitchen, he leans against the banister, careful to avoid the laundry drying in the morning light. 'You'll be suntanning up here by August.'

Through my chapel window, we study the ridge of the Downs. The hills, the grass, the salt-bitten edges seem lit from within.

'You're going to need binoculars,' he adds.

The sea today is lagoon-green near the shore, turquoise where the shelf of England drops off and – deeper still, farther out – the fierce blue of the open Channel.

He is about to make a start on the drainage when it appears: the Portsmouth-to-Caen ferry, edging into view like a phantom ship. In outline, it looks too big, too bloated to be so close to shore.

'Shouldn't that be in the Solent?' he asks.

I nod. 'It passed the West Pier a few hours ago, adrift apparently. They were saying on the news. Just a skeleton crew. No passengers. I suppose it must still be going, carried on the tide.'

He squints into the day. 'Sounds like someone's big-whoops to me.'

'French ferry strike today. So the berth in Portsmouth is overfull, and they put this one to sea. No engines – to save fuel. They're calling it a "calculated drift".'

His smile is half grimace. 'Next time someone asks me what I'm up to, I'm going to borrow that. *Calculated drift*. "I'm in a calculated drift."'

We watch the lonely monolith of steel.

'Perhaps your girlfriend *should* know,' I say.

Two hours later, as the ferry drifts beyond my chapel arch, I call down the stairs. 'Almost gone.'

'God bless her,' he calls over his soldering torch, 'and all who forgot to sail in her!'

The stink of burnt metal rises. I heave windows open. 'Toby, you couldn't give me a hand, could you?' I forgot. Fresh laundry is everywhere. Sheets are drying over chairs, railings, my sofa, the kitchen table.

'I did warn you,' he calls.

'You did. So much for Lemon Fresh.' I reach for a sheet from the banister, pulling it up and across.

He goes to the stairs below, gets hold of the far edge and travels up, sparing it the dust of each step. 'My girlfriend can't keep house to save her life, but she's good with the kids and that, and she says they'll fuss in a few years if we're not married – sticklers for rules, kids are – so I did it. I booked the Registry Office.'

'Congratulations,' I say, beaming for him. 'That's lovely news.' I think of his broken mouth filled with vows.

'Second time round for me. When you're a marine, they say: marry desperate. Because anyone truly sane would have to be desperate to marry a Royal Marine. Anna, my ex, was out of my league. My own father said as much, but I ignored him. I was doolally for her.'

We shake out the sheet and pull it taut between us. Then we begin a quadrille of meetings and separations, slow at first, halting, until we find our momentum – reaching and folding, reaching and folding. When the sheet is reduced to a compact square of linen, we find ourselves stopped, hand to hand. 'They don't look it,' he says, 'but my hands are clean. The nails are only black where they didn't heal right after they were pulled.'

I blink. 'So you've set a date. That's wonderful.'

'She wants me to get dental implants first. She says, you only have one set of wedding photographs. I've told her about the last time, but she forgets, you know, on purpose like.'

I lay the folded sheet on the table, and he reaches for the next. Meet and fold. Meet and fold. 'I keep trying to explain there won't be any date if I have to pay for implants. And when I see my mouth, I'm fine with it. It reminds me – I got off easy.'

He turns his face to the vaulted ceiling and wooden beams high over our heads. 'Original, those.' He points to the iron truss that runs the length of the kitchen and living room. 'And that. A single blacksmith made that. Not a foundry. A single man. Look at those iron knuckles. You could swing from that truss, and it wouldn't budge.'

'Sometimes,' I say, 'I stand here and imagine all those prayers downstairs in the old nave, a century's worth offered up.'

'It's peaceful here.' He nods. 'Solid.' Downstairs, among his tools, his phone buzzes but he ignores it. 'She was only ten in 2003. She knows I was a marine but she doesn't want details. The past is passed. Fair enough, I said. She said she thought she remembered it being on the news. The Invasion.'

We begin our quadrille again. The sheets in our hands hold the warmth of April. On my kitchen table, the tulips are risen. At the top of the chapel window, the circular panes cast mandalas of light. A breeze moves through the skylight windows. Prayers roost in my roof space. Together we are Methodists.

Then Toby passes me the last sheet, grabs a blue corner and glances over the banister to check the drain-off hose downstairs. 'Your teeth,' he says, 'they're beautiful.'

That evening, the call comes around nine.

'Hello?' I say. I press my ear to a burble of voices and tinny, distant music. I wait, staring at my bedroom ceiling. 'Toby?'

The phone must be in his pocket. He's sitting on it. Down the pub.

I end the call.

In the night, beneath my chapel window, yellow sand drifts against the whitewashed walls. It piles high under the staircase.

At first light, I find the broom.

The new day brings taps and showerheads. Toby's been to the wholesalers'. I show him to the en suite where he checks the old taps a final time. 'Limescale, end of,' he says.

No speech today. He's broken free.

'In Stoke, where I grew up,' he tells me, 'the water is beautiful and soft.'

'Miss it?' I ask.

'Couldn't wait to get away, to join up.'

'And now?'

'I was married for years up there, and like I said, I've one teenage boy. I'm only down here because my girlfriend is a local girl. We met online. But being away seems to get harder, not easier, as you get older. Funny that.'

I nod. I see him as a boy, scrambling down the steep, stern valleys of the River Trent with his rod and box of bait, when he dreamed of seeing farther than the next valley.

'You? Family?' he asks.

'Not here.'

'Husband?' he asks.

'Divorced.'

'Significant Other?'

'Dead,' I say, '2003.'

'That bloody year again.' He unscrews the limescaled taps. 'Other Persons of Interest?'

I pass him a towel. 'That would be telling.'

He nods and turns to study the blocked showerhead. 'I thought you must be lonely. Betwixt and between. Now, me, I'd *pay* to be lonely. When I get home each night, like I said, it's a madhouse. And at weekends, my boys don't want to go out to fish with their old dad, not even when I say we'll put the boat on the water. I try to tidy up and join in with telly nights and that, but mostly I look around my house, and I think where am I? *Where the hell am I?* I go sit in Madison's room with a cup of tea or a brew. Sanity. You have to take it where you find it. Like yesterday. A customer in Lewes – you know Lewes? – he forgot to leave the keys.' He looks back to me and smiles shyly. 'Guess what I got up to?'

'Burned a cross?'

He looks at the floor and laughs. 'You're peculiar. I like that. I went to Anne of Cleves's House. No one else there. Had the run of the place. I like History. You like History?'

I smile. 'I like History.'

'Teacher? Lecturer?'

'Lecturer.'

'Thought so. No telly. All the books. Your moving men must have been glad to see the back of you.' He whistles. 'Lecturer. That's brave. If I had the choice between having to speak in public or having my fingers broken all over again, I know which I'd choose. Why do you think my teeth are like this? I asked someone once to smash them in, just to get me out of a job interview.'

My eyes widen. 'You didn't.'

He laughs again. 'Your face is a picture.' He looks away. 'A picture.'

In the en suite, we negotiate the narrow space. I look down, he looks up, we lift our ribcages and shuffle. I demonstrate the problem with the showerhead, the paltry spray. 'Low water pressure?'

We trade places and he clambers into the shower space. As he reaches up to the fitting, he appears, briefly, naked in my mind's eye, ready to soap an armpit. He's thirty-six. I did the maths. Younger than I realised, and older in himself than anyone should be. For a moment, he is a still photograph. A freeze-frame. No longer my plumber. I see the solemn gravity of his body, the dark energy of his pupils, the tenderness of his eyelashes and the truth in the unsteady line of his throat.

Toby strains higher to get a grip on the showerhead, but just as his spanner clamps on, his phone goes off. He passes me the spanner, hits 'Decline Call' and mimes, for my entertainment, the cutting of his own throat. 'My girlfriend. Who else?' When it rings again, a minute later, he climbs out of the shower, takes a seat on the loo and buries his eyes in his hand. 'No, love. Not yet. I'll be here a few more hours.'

I tidy the towels on the rack.

'Yes, it *is* a big job.'

I begin to slide past him, out of the room, but he shakes his head at me.

'Of course I haven't forgotten.' He murmurs into his phone. 'Yes, I *have* told her.'

Then he slides the mobile into his pocket and looks past my shoulder. 'Forgot to say. Doctor's appointment tomorrow. Not sure when they'll see me. Apparently, I just have to go along and hope.'

'Nothing serious?' It's what you say.

He massages a spot near his sternum. 'I've been hoping for months it would just go away. Right here. A lump. As big as fuck – sorry.' He looks up. He's spooked himself. 'Had a good look in the mirror the other week. I call it Saddam. It looks like him in profile.' From his perch on the toilet, he studies the showerhead again. 'I reckon somewhere in Basra there's a bloke with a tumour called Tony.' He extends his palm; I return the spanner. 'I just hope to Christ it's not breast cancer. My old navy mates would never let me live that one down.'

In the night, later than last time, my mobile rings. I hear a TV, a door closing, the scraping of a chair.

'Hello?' I try.

'Are you the one at the church?' a girl says.

'Who is this?' I say.

I know who it is.

'Is he with you? Is he there now?'

Outside my window, there's no moon. You wouldn't know there was a sea.

Bearings. Such delicate things.

I end the call.

In the morning, I rub the sand from my eyes. It crunches in my molars. Under my new showerhead, I rinse it from my hair and rub it from my scalp.

When Toby returns three days later, for the final job, the installation of a thermostat, he lowers his gear and a cardboard box to the floor, climbs my staircase and seats himself on the uppermost stair.

I follow him up and cock my head. 'So?'

'So?' he says, his face blank.

It's none of my business. 'What did the doctor say about Saddam?'

He bites the plastic packaging off the box. 'Moobs, yes,

deffo. Breast cancer, no. No lung cancer either, as it happens.'

And the lump? I want to ask. *What about the lump?*

He opens the box, lifts out my new thermostat, and fishes for the installation instructions. He rummages in his toolbox, lifts out a glasses case and waves his specs. 'You'd never know I used to be a sniper.'

Watch.

A sniper is an expert marksman at a thousand yards. His vision is perfect or near perfect. When he isn't shooting, he is able to run three miles in eighteen minutes. He can perform a hundred sit-ups and twenty pull-ups in two minutes. He can execute the low crawl, medium crawl, high crawl and hand-and-knees crawl while carrying a hundred-pound pack, an L115A3 rifle and a 9mm pistol.

He can navigate by day and night. He can draw an accurate field sketch. He understands the vanishing point. He knows the imagination can distort. There can be no history of mental illness.

A sniper must move undetected. He must not smoke, move suddenly, use soap, wear insect repellent or arouse birds or wildlife. He relies on his spotter. The spotter will calculate wind velocity, the position of the sun, the grid coordinates and the range of all weapons prior to each shot.

On that searing March day in 2003, four men landed in the Drop Zone of Umm Qasr. 'Two teams,' Toby explains, 'in all that light. Two men too many.'

In desert areas, camouflage must be tan and brown.

A sniper uncovers his riflescope only when aiming at a target.

A sniper must not shine.

That day, Toby shone. While the four men lay prone on a rooftop across from the corner shop from which the target was about to emerge, Toby's St Jude medal slipped outside his T-shirt, outside his combats, and glinted in the midday light.

Later, in the concrete courtyard, the butt of an AK47 would break his skull and knock out his teeth. It would crush his fingers, break an arm and smash his ribs. Each day, the four men were pushed into the four chairs.

His first tour, his first assignment.

One morning, a bird, a warbler of some kind, sang overhead. *Kaka-kee, kaka-kee, kaka-kee*. Toby didn't hear the footsteps. Two shots rang out. Only when he opened his eyes did he understand that he wasn't dead.

A scan revealed the lump on Toby's sternum to be a protective scar of bone; a final, slow mending where the ribs had rejoined the sternum.

I take a seat on the stair below him and stare straight ahead. 'How did you get out of the courtyard?'

He stalls, choosing his words for me. 'The two of us fought our way out.'

I understand what cannot be said to a stranger, in a stranger's new home. They killed their way out.

I don't turn around. 'Your girlfriend calls me,' I say, 'on your phone.'

'Ah,' he says. 'She say anything?'

'Not really.'

'Right,' he says.

'I suspect she knows you're keeping something from her.'

Behind me, he's nodding. Without turning, I know he's nodding. And staring at his hands.

'Another woman?' I try.

'Almost,' he says. I can hear the smile in his voice. 'Fatboy Slim.' He shifts on the stair. 'At night when it warms up like it has, I sneak out, pull on my waders and fish from his surf. No bathers to bother you, no one to see, and the bass bite best at night in spring and summer. I'm pretty good now at casting, hooking and landing them in the dark. Nice bloke actually. Don't expect he'd mind. I don't bother anyone. Before I leave, I hide my fish on the public side and return first thing to collect them, before work.'

'It seems you've been spotted. At home, I mean.'

'Point taken. Yep. After the kids are in bed, I slip out our back door. With her friends being over, I didn't think—' Behind me, I hear him rub his whiskered face. 'I leave my phone. I mute it and hide it under Madison's mattress. Can't risk it lighting up in the surf in the dark.'

'I'm fairly sure it wasn't Madison on the line.'

'No. Sorry. I'll sort it.'

'Maybe she knows you're keeping something more from her. More than the outings in the dark.'

'I am. As you know.' He hesitates. 'And it can keep. Now it can, I mean. That's what I mean. Now it can.'

'Right,' I say. 'That's good,' I say.

I feel his hand, light, fleeting, on my shoulder. 'You're a fine Methodist woman.'

I turn and peer up. His grin is broad.

'That's a comfort.' I bite back a smile. 'But I forgot to say. Our tulips are dead. I mean, totally dead this time.'

He sighs. 'Total death. It comes to us all in the end. Including the two *beautiful* bass I landed last night.' His smile breaks out again. 'They're on ice in the back of the van. Not gutted yet, but I could give you one if you like.'

'You're all right,' I say. 'Next time maybe.'

I look away again.

And together, beneath my chapel window, we sit in pools of morning shadow while, somewhere beyond the bright panes, the Portsmouth-to-Caen ferry is slowly returned to port.

ADRIAN SLATCHER

LIFE GRABS

ELVIS WAS IN tears. The big man had watched the film time after time. It had been given to him by the police, who either had no need for it any more, or had finally remembered that the father should get a copy.

His son's last movements, caught on CCTV, first as he leaves the school, then, just briefly parking his bike up outside the shop, and you can see him walk in the door, move purposefully to where the sweets and ice creams are, and just a glimpse of him at the till, with a bag of sweets; then, finally – and you wouldn't know it was him if it wasn't segued into this montage – cycling away past the blue car, back on the pavement and round the corner, out of the way of the CCTV for ever.

Little Magnet he used to call his son, sticking to me like a little magnet. He'd called him Malcolm, an old-fashioned name that he hoped he'd grow into. Little Mal, smallest boy in the class, but not afraid of anything or anyone.

The earlier part of the film shows him clearly. He is at a wedding dancing with the little girl from next door who isn't that little and towers above him, and then there's a short panned shot of him caught in the front row of the choir, dressed like all the other little boys and girls, but fidgeting more than most of them. And the latest bit of footage, the bit that Elvis prefers, just taken that last Christmas. The neighbour had brought round the video camera, and it's Mal speaking to camera, 'I am Mal, and this is my daddy . . .' and collapsing in laughter as Elvis comes into the picture and grabs him. Shrieking with joy as he whizzes through the air, head spinning.

They said it was a man, aged perhaps fifty, with a beard. There's no CCTV footage of this, just the grab of the blue car, which was later abandoned. The case had never been closed.

Elvis has the tape in his hand. It's a precious thing, but tapes aren't much use any more. The shop said they'd do a tape-to-DVD transfer.

'Be careful,' he says, handing it over, 'it's the only copy I've got.' The boy behind the counter is about Mal's age. Mal's age as he would be now.

When he goes back in the shop a couple of days later Elvis is worried, worried that something will have happened to the tape, but the assistant hands him a bag with two DVD copies and the tape.

Elvis hands over the money, and says thank you. He doesn't quite know what to say, but suddenly it's very important that he knows what precisely the boy has seen.

'Do you watch them?' he asks.

'What?'

'When people give you tapes do you watch them?'

'I have to watch some bits. The start. The end. If there's some edits. But those wedding videos!' He rolls his eyes. 'Some marriages don't last that long.' It's a joke that feels out of place, and the assistant appears to regret saying it.

'Hi, I'm Simon. I watched it. I remember,' he says.

'Remember?'

'Remember the disappearance. I was in his class. Actually I was in the year above, but they sometimes put us all together when a teacher was ill.'

'It must seem a long time ago to you. He was only . . .'

' . . . eight. He was only eight. I was nine. They called us all into assembly and said there had been a terrible thing happened and that if anybody knew anything, anything at all, then they wouldn't get into trouble but they'd better tell a teacher.'

'I think about him every day.'

Simon looked a bit embarrassed. 'I'm sorry, for your loss – you and your wife – it must have been . . .' His sentence tailed off.

'It's just me. It was just me and him. That made it worse. She never forgave me.'

'For what?'

'For losing him.'

The big man was close to tears, but he'd been close to tears ever since that day. Time dulled the pain, that was all – or rather, it made the pain the one familiar thing. He'd miss the pain, he realised now. There were those soldiers who had their leg amputated and they could still feel the leg there even though it was now just a 'phantom'.

Malcolm was just a phantom: they'd never found him and never found the man.

'I remember him, from the video,' said Simon. 'All these things came back to me, that I hadn't thought about in years.'

'Were you friends?'

'Not really,' he said, 'it didn't work like that. There were gangs and you were with one gang and then with another gang, and sometimes it was one big gang, but only for a day or two and then it would break up again.'

'I didn't know. He seemed to be on his own a lot of the time.'

'We were all alone a lot of the time,' said Simon. 'What do you think happened?'

'I think he's dead', said Elvis, simply. It was a lie. But it was easier than the truth. The truth might be that there would be a knocking on his door late at night, with someone from the porn squad, with a load of other videos, showing some men buggering his Little Magnet. For a while, he'd started researching child abductions, even visiting paedophiles in jails. Once he'd shown a picture of Mal, on the beach, to one of these monsters, and the look on his face had been enough for him never to go back. Had he been able to get on his own with him he was certain he'd have broken the man's neck. He even started looking for pictures on the internet, himself. These were the days when you had to dial up and a photograph would take a few minutes to download. He'd watched agonisingly as his request to one of the newsgroups had come up with his specific request, 'mixed-race boy, aged between 6-10'. Each time it wasn't Malcolm, he'd felt both relieved and sad. The tension of waiting for the picture, not knowing if you were going to see something abominable, or just a normal, healthy picture of a boy on the beach, was what made it worse.

Then they changed the law, so that even looking for these pictures was a crime. Every now and then, late at night, with his much faster connection, having had a few too many drinks, and unable to sleep, Elvis would go searching again.

The online world had become more complex, more depraved, it seemed; but the ways into these sites where men traded pictures and videos of young boys weren't so easy to find, and Elvis wasn't really looking, he just wanted to find.

Elvis worked as a security guard, doing nights, and would come in before his shift started. If he came round on a Friday afternoon, it was pretty quiet, and Simon could shut half an hour early and take him round the back, show him all the equipment, the rows and rows of recorders and duplicators.

'Everything's recorded now,' marvelled Elvis, 'and I've only so little of Malcolm. It doesn't seem fair.'

'It's all digital now – storage – endless,' said Simon, in the chopped-up way that his generation talked. Elvis realised that his son would speak like a text message if he had lived. Yet, when he'd disappeared there wasn't such a thing. He marvelled at that as if it was another mystery, almost as powerful as the mystery of the disappearance.

'They used to wipe the tapes – or rotate them – look . . .'

He pulled out some footage, similar to the footage on the tape the police had put together, a grainy image with a time-stamp at the bottom.

'I collect these from car boots,' said Simon. 'I'm making a montage – of stuff.'

Elvis laughed. 'I'd like to see it some time. More interesting than all those wedding videos.'

The next time Elvis came round, Simon called him into the back and sat him down.

'It's not finished yet,' he said, 'but here's our street . . .'

He clicked a mouse and the screen started running a film – or rather a series of short films spliced together to tell a somewhat jerky story. Elvis recognised the walk he'd take from his house to the video shop, then it moved off, and took him past the place where Malcolm had gone missing, and over to the school. It was like the footage of the police tape but more complete somehow.

'I've split everything up,' said Simon, 'and then keep filling in the pieces. Watch again.'

And this time there were some subtle differences. Where Simon only had one piece of film it was repeated but, where he had more than one, the scene changed subtly. Instead of two boys parking up outside the sweetshop, there was an old lady. The trees changed from summer green to winter brown.

'Can you put him in there?' said Elvis, suddenly excited.

'What?'

'My video. Malcolm. Can you put that in there?'

Simon nodded, looking uncertain.

'Do it, please.'

'I'll just realign the sequence – and pull in – yes, I've still got that on the server, Elvis McCardle, got your file here . . .'

And in it popped. The familiar footage but this time the day seemed different, the world seemed different.

'It's at this point he comes out of the shop . . .' said Elvis, and sure enough he did, 'and past the blue car . . . the blue car's not there, Simon. The blue car's not there!' He sounded delirious with happiness, as if somehow the change of sequence had changed the past.

'It's a different scene,' said Simon. 'I split them as small as they can go.'

'There it is again,' said Elvis, sadly, as the scene jumped again. The blue car was there and round the corner went Malcolm. 'I have to see where he goes . . .'

Simon nodded. He changed the route so that the video now followed round the corner. There was nothing there. The scenery had changed, even the road markings. There was a new speed camera and some speed bumps.

'Re-run that . . .' Elvis implored.

Simon did so. This time the footage was older, closer in time to the day when Malcolm had gone missing. It jerked forward. There were two boys on bikes coming the other direction.

'I've not seen them before . . .' said Elvis, 'maybe they knew something . . .'

Simon paused the film. The time in the bottom right-hand corner was six months after.

Elvis sat back in his chair and asked Simon if he could have a copy.

'It's just an experiment . . .' said Simon. 'It only exists on my computer.'

'There must be more clues . . . more things. I need to see him change, grow older, I need to see what happens to him when he leaves the camera,' he said. 'I can pay you . . .'

'I'm not sure . . .'

'I might be able to get you more film,' he said, 'more old film.'

The next week he was back with a large holdall full of films.

'Old CCTV footage,' he said, proudly. 'Stuff from cases, all copies, just don't tell anyone where you got them.'

Everything was on camera these days. He'd read somewhere that there was a CCTV camera for every five people in the country. Had Malcolm gone missing today they might not have found him, but they'd have seen a lot more of him.

Everyone had video cameras on their phones, kids taking selfies. As Simon worked on expanding the footage, and putting it into his computer model environment, Elvis stood outside the schools, next to the shops, all these places with cameras. He noted down names and numbers.

'If they're digital, they're stored,' Simon had said, 'we can probably get the direct feed – we just need to know which systems they are using . . .'

Elvis got a job as a night watchman for the security company that looked after the area. There was a little room at the top of one of the office blocks where CCTV feeds from private houses, businesses, factories and schools came in. His job was to monitor activity. He took down the information that Simon had asked him for and passed it on; the feeds were now being sucked directly into Simon's model, making it more complex. Simon had begun applying some other touches taken from computer-gaming environments. He could take a car from one place and move it around. At first it didn't look realistic, but he soon improved on it, until it was perfect.

Both of them wanted more. Simon realised that it was still only an approximation of the real world. He overlaid street data, he overlaid map data. Eventually there was nothing more he could do to his structure. Elvis wanted to see his little boy outlive the frame, move beyond the confines of that fateful day, and the few surviving images. The first time they were able to take Malcolm's bike and transpose it, Elvis cried. His son – or what looked like his son – was choosing to go a different route, away from the blue car, to safety.

At home that evening he watched the footage that Simon had quickly copied to a DVD. The film was the familiar one, but different.

'What happened to you?' Elvis wondered, as the footage dissolved. He wondered what his son would look like now. He couldn't even begin to think.

Elvis knew what he had to do. He was due on shift in fifteen minutes, the early evening one, a similar time to when Malcolm had gone missing. The night watchman's job wasn't just to watch the screens, but to check that the screens were doing their job correctly. Every now and then a screen would blow and whoever was on duty needed to go and investigate. The CCTV cameras would continue to take their evidence.

He had a plan. It took him three attempts, but eventually he managed to throw a sack over the CCTV camera that was furthest from the office. He knew that whoever was on shift before him would have to investigate.

Elvis ran quickly across to the shop where Malcolm had gone missing. He lingered outside, cautious of the time. He was lucky. There were two boys on bikes, about Malcolm's age when he disappeared. Boys on bikes had been stopping at this shop since Elvis himself was a child. It wasn't perfect. There were two of them, and they might not go the way he wanted. He lingered outside the doorway.

'Here,' he said, to the first kid as he came out of the shop, 'can you do us a favour? My boy's supposed to be here at five. Ryan. You know him?'

He'd picked the name at random, but he figured there had to be a dozen Ryans in their year.

'Think so, mate,' the kid said, looking him up and down. 'Waddayawant?'

'I've a dickey leg,' said Elvis, pointing down. 'Can you pop round the corner and see if anyone's coming? I'm in a bit of a hurry. He's your age, blue coat, racing bike a bit like your mate's. There's a pack of smokes in it for you.'

And Elvis dangled the contraband.

The second kid came out as the first had biked out of sight.

'Your mate's gone that way . . .' said Elvis, pointing in the other direction. He didn't need the fake hobble now.

He rushed to where the blue car was parked. He got in the front, and slowly drove out from the spot.

He turned round the corner.

Where was the kid?

Then he saw him. Sat down on the roadside. Bike beside him.

He drove towards him.

'No sign?' he said winding down the window. 'I'll kill the bugger.'

'Where's me fags, mate?'

'Oh yeah.'

Elvis held them out and put them on the passenger seat.

'Door's open.'

The kid came over to the door, and reached over. Elvis was too quick.

'Hey, mister, let me go.'

Elvis pulled him over and slapped him in the mouth. The kid started crying.

'Be quiet, and you'll be all right.

'What do you want?' the kid shrieked.

'I just want to know what happens next.'

Elvis, in the blue car, drove away, looking up at every speed camera, every CCTV camera. He knew them all. They all fed into Simon's model. Updating every few seconds, or live, with the slightest delay.

I just want to know what happens next, he texted to Simon. The car moved slowly away. It could no longer be observed by any camera.

M JOHN HARRISON

DOG PEOPLE

I MET MYRA at the Arts Club. It was lunchtime on the sort of summer day which makes you want to eat outside, off a table with a luminous white cloth. The girls touch the statue of Aphrodite for luck, imagining her to have blonde hair and bare arms like their own. They look down admiringly at the healthy balding suntanned heads of the men who have signed them in. My own date had failed to appear.

The Arts Club isn't a good place to be blown off in, especially at lunchtime. People who have also been blown off, or are about to be blown off, or are about to admit to being blown off, eye you with hatred as you walk past. They want no reminders. Among them that day was the ugliest woman I had ever seen. Her head had the qualities of an ethnic bronze, massive and massively proportioned, all the features of which overstate some powerful but recently obsolete cultural dictum. She swung it slowly left and right. She stared at her watch, ordered a glass of house red.

'I'm waiting,' I heard her tell the barman, 'for this wretched person I wouldn't even recognise.'

I asked him if I could have a club sandwich. Recently he had stopped cautioning me, 'And you are a member, aren't you sir?' every time I ordered a drink. I told him I would have the sandwich outside. 'The table nearest Cupid,' I said. Cupid, a rational little deity, perches out there in the Arts Club garden, on a mossy clam shell between two terracotta urns, shooting his arrow of water into the air above a black pond decorated with green weed. He presides over affairs, one night stands, change. He serves the club members with the endless debacles they mistake for an emotional life. I was ignoring him when the woman with the massive head came and stood by my table.

'You don't mind,' she told me, 'if I sit here.'

In a way she was right.

'These bloody people who say they'll meet you,' she complained. She pulled my *Telegraph* apart and began to read the food page. 'I can't stand octopus,' she said, as if she had caught me eating one. Then: 'You don't say much, do you?'

'I'm sorry?'

'I can't stand fish of any kind. I suppose you're doing something this evening?'

We went to my flat. 'Flat' is perhaps the wrong word. I was renting a room from some friends of mine who lived in a maisonette on a council estate in Bow. The estate was constructed like an open box, so that it captured every passing sound. Even the silence was full of ghost aircraft descending far away, a shim or resonance of cries and traffic. At night you could hear young Asian men having their heads kicked in outside Mile End tube station by cheerful BNP members over from Leytonstone for the dog fights. I was as far east as the Arts Club is west, but I could come and go as I liked, and I was never uncomfortable there until Myra said:

'They're very tidy, aren't they? Your friends?'

Then she said:

'My god, is this actually a futon?'

She was wearing a white linen suit, the skirt of which she soon pulled up round her waist to show me the sandy-coloured fur between her thighs.

'What do you think of that, then?' she said.

As soon as I got close enough to have an opinion, she turned away from me and lifted her great haunches in the air, laughing.

'Come on.'

'Can't we talk first?' I said.

When we had finished – or rather, when Myra had come, with a sudden series of barks and groans, shaking her head from side to side and looking back at me over her shoulder – she seemed to expect something else. There wasn't anything else I could think of. That was the first and last time Myra ever came to Bow. If I suggested it thereafter she made excuses, and we always went to Chiswick, where she owned a garden flat thirty seconds away from the Thames. There she had, as she put it, La Trompette for evenings, Richmond for Sundays, and the kind of neighbours who can easily afford an Audi cabriolet. In Chiswick, sex was noisier. I wondered what people made of us. 'So long as you can avoid Hammersmith,' Myra said, 'Chiswick is heaven.' To her, Hammersmith was less a place than a condition.

She was already anxious when we were apart.

Is 'anxious' the right word? It was an anxiety which revealed itself, like most of Myra's emotions, as irritation. Where it proceeded from, I don't know. 'You'll go to seed in that place,' she would warn me, if I spent a day working at home. 'I'm your last chance at a normal life.'

Eventually I gave in. After Myra's remarks, Bow had lost its gloss anyway, though I still quite liked the strange shop signs along Roman Road – Spoilt Bitch, Blisters, Shuz-A-Go-Go. (For a while there had been a lingerie shop called Bare Essensuals. It didn't prosper, and though the sign remained the shop began to sell mirrors instead, as if its owner had decided to cook the impurities out of the narcissistic act and leave only the really good stuff.) Myra hardly seemed to notice when I moved in with her, except to warn me, 'Don't get in my way in the mornings.' The only other thing she said was, 'Don't offer to do my washing and I won't offer to do yours.' She could see I had been tempted by that. The bedroom smelled of overused bath towels, Myra and Nonoxynol-9. On the bed, the sheets were always pulled about untidily into heaps. Perhaps that was because we were always having sex there.

Myra hated it if we didn't have sex, or if I seemed to lose interest in her for a moment. I could see there might be problems with that. Around then my mother, who was seventy three and lived with mixed success in the Midlands, had a small stroke. Unlike Myra's, my mother's anxieties had always revealed themselves as anxiety: when she saw the ambulancemen in her front room, she fought. Just as she feared, worse was to come. Her struggles brought on a further stroke, and a coma, and then, for a month or two, Bramley Ward in the local hospital, which she shared with a transient population of equally unconscious but always slightly younger women.

Most of that time, my sister watched over her. My sister, like many relatives of stroke victims, had convinced herself my mother was still somehow there. The nursing staff explained to her that passing expressions don't signify awareness, but she couldn't accept it. My mother wasn't helping with this. She was smiling as happily as a girl. Some of those smiles were surprising to me, they were surprisingly sexy. It was as if she wanted to share something with us. Sometimes she wanted to share it so much that she was practically winking at us. I didn't want to know what it was. These were the opposite of a baby's practice smiles, they were what you got when there was nothing left to practise for. But my sister kept saying, 'We can't give up, we mustn't give up.'

I didn't know what to feel about it. I had my own difficulties, sitting by the bed on a plastic chair for an hour in Bramley Ward trying not to interpret that smile, so all I felt was my sister's need. It pressed me into the walls. She had me cornered there twice a week in the hospital smell and the light of an internal window with a kiddie's picture taped to it, entitled, probably, 'My Gran doesn't say anything any more.' There were other issues. I had been looking for a better family than ours, my sister said, since I was thirteen.

'Something's the matter with you,' she said.

There was some justice in that: as soon as she spoke, the world had tilted to one side and started to rotate slowly.

'Look,' I said, 'she's not going to wake up.'

The vertigo wore off in the cab on the way to the railway station, but though I felt fine by the time I got back to London, I'm not sure I was ever fine again.

The hospital gave fruit and flower names to all its wards. Bramley Ward. Daffodil Ward. Cherry Ward. Wards were grouped into wings which had the names of famous local people. Despite that, it had no integrity, it wasn't even itself, and was run as a satellite from some other hospital in the nearest big city. My sister explained to me they were always threatening to close it down; it was probably another thing we shouldn't give up on.

So that was the way things worked out. I went up and down to the Midlands, sometimes by car, more often by rail. Each visit, I tried to avoid my sister and catch the early train back to London. At night I lay in the dark imitating my mother's depthless, lively, transient expressions, thinking we were more alike than I preferred: both of us were afraid of death. As a result my dreams were full of the surprised humiliation I used to feel as an adolescent when forced to see things from someone else's point of view. I would wake up to find the room rolling slowly to the left and Myra staring intently down at me as if she knew something I was keeping from myself. Whatever it was, it still didn't enable her to understand me.

'Can we not fuck ?' I would hear myself beg.

It was another climate-change summer. The light, like seaside light, seemed to make the streets wider and more spacious. Even London streets had a promise about them in that light. They became esplanades luring me upriver towards Richmond, or, less advisedly, north through Turnham Green until I lost myself in the tissue of residential streets which had worked its way into the fabric of Acton then died; a place neither clean nor dirty, new nor old, inhabited by mid-day joggers and almost defunct pigeons, organisms like me. One afternoon I got back early and sat out under the cherry tree in Myra's garden. Chiswick Eyot smelled of exposed mud. A dog barked, an engine fired two streets away. A man was saying 'Yes,' and 'Hm,' into a cellphone, his voice close and slightly hollow, as if he were talking from an empty bath. It was another afternoon of hyperaesthesia. A breeze started up and though the sun was still beating down, the rustling cherry leaves made it sound like rain. Lulled by this, I fell asleep. When I woke up ten minutes later, a rhythmic sound was coming from the garden next door. It had a shuffling, plodding quality, like the sound of someone exercising on a treadmill. The rhythm of it was metronomic. Then a voice said: 'Venice is nothing but souvenir shops. You wonder how they make any money, with such a high ratio of shop to customer?'

It was Myra.

Instead of calling over the hedge, I went upstairs to look out of the bedroom window. Two people were down there, but I couldn't get enough of an angle between the hedge and the wall to see what they were doing. 'Mind you,' Myra said, 'I did hear of a blind man who, whenever he was abroad, went into souvenir shops to touch the goods. He would run his fingers over a Tower Bridge or an Eiffel Tower, whatever, to get some idea of the shapes of the city he was in.' There was a pause. 'On the other hand,' she said, 'I don't suppose there are enough blind people to keep Venice above water.'

Later, when I asked her, 'How was work today?' she answered, 'Oh, the usual bloody grind.' Then she added, in a voice not quite like her own, because sympathy was a difficult thing for Myra, a response drawn forth only with the aid of deep resources of patience and stamina:

'And how do you feel?'

I wasn't sure. In one way at least, I said, I actually felt relieved. Once my mother had suffered this disaster I could embrace it as a possible fate of my own. In a sense I could even look forward to it, because prior to that I had only my father's death as a template. For years I'd expected to die suddenly and be removed without warning from other people's lives, the way he had been when I was thirteen. 'I'm not sure you'll understand this,' I told Myra, 'but now I can imagine something different for myself.' I had something new to look forward to.

'Jesus,' she said. She said that if I needed to see someone, she could get me a recommendation. She said, 'Look, do you want the rest of that?'

We were at Le Vacherin in Acton Green. It was late. Our waitress had an inturned look. Outside, Acton Green Common lay in a moonlike trance all the way to the tube line. Apart from ours only a single table remained occupied, by a young couple who had brought their very small, quiet baby with them. It didn't look more than a day or two old, and they were obviously delighted by it. Every ten minutes they lifted it out of its carrycot as if they had just been given it, passed it to and fro across the table, then settled it back again. Myra had lost patience with this pantomime early on, but seemed undecided how to respond. Now she put down her spoon in the remains of my prune and Armagnac tart and said in a loud voice:

'Did they order that? Only I can't find it on the menu.'

They stared at us in surprise. Didn't we like their baby? No one disliked their baby.

Myra shivered.

'They hate me,' she said. 'I'll see a cat when we leave here. There'll be a cat out there now.'

Myra hated cats. She claimed they were sly and untrustworthy; their love was cupboard love and without looking hard you could find something flat in their eyes. A dog's eyes, on the other hand, had depth. A black cat crossing their path, some people think, brings luck. Myra wouldn't walk down a street if any kind of cat had crossed it that morning. She said they smelled.

'I don't know how you can bear the touch of them,' she said with a shudder.

At a loss, I could only tell her the following story—

'Things were chaotic and miserable during Adam and Eve's retreat from Paradise. The children squalled endlessly. There hadn't been time to pack. Adam, who regretted the whole episode, blamed Eve; Eve realised for the first time that Adam was a wimp. Jacob, the third son, was particularly upset. With the whole tribe cowed and disoriented, less by God than the weather outside, only the family cat Mau had the presence of mind to memorise the route. A few years later, driven by her love for Jacob, who had allergies and never came to terms with the world, the cat led him back. Impressed by the boy's obsessiveness, the angel on the gate that day offered Jacob a piece of the maternal fruit. But as a reward for Mau's loyalty, he franked the route permanently into the blank back pages of her DNA. From that time on, there has always been a cat who remembers the way back to the Garden of Eden.'

'I heard it was their dog,' Myra said.

Talk to someone in a coma and you are talking to yourself. When it's your mother there are further complications. What do you say to her? I really liked your meringues? That time when I was eleven and threw up on the tea table from eating Heinz spaghetti on toast - do you remember? - sorry about that! The things you expect to say, you don't. The things you want to say don't seem quite right. Eventually I began to talk about myself. I gave her progress reports dating back as much as twenty years, from the parts of my life she had missed. I listed my divorces. 'It took a long time to learn to like myself,' I concluded, 'but I'm doing quite well now. I don't think I'm as angry as I was, not as angry or as scared.' It brought her up to date and it was therapeutic for us both. I used all my charm on her, son to mother, and she used all hers on me, mother to son, staring coyly up at the ceiling of Bramley Ward, bursting with the secret no one wants to hear.

My sister left a message for me with the nursing staff.

'She does seem rather anxious to get in touch with you,' they said, handing over the damp, heavily folded piece of coloured paper on which was written, 'You'll have to talk to me in the end.'

I stared at these words, then out of the window of the 1.50pm to Euston. Now, I don't know. Or do I? What I would say now is that until the thing with Myra happened I didn't feel enough terror. I would say that like everyone else I ate too much; looked forward too often to the evening bottle of Chilean red. That's what I would say now. But that afternoon all I could do was smooth out the paper until you could barely tell it had been folded, and leave it behind me on the table when the train got in.

Back in Chiswick, someone was in Myra's house. The truth of this visited me not experientially – as a smell or faint sound, a sense of occupation, of usedness, in the air – but as a kind of prior knowledge validated by my sister's note, the moment I opened the door. I stood just inside the hall, the way we all have done at one time or another, and called:

'Hello? Myra?'

They were in the bedroom. She was on her hands and knees and he had got up on her from behind in the gloom. They were panting harshly, and their faces had a stunned look as if something was happening they didn't understand. He had a thick ginger beard. She seemed to have one, too, but I suppose that must have been an effect of the shadows in the room, the few thin slats of river light angling in through the blind. As I watched, he began to turn round so that he faced in the opposite direction to her. It was a slow, awkward procedure if he was to keep his cock inside her. But he did it eventually, and they remained like that, motionless and uncomfortable-looking, until I closed the door on them. They hadn't seemed to notice me.

That had to be the end of it.

'I hate dogs,' was my parting shot to Myra. 'I hate their shit. The smell of it makes you heave.'

When I'm in Chelsea I still look for her, listen for her voice, watch for the swing of the head slowed by its counter-weight of vanished meanings. I see her there sometimes with other men. They're over-attentive, but then this is the Arts Club. Myra's sitting at the same table she sat at with me, staring at the Cupid fountain. 'You've got to understand,' she's telling someone, 'that other people are as confused as you. Just not so self-involved.'

My mother clung on for a while then died. The funeral went well, in that none of the relatives fought; although one or two refused to attend. Perhaps to help make up the numbers, my sister brought her dog, an English bull terrier with a big white blind-looking face. Two months later she was telephoning me every other day to ask for money; once a week she would write a letter summing up the injustices done her by the remains of the family.

She lived with the dog, on one of those estates financed by the optimism of the late 1940s, a hundred and ten company houses in light-coloured brick set down around bleak flat squares and triangles of grass. She made some sort of life for herself there. Eventually I drove up to visit her, and we leafed through the family albums. There was my father, Guy Fawkes night 1968, thirty three years old but laughing as fatuously as a boy, in a boy's red-and-white football scarf, with the bonfire lighting up one lens of his spectacles. I never liked him. He died not long after the photo was taken, and that only made things worse. It reduced the chances of settling anything between us.

After his death my mother couldn't stand mess. She decorated often, bought new furniture and carpets; cleaned and cleaned. I can't stand mess, she would tell us, meaning, I can't stand the mess you've made of my life. I don't think there was any doubt she loved him, and adored him, and depended on him. She grew roses in the garden he had measured out so exactly with pegs and twine. She grew them in the way he would have approved, pruned to stumps in severely rectangular beds, surrounded by grey, cloddy, heavily weeded earth. Even at that age I could feel her looking around in a numb way and wondering how she would make sense of it all, which I don't think she ever did. It all fell apart when he went. Things were too much for her. That was the feeling I had from my mother around then, that her hold on things was marginal, that we were a difficulty hard to contend with: things were difficult enough without the demands we might make.

'Our mother always preferred you,' my sister said. 'We need to talk that out. We need to talk about it.'

I asked if I could go to the toilet.

She looked puzzled. 'Of course you can,' she said. 'Of course you can go to the toilet.'

It was another greenhouse Sunday, high humidity and temperatures in the 30s. Every so often she coaxed the bull terrier on to the steps outside the kitchen door and poured a two-litre bottle of Evian water over its head. For the next few minutes it sat in an evaporating puddle with its tongue lolling out of the side of its mouth and an expression of bliss on its face, while its pinkish eyes remained as hard as marbles. The back yard was full of dogshit, and stacked up on the hard earth was all my mother's furniture – two double mattresses, a thirty-year-old Creda gas cooker, armchairs and sofas the vinyl of which had already faded and split in the sun and rain. My sister was in dispute with the council over this. She was in dispute with her neighbours over it. 'But be honest with me,' she said, 'where else could I put it all? I ask them that and they can't answer.' She was in dispute with almost everyone about almost everything, and in addition genuinely disabled by asthma. The house smelled of the dog, which rarely took its eyes off me.

Driving back down the M1 an hour or two later, I spotted a couple and a child in a splash of sunlight, waiting by their car for the breakdown service. The woman and her little boy smiled at every passing vehicle; the man only seemed embarrassed. You often see families like this, poised on the hard shoulder of the motorway where woods and wildflowers spill down a shallow bank to the edge of the tarmac. Their afternoon is already ruined. The AA has been called, the outing postponed. It's a cracked radiator, it's electrical, it's something none of us, any more, can fix. There's nothing left to do but wait. At first they stand awkwardly in their careful high street clothes, unable to find a body language for the situation. Then, after five minutes, something happens. They move away from the vehicle, shade their eyes, peer at one another or back at the motorway, torsos moving one way, legs another, in the long grass. From the nearby woods a bird sings, there is a flicker of movement. The child tilts its head alertly to listen; the parents look at the child. Suddenly they hang between choices, up to their calves in moon daisies and cornflowers, surrounded by a froth of elder blossom and pink dog roses. Possibilities stretch away in the form of field and hedge. Scents, sounds. For a moment it's likely they will abandon the car and disappear, having mistaken this strip of woods between the motorway and the low-lying pasture for something they can run off into for good.

JO MAZELIS

SKIN

IT WAS THE coldest day Clara had ever known. The wind coming from the north; a freezing airstream from the top of the world where there is still ice, and she feels it in her bones – an arctic crack.

She's wearing tights under her jeans, thick woollen socks over the tights, heavy, thick-soled, low-heeled black leather boots. Then two T-shirts, a wool jumper, a jacket and, over it all, a black wool coat. Knitted hat, a scarf and fleece-lined leather gloves, yet she still feels the wind whistling through her, tracing its breath over her skin, sending up goosebumps. So cold. So, so cold.

Clara is meeting *him* at ten at the Metropolitan Museum of Art. They have decided to meet inside. Not at the entrance. She is walking fast, though there is no need to. No need to hurry at all, except for the cold.

'Meet me by the screaming man,' he'd said earlier on the phone.

'The painting? By Munch?' she asked, though she was sure Munch's *Scream* wasn't in the US.

'No. It's a sculpture. White marble. On a tall column. Forget who did it. But there it is, this head in agony, life size or bigger, disembodied, on a white pillar. God, who's the artist?'

'Um, is it a twentieth-century artist?'

'No, don't be so stupid. What's the damn name?'

He can't remember, but *she's* the one who is stupid.

She says nothing. Stops listening, though she can still hear his voice going on and on. In German there is no difference between the words 'listen' and 'hear', Clara remembers. She is glad that English allows her this distinction.

She likes pictures with words in them. Liked Ed Ruscha's large-scale paintings of traditional nineteenth-century-style landscapes with added text in the sky: WAR FAMINE PILLAGE. Was it Ed Ruscha who used to live at the Chelsea Hotel and paid his rent with paintings? Or was that someone else? Larry Rivers? And does it matter?

She was on the phone to Kaspar. Hearing and not listening. Sitting on the edge of her bed holding the receiver to her ear and gazing out of the window at the building just across the way. Fire escape zigzagging up. A pair of trainers on one of the window ledges. They must smell bad, she thinks. On another ledge, a carton of milk.

The steam heat has been on all night so she is not yet dressed after the shower. As if she were at the beach, she's wearing a bra and panties. She must look like someone in an Edward Hopper painting. Or a photo by Nan Goldin. Or a still from a movie – Gus Van Sant or Larry Clark.

Sex and art.

That's what she and Kaspar do together.

Sex and art.

The art in order to make both of them feel that there is a real relationship going on. Even though there isn't. The sex because . . . well . . . just because.

She gets up still holding the phone to her ear, *parades* around the room.

Clara is twenty-six years old. Body lean. Her bra is flesh-coloured; nipples can be glimpsed, flattened disks rosy behind the sheer nylon fabric. The bikini pants are sky blue with a pattern of pink flowers. She bought them at Macy's. The blinds in the room are drawn up. She imagines someone watching her from the building across the way. Imagines them filming her. Months later, she'll go to MOMA, to a video installation by a hot new artist and wow, what do you know, it's her projected onto the white gallery wall, larger than life, twelve feet tall. Her, as she is now, in her underwear, gracefully insouciant in her anonymous room, filmed from outside, the window an effective framing device.

Her cat lay on the bed regarding her slyly, folded in upon itself and looking, apart from the green judgmental eyes, like an old-fashioned white fur muff that had been flung down by a petulant child.

Inside, outside. The private and the public. *Rear Window* revisited. *This is no dream, this is real.* New York films, New York apartments. *Rosemary's Baby.* But the artists' films are different; there is no narrative thread to follow. The woman in the film Clara imagines isn't acting, didn't even know she was being filmed.

Except that now she, Clara, is betraying a certain self-consciousness, striking casual poses that are designed to show off her body to the best effect. She is sucking in her tummy, holding the muscles taut. It is pleasant to imagine these things, her presence here, now, translated into something that is more than herself. Her loneliness becomes mythic, no longer hers alone, it belongs to everyone.

But wouldn't the artist have to ask her permission before he showed the work? Wouldn't there be a release form she'd have to sign?

On the other end of the line Kasper's tone of voice has changed, there is a falling-away sound to it and so she pays attention. Listens.

Kaspar is saying, 'Okay then, so I'll see you there?'

'It's cold out,' she says.

'Yeah?' he says, his voice rich with sarcasm.

'So why don't you just come here?'

'See you by the screaming man, ten o'clock.'

He hangs up.

Time to dress. Time to go back to the start.

Kaspar. Sometimes she suspects that's not his real name. It's probably Brad or Henry or Edward.

He told her his age was thirty-two, but she suspects that's a lie too, that he's younger. His hair, though, is thinning on the back of his head. She believes he is not aware of this. She won't tell him, not now, not yet. She'll save that for some future time when she is angry with him. When they are throwing insults at each other. When they have run out of art, exhausted desire and are left with nothing except the capacity to hurt one another.

But not yet. The sex is still good. It's good and getting better. The way it always does. Or at least, that was how it seemed to her.

So she has to schlep across town, find the screaming man, find Kaspar, see art, talk art, debate it, drink coffee. Debate whose turn it is to pay. He always says it's her turn.

Would it be petty of her to begin to keep a record of all the coffees, the pastries, the Cokes and beers and hot dogs she's paid for?

Yes, it would. Though she keeps a rough tally in her head. For example, the bottle of wine from the deli; Californian Merlot, he'd suggested it, picked it up from the shelf, then while they were queuing at the till (there was only one other person in line) he'd said, 'Hang on' and disappeared into the back of the shop where they kept all the fancy imported tea and coffee so she'd had to pay. The cashier was already handing her the receipt when Kaspar reappeared with a packet of crackers. He paid for the crackers, seventy cents' worth of crumbs in her bed, and he'd drunk most of the wine too.

What was he? A gigolo? He was certainly arrogant enough to be one, but what did that make her?

So she'd dressed putting on layer after layer like some mountain climber.

As soon as she left the building the icy wind hit her. A hard cold wind, implacable as a rock face. After five minutes of battling against the elements she gave up and instead of cutting across the park as she'd planned, she hailed a cab that deposited her outside the museum at twenty minutes to ten.

She stood in line to check her coat, her hat, her scarf and gloves. It was still early. An older woman ahead of her was theatrically slinking out of a sable coat like a butterfly escaping its cocoon. The animal fur was glossy and alive in a way a fake never was. Except that the animal wasn't alive. Not any more. The woman was offered a biro to fill in the insurance form, but shook her head *no* and, her face showing disgust, she dug a fountain pen out of her Hermès bag instead.

There was money, and then *there was money*. Oh yes. And then there was no money whatsoever. It was always so.

Clara had money. The consolation for being an orphan at the age of nineteen. As a student at Columbia, seven years ago, she had, after getting the news of her parents' death in an automobile accident, lost all focus. She could not sit in the lecture halls or in the library and concentrate. She had been the sort of daughter whose chief motivation in life up until then had been to please her parents. As their only child, they had equally sought to please her. Wished for her happiness and assumed that a part of that must be academic success. It was not something either of her parents had had, and they regretted that – despaired at their early lives, their bright potential squandered on exhausting work for little pay. Their immigrant parents – her grandparents – Italian on her mother's side, Irish on her father's, had stressed the necessity of work and money. Money first, then education.

But with all of them gone – mother, father, all four grandparents, no brothers and no sisters, no aunts, uncles or cousins – she'd found there was no one to please any more. Except herself. And it pleased her to visit the city's museums with a head almost empty of the desire to learn; to wander about and sometimes gaze in an unseeing way at the objects before her. As if she were in a perpetual dream. Outside of herself. Waiting to awaken, but with no sense of urgency, nowhere to get to.

This was how she had met Kaspar. Kaspar, tall, broad-shouldered, with richly glossy chestnut-coloured hair that he wore brushed back from his forehead (though wilfully it fell forward). Well, that gave him a chance, an excuse, to run his hands through his hair, which when she watched him, made her aware of a sensual and fatalistic and dark *something* stirring within her.

At the beginning she had thought that they would start to see one another with increasing frequency; that they would become a couple. But instead it had become this sporadic, this nameless thing – not quite a relationship, nor a secret affair as neither of them had anyone to cheat on. Once or twice a month they'd meet at a gallery or museum, then he'd come back to her hotel for a few hours. He didn't stay the night and they never went to his place, which he said, somewhat vaguely, was somewhere in the Village.

She didn't know it but Kaspar regularly got his body waxed. At least she didn't know it until one day she'd felt the sharp nap of sprouting hair on his back and had to draw her hand away as the sensation was so shocking, almost frightening.

The woman with the sable coat made a mistake filling in the insurance form and had to redo it. Her companion, a handsome, silver-haired, expensively groomed fox of a man, touched the woman's shoulder tenderly as if to convey to her that she should take her own sweet time, he'd be there no matter what and to hell with the line behind them.

But the woman shook his hand off impatiently and turned to glare at him. He looked hurt, then when he saw Clara looking at him his expression turned to something like anger. *How dare you pity me*, his eyes seemed to say, *you who are nothing, no one*. The moment was chilling and Clara looked away quickly. When she turned back they were gone. She stepped forward with her coat, her scarf and hat ready. The attendant took them, his face impassive, dead.

He put her coat on the hanger, arranged the scarf around the neck tenderly as if he were dressing a small child.

'You like cats,' he said.

It was neither a statement nor a question. His accent was strong, straight out of the Bronx, the 's' at the word's end had a hard 'z' sound.

'Sorry?' she asked pleasantly, half smiling, wondering if she had misheard him.

He slapped her ticket on the counter. 'Next!' he called, brusquely dismissing her.

Feeling she could make no sense of anything today, she went off in search of the screaming man.

She stopped to ask a guard if he knew of a marble portrait bust of a man in agony, in some kind of demented torment.

'Marsyas? He's in the Petrie Court,' the guard said.

She set off through the galleries. Over and over she thought about the cloakroom attendant's words. 'You like cats!' 'You like cats?'

He had spat the phrase out of his mouth, like a dog giving a warning sign, baring its teeth and snatching at the air with a growl.

What on earth had he meant?

Then she realised – there must have been stray white cat hairs clinging to the surface of her coat and what he'd meant in effect was, 'Hey ya filthy whore, you don't brush your coat down, but ya wander in here to look at art like you own the place? Whaddya take me for – you think I wanna touch ya filthy clothes?'

She felt ashamed. Deeply humiliated – as had been his intent.

Actually when he'd said 'You like cats' she recalled that she had grinned at him in a confused way, thinking his words were a pleasantry, that he was being nice.

How stupid she must have looked.

At last she found herself in the Petrie Court, hesitating as she searched for the sculpture Kaspar had mentioned. Hesitating over everything at that moment.

Straightaway she saw Kaspar, his back turned to her, standing in front of what was the white ghost-like head of Marsyas.

She read impatience in the set of Kaspar's shoulders, recognised the increasing coldness he seemed to radiate towards her - even now when he couldn't see her. The sculpture's head peeked out over Kaspar's left shoulder so that the real man and the marble man seemed to be in some kind of terrible embrace. The marble man's face was twisted away from Kaspar's in agony and she saw at last that Kaspar hurt people.

Would always do so. Would hurt her in particular.

Not by any tangible means, but by the stripping-away of those last tender, hopeful parts of her she still held onto. Kaspar kept her at arm's length. He revelled in her occasional ignorance. He was cruel. She had tried to please him, and in doing so, she had stepped outside of herself, but she'd failed to see it until now.

The subject of the sculpture, Marsyas was a satyr who had been tortured. He'd suffered a hideous punishment for some insult to the gods. Yes, that was it, she remembered now - she'd seen the painting by Titian which showed how he'd been flayed alive, the skin slowly stripped from his body as he hung upside down from a tree like a slaughtered deer.

She would have liked to move closer to the sculpture to study the carved stone into which human pain was given a hellish eternity. But Kaspar with his thinning hair was blocking her way. Was waiting for her and would wait for her.

She turned on her heel smoothly and went back the way she had come. She pictured her journey as a tracked shot down a long corridor, then as one long unedited shot - a woman walking swiftly, without hesitation or interest past statues, glass cases, paintings, to the cloakroom where a different man returned her coat.

Then out into the cold, clear air where the camera would tilt up until the screen was filled with nothing but sky and the only sound would be one long repressed and exultant sigh.

Escape.

CONRAD WILLIAMS

CWTCH

SALTER WOKE IN the night and this time the screams were real. Raw, lusty, the kind of scream only an infant can make. It seemed so close as to be just the other side of the canvas. This was his first night on the camp site. The family had turned up to their pitch late: Salter had eaten dinner and was reading by torchlight as a middle-aged man in shorts and a waterproof coat cursed over a jumble of poles and pegs. His partner switched on a radio tuned to old pop songs despite the camp rules stipulating no music at any time. Salter had purposefully selected this camp site because it was not child friendly, it didn't allow pets and it placed a premium on silence. Why couldn't people adhere to simple rules? Why was there this constant flouting of regulations? It might seem trivial to them – *it's only OMD, lighten up, Grandpa* – but this was his holiday, a rare chance to enjoy some rest and recuperation before returning to the grind.

And now this infant, shrieking [greeting, skriking]. Salter checked his watch. Just shy of five a.m. He rolled off his mattress and flexed the muscles complaining in his back before pulling open the tent flaps and sticking out his head. Folds of drizzle [mizzle, Scotch mist], colour low in the sky: green and pale gold where dawn threatened. Opposite, screaming miles of black. The cries became muffled, as if the parents had noticed his appearance and were trying their best to soothe the child. The poor thing might be teething, or suffering a cold. Well . . . they could have chosen to not bring it here, he thought, knowing that for a few pounds more he could have stayed in a B&B and not been disturbed at all. But part of the reason for this holiday – for these holidays – was because it was what he had done as a young boy. Abersoch, Dolgellau, Port Eynon. Each summer his mum and dad had loaded up the old Austin Princess with tents and fishing rods and they'd follow the M56 to Wales, him in the back seat with a *Beano* and a quarter of aniseed twists, especially for the trip. *Save one for Mo*, Dad would say. And he did, every time. His mum and dad would bicker good-naturedly about what they listened to on the cassette player and it was usually his mum who prevailed. Everyone she liked seemed to be called Joan or Joni and all of the songs seemed to be happy and sad at the same time.

At the end of all this road there'd be the usual bellyaches [gripes, protests, whinges] about pitching the tent in the wrong place, or getting the groundsheet pinned down incorrectly . . . but the bad tempers didn't last long. He would find a nice spot and bury that final sweet for Mo, Mum would get some pasta going on the camping stove and Dad would tuck into a couple of cans of McEwan's. There would be rain, and complaints about bad backs. Fish would be caught or, more likely, wouldn't. They played cards. They told jokes. He had loved these holidays.

Now he rolled up his night things knowing that he wouldn't be able to catch hold of the tail of sleep [shuteye, kip, slumber] so there was no longer any point in trying. He dressed quickly and reached for his raincoat, unzipping the tent at speed in order to make as much noise as possible. The violent sound of it was close and waspish in the dark. He would have words with the owner when the office opened at nine. He needed rest and no distractions. So much of his normal everyday life was riddled with noise that he craved these oases in the year, rare and precious holidays that allowed him to reflect and, yes, heal [repair, recover, mend]. He believed he was still coming back from that childhood insult - the shock and the unacknowledged pain; a grief that would not hatch in him - and only silence could provide the environment in which he might achieve that release.

He walked to the far edge of the camp site where a perimeter fence gave access to a track through the woods. Beyond those trees Craig y Cilau rose like a sheer grey wave. Pockets of golden light opened up on the rock face as breaks appeared in the cloud that had clung to the base of the mountain all night. Already there were climbers arranged upon the limestone.

Crossing the track he entered the woods at their thinnest point. Sunlight was filtering through here too, gilding the whitebeam and adding varnish to the boughs of rowan and hawthorn. He had no idea where he was going. Away was enough: he could still hear the child's agonised, red cries rising in the trough behind him. Three hours until Davis, in his self-important tweeds and his moisturised beard, came down from his nice stone cottage to open the office and treat everyone with an air of amused indifference.

The crack of a twig underfoot highlighted the depth of quiet he had stumbled into. He could no longer hear the child; its shrieks had been replaced by the soft suck and blow of a breeze sifting through the limbs. It was as if the wood had lungs and he had detected the rhythms of its breathing. He could smell moss and fungus, a mix of the clean and the corrupt, and, he was sure, the mineral aroma of the warming rock face. He felt the tension of the last few hours lift a little.

The family must have been unaware of the regulations, as unlikely as that sounded. Salter was not a father, but he tried to put himself in the shoes of those people now. They'd be more stressed than him, that was for sure. At least he could have a nap this afternoon when fatigue [lassitude, enervation] inevitably caught up with him. They would undoubtedly be asked to move their pitch to one of the neighbouring camps where families were tolerated. He'd help them relocate if that was the case. Everything would be fine.

He was a little out of breath by the time he broke through the far stand of trees into full sunlight. Since observing the climbers on Craig y Cilau Salter had seen no other people. He craved that sense of being alone, the illusion of the last man on Earth, to the extent that he felt cheated and disappointed [crestfallen, despondent] whenever he spotted a figure clinging to rock, or a car winding along the A465, or the peal of a distressed child in a badly constructed tent. Now though, he was here for a different reason. Mo. Though he couldn't work out the impulse for it. Could it just be as simple as a need to tidy up the strands of his life now that he was closer to the end than the beginning? For so many years he had avoided coming to the Brecons, but why? It was not as if he could remember much about his sister. He felt that those memories he did have of her were informed by the photographs in his parents' old albums; Kodacolor prints he had picked through only once since their death. Invariably, the photographs of Mo displayed a toddler with long, fine blonde locks (from birth until her death, they had not cut her hair), her hands outstretched, begging a hug, or for someone to pick her up. Salter was never in these pictures, which was another reason for the buffer between himself and his grief, if grief was what it could be called. How could you grieve for what you had never consciously known? How did you love a sister who had been in your life for only two years?

He stood at the edge of the trees and opened his arms, opened himself to a feeling that would not come. They had been twins, but there was never any of that rumoured synergy. No telepathic communion. No phantom muscle recollection. The breath in the trees intensified as if in sympathy. He watched the canopy wave. The moment moved on; he came to his senses, feeling self-conscious, foolish.

Three sheep paused in their cropping to watch as he picked a route across stony ground. He angled through another field, though a sign on the gate asked that ramblers restrict themselves to the edges. Lines of blue mould in a cracked plastic bathtub drew a map of a world he didn't understand. He'd always felt apart, on the edge of things, as if life was filled with codes he didn't have the key to access. He resented his parents for that, believing their withdrawal from the public eye in the wake of Mo's death had included him too. Their protection of him became smothering, but he never felt it was motivated by true love, more out of guilt, or some misplaced effort to atone [expiate, recompense]. His father had slapped him across the face when he suggested it was a little too late for that.

They used Mo as a stick with which to beat him. So many times over the years to the point where they no longer had to use euphemisms to suggest that if any child should die, it ought to have been him. It was in the cast of their faces; the language of their ever more stooping bodies.

Salter had trained to become a teacher, anticipating that spending time with children might help him cope with his suite of insecurities, but all it did was trap him in a prison of 'what if?'. He daydreamed elaborate fantasies in which he somehow managed to rescue Mo, prevent her from falling into the pond rather than being the one to find her. He set his class exercises and then watched as they frowned over their books, wondering if Mo might have grown up to talk like Susan Webb, or laugh like Debra Barker, or would she have been naughty, like Kathy Bowden?

He mythologised the discovery of her body, unable to remember what had happened, conscious [aware, sentient] only that he had discovered her because of second-hand stories, heavily censored by parents who did not want him to have to deal with the trauma. Instead he internalised it, torturing himself with any number of death scenes. It was a wonder he didn't drown too; the pair of them were little older than two, realtively new to the task of walking.

The image that stuck in his mind more than any – which persuaded him to believe it was authentic [bona fide, genuine] – involved the slow roll of Mo's head in the blue/black water of the pond as her face returned to the surface. Her fine hair was arranged around her like glass noodles left too long to soak. Her mouth and eyes were open, and he always recoiled from that part of his recollection, the infant part of his mind upset that she was swallowing dirty water and would get a poorly tummy. Her arms were outstretched; even in death she was keen for a cuddle.

Salter exhaled in the silence and it was a ragged, unnerving sound. He gazed back in the direction of the campsite and saw the route he had carved through the deep grass, a dark green oblique bisecting the field. Beyond that he could just make out the small parallelogram tents peeking over the tops of the trees. He could see now that his quickening breath was as much to do with the gradual incline he was ascending, as any delayed childhood shock. The early morning sunlight persisted, but grey cloud, like the edifices of stone they towered over, was gathering. He would walk as far as the river and then return for breakfast and a reckoning with Davis. He shook his head clear of unpleasantness; enough thinking about Mo for now.

He stretched his legs and strode hard along a path under the rockface, enjoying the heat building at his back. Muscles in his legs sang; he knew they would ache later, but it would be a good ache, telling of honest exercise. His thoughts returned to the classroom. He'd brought a little marking with him that he would enjoy: stories by his pupils written without fear, something he found common to primary school children in the main. Something that sadly would be unlikely to last as self-consciousness kicked in and distractions mounted. There were some children who had natural skill [expertise, adroitness], a real feel for words, as he had done as a boy. He remembered being teased for taking a dictionary with him on a school trip. His peers nicknamed him The Saurus because he was constantly getting his pupils to come up with synonyms, a habit that he couldn't shake himself; he was often consulted in the staff room regarding a crossword clue, or a letter that needed to be precisely worded.

He reached a stile almost fully concealed by bright green lichen. Over that, a field of what looked like stubbled barley dipped away to a barn in the far corner. By the time he reached the building – little more than a weather-thrashed lean-to built from asbestos cement and corrugated iron roofing – it had begun to rain. Now he could see a series of single-storey outbuildings hopscotched amid the green beyond. Salter pulled up his hood and watched the thick grey clouds spend themselves. Black nets of rain hung across the sky like dirty curtains in a terrace filled with secrets. The only sound was a stippling against his waxed jacket. It felt as if he was at a moment of poise, or pause. It felt as if something would develop imminently: he was tensed for the explosion of wings as a heron broke through the tree line or a rabbit shot out of clover. Nothing like that transpired, but the feeling remained and his heart rose to meet it.

The sound of running water turned his head. For a moment he thought the downspout from the gutter was blocked with hair, but it was only water, hurtling from the mouth in a shock of white. Thin veils of cloud sank from the top of the mountain and removed sense, softened edges. A cow despondently chewing its cud became a sepia stain on blotting paper. Cold found its way past the toggles of his jacket; he wished he'd taken the time to prepare a flask of coffee, but anger had ushered him from his tent. It was time to go back. The sun had threatened enough and retreated quite possibly for the rest of the day given the thickening shroud and the absence of any breeze to shift it along.

A single magpie ducked and fluttered, washing itself in a dip in the barn's concrete apron. The ancient shadow of an oil puddle. Rust ghosts in the wall told of defunct, removed machinery. There was an old wheelbarrow inside the barn, and a tyre torn through to its steel belts. Dead nests of things long gone. Water lipped troughs and gutters. It spanged off the metal roofs.

Salter did not drink water; not in its purest state, not any more. It had to be blended with some other beverage: tea or coffee, an ice cube in his gin and tonic. His parents had to fool him into imbibing water by disguising it in a cordial of some kind, or topping up his cocoa from the kettle. They had always shielded him from the truth, perhaps believing that to protect him in this way gave them licence to take their anger, frustration and guilt out on him. Not that they would ever admit as much. How could they? How could any parent acknowledge such an egregious transfer? He trudged back, raking the burning embers of his resentment; every little spiteful episode. The pointed fingers. The heated asides.

His route took him alongside the river, now swollen and fast, groaning under the weight of itself. It was unlikely to remain clear for much longer as the muddy banks were encouraged to became part of the flow. For now, though, he could see into the heart of the river, and the reeds trapped there, like slender arms waving in the current.

She could not say his name. *Trevor*. He seemed to remember her trying, but she got the name twisted in her mouth. *Rover*, she used to say. That was it. *Rover*. 'Mo,' he said now, in response to that memory, and the simplicity of it, the stark snap of it in the relative quiet shocked him. He had not uttered her name in twenty years, at least. The trees murmured again, as if he'd spoken too loud. Already he suspected he might have done. His breathing would not settle; he could feel, see, even, the torment of his heart in the materials layered across his chest. That sense of imminence. Perhaps he was anticipating thunder in some lizard chamber of his back brain, as other animals were able. But there was no such rumour in the colour or shape of these clouds. Panic gnawed at him. Heart attacks were a shadow in his bloodline. He had stumbled upon a dead rabbit on one camping trip, its splintered [fragmented, spillikin] ribs splayed to allow access to the soft vitals within; it was too easy to imagine himself become much the same. Perhaps under the beak of that magpie, and whatever else hunkered in the undergrowth with a nose for carrion. *Please don't let me die out here, alone.* The hiss of the trees. Had he spoken aloud again? Despite everything, he laughed.

He came back along the bank until he could avoid it no longer and strode into the stand of trees. Gloom and sullen silence under the canopy now. Odour of petrichor. He felt swaddled, but there was no comfort in it. When he reached the edge of the trees he saw his tracks in the field again, those deep green furrows, but now they had been supplemented by another set of narrower tracks, weaving in and around his determined pattern like those of a dog, or a small child. The rain intensified and he couldn't understand if it was the hiss of that he was hearing or those incessant trees. A sharp intake of breath at the witnessing of atrocity. The cusp of something. It was like that game he had played as a child. When someone hid something and you went looking for it. Warm, warmer, colder, cold. Hot now. Very hot. Boiling.

Nothing had ever been cut and dried in his life. There was always doubt [uncertainty, confusion, hesitancy]. It might have had something to do with his never marrying. He didn't feel comfortable taking that risk with someone, a person he could never know as well as himself. And the fact he didn't know himself all too well meant that any chance of intimacy was stymied from the start. 'Buggered every which way', as his dad had been fond of saying.

He stumbled into a clearing. He knew this place. This arrangement of wood and water. The peculiar sweep of land. He saw the pond and cried out at the pale oval turning slowly within it. But it was only a soft glancing of light finding its way between the cradle of branches. He heard the cry of the child again, and knew there was no such thing. There was no child on the campsite.

'Dad,' he said, and steadied himself against the bole of a tree. It was as if, viewing it all again, fifty years on, a match had been made in his head, like a copy on tracing paper aligned with the original. 'Mum.'

Dead a dozen years now. He was the last of the Salters. And their name would die with him.

He crouched and placed his hand in the cold water, wishing his infancy back, a crucial few seconds in which he might have made a difference. Everything could have changed since that pivot in time. All of those holidays he remembered since Mo's death. The sham of their routines. The jokes. The games. They were told and played behind masks. Nobody was who they had been before. He had hated these holidays. Yes, he had hated them. The last sweet for Mo? He had eaten them all.

He thought of the way his parents regarded him as he grew up. That barely concealed mixture of revulsion and guilt. Laced with something else, he thought now. Fear, was it? What if? What if?

He heard movement in the undergrowth. That moment opening up again. That bubble of imminence. He dredged his hand through the water, ruining the calm of the pond. He fancied he felt something winding itself around his fingers, but when he pulled them clear, there was nothing to see. He stood up. All his life he had been pushing people away. Always pushing people away. Always pushing. He didn't have a word for what he had done.

The trees hissed as he closed his eyes and Mo coalesced there, reaching out for him as he had done for her half a century ago. The arms that tried to encircle his body were much too short for the task.

KELLY CREIGHTON

AND THREE THINGS BUMPED

I THINK OF Stephen Kent and I remember the first time he ever collected me in that taxi of his. His name and number on a laminated card swinging on the rear-view mirror. You know the type of thing I'm talking about. He told me a fill from the moment I got into his car at the airport pick-up zone: Stephen had been a *transplant* in Chelsea until he'd come back home where, all over the province, he bought houses as investments, apart from the one he was renovating for his family. Sitting good-naturedly in Friday dinner-time traffic, he'd boasted his wife was living with her parents until the new homestead was shipshape. Stephen used to work in stocks, making money from money. Back then I toyed with writing: making something from nothing or stories from stories. I suppose there are more than two ways of looking at the one thing.

Outside my home he said, That's a nice wee house you have there.

Cheers, I said, about to leave.

Stephen said, This place is overrun with kids. How many have you got yourself?

One, I told him, and one on the way.

He turned the radio off completely. I've three, he said, two lads and a girl. He sat back so he was looking at me full on in the rear-view mirror. He was somewhere between a pair of eyes and a hard thick neck. You have to give stuff up when kids are involved, don't you? Stephen said.

We only had our daughter then so I couldn't tell if that would catch us up. Trudy and I didn't stop each other doing the things we loved. I thought about her and her surfing, and me and my writing. Stephen and I got talking and lost track of time. Trudy looked out the living room window at us.

Someone wants you home, Stephen said though neither of us moved.

Trudy's easygoing, I told him.

That's good, he said. Then you're a lucky man.

Stephen told me his neighbours were young guys. They invited him to the bar, coaxed him into going to Ravenhill to watch the rugby. Stephen normally ended up driving. He said sometimes he felt they used him for lifts. There was never any point in leaving the Merc at home, which was the car he drove when he wasn't taxiing, and he didn't charge them. They're not a bad crowd, he told me. It's good to have the company of young fellas.

Stephen had a decade on me. Just had his fortieth. He had a thing for numbers which I understood as being residual from his broker days. He talked about being born on the tenth of May, that his daughter had the same birthday. He was one of ten kids.

I think ten might be my lucky number, he said.

I listened quite easily. Always thirsty for a story back then. He elaborated on his living arrangements, admitting he and his wife were on a trial separation he believed they'd reconcile from, especially once she saw this house he was building for her and the children: whom I recall were seven and nine and ten, or thereabouts.

I said, Forgive my nosiness but is there anyone else in the picture?

No, none of that, Stephen told me. He was still wearing his wedding ring. I'll tell you something, he said, and it goes no further. In my experience money is the killer. People can put up with all sorts. Cheating would never do the damage money does.

So let me get this straight, I said, it's having too much money that ruins things?

He squinted in the mirror at me. Money is the killer, he repeated. It always has been with me and the missus. She wanted me to come back here so she could be near the grand-parents for babysitting. She said she was lonely in Chelsea. All those millions of people and she couldn't find one she liked! We used to holiday in Dubai. New York. You sacrifice things, don't you? The house you want, the motors. I came back for her and what happened? If I'm being honest – and what's the point in not being – she was a very selfish person. What she put me through – and I'll not get into it all – but there aren't many men who would put up with the things that I put up with. In the end I couldn't any more.

Yes, you can't be doing with that, I said.

He dried up, so I told him it had been good talking to him. Stephen turned side on and shook my hand. He liked the look of the cufflinks Trudy had bought me: two silver crowns with little jewels set into the spikes. They were flash for my taste. A gift for my thirtieth I didn't have long. I lost one in the airport after a month or two. Trudy never really forgave me. One is, after all, sort of jobless on its own.

Stephen knew they were Westwood, who, as it turned out, was the only designer Stephen wore when he lived in Chelsea. Then out of nowhere he said, My wife did time. You asked so I'm going to tell you. She did time for fraud. Was stealing from me the whole time, and from her employer.

Jesus, I said and sat back, what else could I do?

Ruth, he said, that's her name. When Ruth came to Chelsea she got a job for the Crown Prosecution Service, started writing dodgy receipts. I just couldn't live with a woman like that, not in my profession. If you really want to know, I had to leave the market. I was warned it could have repercussions on me. They did me a severance deal and I took it. I'd be a tool not to. Ruth comes from a family . . . well, let's just say they aren't short of a bob or two, so between them and me the kids are kept right, you know? And Ruth too. And I don't want you to think that I wish her ill, because I don't.

No of course not, I said.

But if I wasn't a gentleman I could tell you a few things, said Stephen.

How long did she do?

Where? Inside? Not long. He rubbed his eye. A good solicitor, if you ever need one, is all you need. Remember that, pal. If you ever find yourself on the wrong side of the law, a shit-hot solicitor will seal the deal. And keep your mouth shut. It does you no good if you can't hold your water, do you know what I'm saying?

I presume you get what you pay for, I said. In terms of legal representation. Same as everything.

Absolutely, he nodded. It is the same as everything.

Especially in money issues. A good solicitor will talk it all around and before you know it, you don't know what end of you is up. Well, Joe Bloggs doesn't know. People who aren't used to money chat. It has its own language. I don't need to be doing this, I live in a real nice place, nice but small, I like working with people. You couldn't beat it really. He yawned. Look, it's been good talking to you but I have to get back now, the kids will be calling me. I like to tell them I love them every day. Even days I don't see them. Make sure you do that too. Especially when the next one comes along, Stephen added letting me know he had been listening. Don't let the wee child feel left out. It's not a nice thing. I'm saying this as the eldest of a large family. And you're on the right tracks too, going away to do your own thing, maybe me and Ruth should have done more of that. You get out of the way of it. Don't end up like us.

Okay, I said and we reenacted our handshake.

They are nice cufflinks, he said, nearly longingly and he turned to put his hands back on the wheel.

They are quite nice, I said and I finally got out.

He was some talker, I said. Trudy shook her head and said she'd made something in the restaurant and there was plenty of it left in the fridge.

That night we lay in bed discussing Stephen. She was sceptical, like I had been, like anyone would be. Why would he be taxiing if he's so loaded? she asked.

He turned the meter off all that time we were sat outside.

I should hope so too.

He did say something good, that we should never stop doing the things we love.

Well then, Trudy said, maybe he was worth listening to.

We put ourselves aside for a couple of years. It happens, even though you vow it won't. Having a kid is a whirlwind. The house needed doing up. That fell by the wayside too. We slept together once, maybe twice a month, if we weren't exhausted. Having a second child was twice the work. It makes sense but somehow I hadn't bargained on it. At times it seemed we might crack.

We went to Paris for a weekend. Trudy's dad minded the kids. He hadn't a clue, poor man. Their clothes hadn't even been unpacked when we returned. God knows what he was doing. Potty training the youngest had to start all over again, but at least we got away. We had a good time but it felt cultural, like a school trip. Our feet were wore to the bone with all the walking, then we fell asleep watching the show at the Moulin Rouge.

A week after we came home we spoke about it, how we should have been unable to keep our hands off each other, in Paris of all places. We wondered aloud if we were done. And what we would do with the house. How would we tell the kids? It happened in a blink.

I looked at Trudy and she looked at me and started crying, saying we were like passing ships. I'm so busy I'm meeting myself at the front door, she said. I'm going to miss you so much.

It struck me how ridiculous we were being, how easily we were prepared to tear our little family apart. I don't want this, I told her.

Nor do I, she said in a heavy wet voice. You're my favourite person in the world. All our friends always say we're perfect for each other and we are.

It was then Stephen came into my head, and everyone else I knew who had split up with their partners, especially where kids were involved, and I knew Trudy and I could hold it together. I told her she should go back to surfing and I should go back to writing. It would mean that our time together would be less, but quality.

It must have been three years on, I was coming home from a writing retreat and Trudy had the car. She needed it because she was working nine to five. The kids were both at school by then and we had finally found a good design in the way we lived. We were at a good stage. The kids liked to learn and you could have conversations with them. And me and Trudy laughed together lots. It was then we were at our happiest, together and with the kids, but then I wondered, because we never *really* spoke, what was on her mind. We were like colleagues, in the many revolutions our relationship had taken. Although we were connected more in bed, but it was all a bit predictable. Then once in a while we would have a mind-blowing night and my head would ease for another while.

I got a bit jealous of Trudy's new happiness, I have to admit. She was working in the prisons and I'd expected her to hate it, but she was getting something emotionally that we didn't seem to need from each other any more. I was working too, and writing, but it wasn't really going anywhere. I wasn't putting myself out there. Wasn't seeking publication. Something always held me back.

When Stephen collected me he asked about the retreat. I told him about the lake, how you walked around it for inspiration, how it was peaceful but I wanted to write strong stuff that really was the opposite of how it had been there.

But you did get peace and quiet to do it?

I did, I said.

His name card was stuck to the dash now and it had a photo. I could see his face but still his eyes flitted to me in the mirror. He was driving another heap of junk, working for a company instead of for himself. The radio kept coming through, telling him and his colleagues where to go next. Stephen lowered the volume.

I haven't seen you around in ages, I said to him.

He looked at me in the mirror. His hard thick neck tensed. I realised I wouldn't know him out on the street. You gave me a lift in the past, I said. You were going through some things back then.

Like what? he said.

You were maybe splitting up with your wife, pal, I said.

That's right, he said but Stephen was chary. How are you doing, pal?

Not bad.

And what about this writing? Are you writing a book?

I am, I said. Been writing it for years. I'm blocked.

Ah, he said. I have a story for you. You can have it if you want. It's about a woman who ended up in jail for stealing money from her employer and wrangled her way out of the conviction. You'll sell millions of copies.

He had no memory of me. Had probably told this story thousands of times since I'd last been in his cab. Instead of letting him think I'd spent all that time mulling it over, I pretended I'd never heard it. Is this a real story? I asked.

It's real alright. It's my ex I'm talking about. She spent

time inside, got the conviction overturned, came out and got it fixed on another poor fucker.

Jesus, that's mad, I said.

Are you married? he wanted to know first.

Practically. A very long term relationship, I said.

You'd never believe what they'd do to you. Honest to god, you just never know.

Sounds terrible.

I was living in London, he said. I met this girl on the net, Ruth, and I left there to be with her. She already had three kids. Two lads and one girl. All different dads: that should say it all! I came over here to be with her. She was cute. I'll give her that. Nice little shape to her. I talked her into moving back to London with me. We left the kids with her parents for a while to give things a go. The plan was they were going to come over too. Listen to this for coincidence, her daughter's birthday was on the same day as mine. Tenth of May, he said. I'm one of ten kids and Ruth lived in 10 Gorse Lane. You know, you have to listen to all these signs when they're as powerful as that.

Absolutely you do!

I had my own business over there, a taxi firm – he had excluded the stock broker line – and she was bored so I encouraged her to get out and work. We walked into a registry office one day and got married.

Weren't your family annoyed to have missed out?

Ah, no, I've been married before. They're not bothered. My mother never liked Ruth anyway.

Why not?

All the kids.

He pulled up into town. Fuck sake, there's an accident up

ahead, he said. I'm going to have to turn and go back the long way, that okay with you, pal. I'll cut the meter here sure.

He'd become impatient like the rest of them.

I appreciate it, I said.

I took those kids on like my own, you know. I told everyone they were mine. Now they won't even see me. You got any? he asked.

Two, I said. Seven and five years old. My girlfriend was expecting the little one the last time I was in your cab.

I wouldn't remember that, he laughed. God knows how many fares I've had in here in the meantime.

I'm sure, I said.

No. Ruth hated London. I had a good job over there, making good money, a fleet of motors, holidays to Dubai. The money was unbelievable. It would shock you. I got a bit materialistic, I'm not afraid to say. We were taking out loans and living like king and queen, then it turned out she was being sly.

How so?

Writing fake invoices. Saying they were from court witnesses using my cabs. The cash was going into an account she'd set up. She was using fake names, the lot. She got time and wormed her way out of it. By that time we were back here, and me left with nothing. The shirt on my back and little else. Think how ashamed I was to go to my mother and tell her she was right all along.

Sure you can't help who you fall for, I said. You were decent, taking on her kids and giving them that lifestyle.

He frowned. Yes, he said. Then the bitch got out of it because the taxi firm was mine. She framed me.

God, what happened then?

I had to do time, didn't I! Stitched up like a kipper, you know. Million quid scam. They couldn't account for the whole of it.

That's awful!

He nodded, he pulled into my street.

How long did you get?

Six years, out in three. It's shocking what someone you once loved and trusted can do to you. I hope you have better joy with your missus.

Just over here, I said and he pulled up.

I recognise this house now, he said and he looked it over. Your fascia, he said, don't you find that a ball-ache?

What's that? I said getting my wallet out of my back pocket.

The wood. Wouldn't you be better getting the uPVC? You don't have to maintain it, it's just . . . you paint that, and then in between being arsed, it looks like shite, you know?

I bit my tongue. There you go, hold on to the change, I said.

No, no, he said and searched for a few coins, his hard thick neck tensing.

Trudy was ready to head out to the water, just for a walk. I told her about the accident and she said she'd leave the car at home. Do you remember I met this taxi driver years ago? I asked her. She didn't. Well he was giving me a lift there and he was saying he'd been framed for fraud.

They're all framed, she said.

He got six years and now he blames the wife.

Don't you all, Trudy said and she grabbed her coat and left

without so much as a kiss on the cheek, shouting back that she'd be an hour or two.

The kids were outside on the trampoline. There was a net surround but the zip had never worked from the get-go. I made myself a salad and ate it at the window, waving out to them.

The girl came in straight away. Did you write your book, Daddy?

I wrote a bit of it, I said kissing her on the top of the head. The boy soared out, hitting his head on the corner of the boiler house. It was only a nick but it was deep. Holding a cloth to his head I tried calling Trudy. Her phone laughed like church bells on the counter.

I got the kids into the car and we headed to A&E. I forgot about the tail-backs in town. They were moving the bashed-up car. There was an ambulance at the side of the road, a woman in her seventies sitting with a blanket and paramedics around her.

Trudy, where are you? I said, thinking we might pass her.

You should have left a note, Daddy, my daughter said.

We'll be home in no time, I said.

Once we got to the hospital I managed to get through to Trudy at home. I'm taking a taxi, she said.

I told her it was a waste of cash, that it was a small hole and we were getting seen next.

Okay, she said, sounding emptied.

We were at the hospital for three hours. They put glue in his head and gave him stickers.

What happened here? the doctor asked my daughter.

I noticed the bruise under her eye. What did happen to you? I asked.

A boy in class hit me, she said.

I've been away, I explained. I was only in through the door and my partner had to go out. She never said. She left her phone behind. And to my daughter, What did the teacher say? Did you tell your mother?

She looked at the floor.

Why did this boy hit you? I asked her.

I don't know, she said.

I bet he likes you, said the doctor giving her a sticker too.

I sent the kids ahead, told them to wait at the main door. I said to the doctor, I hope you aren't treating my daughter when she's older because some boyfriend is knocking her about.

He looked at me singularly. I wanted to say more but I let it drop.

At home Trudy came out to meet us in the driveway, she lifted our son into the house. Come here till I see my brave soldier.

The boy sat with us past bedtime to make sure he wasn't concussed. Trudy put our girl to bed and met me in the kitchen. I think it was an accident, Trudy whispered, but I'll go and talk to her teacher tomorrow. I'll find out more. I'm sorry I left my phone here.

It's almost like you didn't want to be found.

I didn't know that would happen, she said.

They're still young, I said. They still need us a lot.

We all still need each other, Trudy said.

And that is what we proceeded to do for the next five years, pull apart and come together. The kids grew. They didn't need us much at all. It was a slap in the face how fast it happened.

❧

I rarely used cabs any more. The last time I saw Stephen I was in the back of his. Trudy and I had separate cars by then. Mine was in getting a new clutch. In his photo he'd aged a lot but his eyes looked the same. I was mindful of the fascia we'd got reconditioned. He never looked at it. We dropped my son off. Stephen watched as he walked into school.

I've three myself, he told me. All getting big now.

Yes, I said, it isn't long in happening.

I hadn't the same time for him. Only as a story, you understand. He had something bitter in him that wasn't pleasant to be around. You married? I asked him.

I was, he said, three times believe it or not.

So you're on the market?

Nah, he said, I've given up on all that. Once I had the ring on my finger I would get claustrophobic, he said. You know how it is.

But sure if you love someone, isn't it worth it?

That's not my experience.

Sure it's hard no matter who you are and what you have, and who you're with.

I'll have to take your word for it, he said. My kids were all with the last wife, Ruth. None with the other ones. Ruth doesn't let them see me any more. Haven't seen them in years.

That's tough, I said.

You're telling me.

What age are they? (I knew they'd be adults by now.)

Hmm . . . (He couldn't remember.) The grandparents won't allow them to see me.

Sure it isn't up to the kids.

But the grandparents have them and they're loaded. The kids know which side their bread is buttered, don't they? Ruth's parents badmouth me in front of them.

Why's that? If you don't mind me asking.

No, I don't mind at all, said Stephen. They loaned me money to start up a taxi firm in Chelsea. They had the kids while we got sorted, then the business went belly-up and they never let off me with it.

Shit!

They fucken accused me of stealing from them, then it was investigated and they found out it was an account in Ruth's name. Their own daughter was doing the stealing.

That's awful, I said.

It was awful. To be honest, it wasn't that bad for Ruth. She got out after a while. It was someone else, someone, a business partner of ours who was really framing her.

Who was this?

I'm not going to name names.

I respect that, I said.

I was very disappointed in him. He was a tool. They put that fella away. He made a lot of mistakes but he did his time.

(Of course I'd looked Stephen Kent up. I knew there was no taxi firm. That he and Ruth had both worked for CPS. That pride of his was so thick it was unswallowable.)

And so were you and Ruth not able to put it behind you, after?

She had someone else by then. She was always gorgeous. People would think I was her da. They'd all look at her when we were out anywhere. I'd be proud as punch.

Wouldn't you move heaven and earth to see your kids?

I have. I always had that fatherly thing about me. My parents had ten kids. I'm the oldest.

That's a lot.

I thought I'd be a dad, but just two kids, because our folks had no time for us you know. They just popped kids out. My father was a prick and my mother, she let him give her dog's abuse, you know.

You couldn't get away with that now.

No, you can't, said Stephen. My mother always hated Ruth. I found it strange when I saw the two of them as being so alike. The shit they'd put up with from men. I wanted to give Ruth and the kids everything. They didn't have much to begin . . . well, the kids weren't mine biologically. They were, I don't want you to think badly of her, but they had different dads.

Ah, no, sure it's not like I know her. I'm not about to judge the girl.

Ruth's parents were very tight with her, said Stephen. She really deserved a lot more than she had. We all do, if I'm honest. We should have more than our lot and not feel bad about wanting that. We give up enough, don't you think? If we ever had it to begin with. I want for nothing these days. He pulled up outside my work, scratched the side of his hard thick neck. Anyway, Ruth has someone else now. I hope he knows what a lucky bastard he is.

WYL MENMUIR

IN DARK PLACES

THE BROWN STREAM *falls into the rocks. Rich water draining in from the limestone heath. The hole is a pinprick eye staring out, wet in the undergrowth. Far above, two buzzards float on a thermal, one following the other. They trace an elliptic path across a sky that is cloudless and of the palest blue. On a branch in the brush by the cave entrance a small bird looks on, its head cocked.*

They pushed aside the branches, shirts stained with sweat, ready to give up by the time they found it. They whooped and embraced and argued over who would get to go down first. They drew lots and the loudest one won. All four of them were loud, but he was the loudest. They sat around and unpacked sandwiches, pasties, fruit and chocolate. After they ate, they lay on the ground, stretched out, their limbs overlapping, looked up at the sky and imagined the depths they were to plumb. They were hazy in the sunlight, shimmering and smiling and young. Here's to being the first, the loudest one shouted and the others raised their water canteens and repeated his words. The first. They may have been the first. It is doubtful. They laid out ropes, helmets and torches, checked and rechecked them all before they descended the rocks, slick and calcifying. They abseiled into the depths, into the perfect darkness. Four of them, disappeared into cracks that opened long ago. They pressed themselves into thin fractures in the crust, just for the sensation of the weight of earth against their chests. Felt the rocks constrict around them and laughed as though it was new love. They crawled and swam in rivers and pools long buried. Pushed through sunken passages and were rebirthed into silent caverns that they filled with their shouts and laughter. They woke us with their heavy footsteps and their echoes, while, far above, clouds that were not there before gathered and rain began to fall.

There were once people who walked lightly. Who heard, in the space between their footsteps, reverberations and echoes of the fissures and caverns that lay below. Otherworlds and underworlds. Places that spoke to them. They did not dive into the openings they found, nor cross too far beyond the thresholds over which might spill a horde of monstrous cats, or ravenous birds, released for a short while onto the thin surface to feed. Depths into which one might be dragged and from which there was no return. They respected this was the case. Ventured no further than they needed. Things change though. It is the only truth.

I want the full works, the man is saying. We've come a long way for this.

The caves here are an ancient house in which no one has bothered to count all the rooms. A house to which there are many entrances and fewer exits. It is a house in which the rooms change shape and location, that flood and collapse, expand, contract, disappear entirely. In which the passage of time and water carves out yet more rooms to replace those that are now gone. Entire wings are cut off from one another, separated by water or by rock fall. The roof's many domes and cupolas are polished into smooth whorls. There are ballrooms here too, state rooms and sunken parlours, forgotten attics and cupboards so small you can barely bury a child in them. It is a house in which arcuated corridors, striated and scalloped, confuse and mislead, run back on themselves or taper into paths too narrow to follow. There are signs at one of the entrances now. This entrance, close to the valley floor, has a café and an office that sells tickets. A man and a woman stand at the turnstile.

The full works? the boy selling tickets is thinking, as though he could throw in some extra caves now he knows it is demanded. The woman cringes. It is the height of summer and the queue is growing. The boy takes their money and asks the couple to stand to one side. They will be met at the gate shortly. The man and the woman stand close to one another but do not hold hands. After ten minutes, during which they read the signs on the walls, a young man with a beard arrives. The guide. He apologises for making them wait. There was a problem with a goat on the cliffs above. He is kind to the goats, this man, and the sheep too. He leads them back to safety. When the guide tells the man and the woman about the goat, he is met with blank stares. He ushers them away from the entrance to a small concrete block set into the cliff, where he hands them boiler suits, harnesses, wellingtons, helmets, head torches to put on. The woman seems confused by this. The man spends an age trying to fit his harness. He exchanges his glasses for contact lenses and he ends up dabbing dust into them. While he is making his eyes sore the woman is overheating on the balcony outside. We hear the word honeymoon. An angry word she repeats over and again in her head. The guide asks the man if he would like to leave his camera in the room. It will be safe there. The room will be locked. The man laughs and says the camera should be strong enough to take whatever they throw at it. They are hard to see in the light, these three figures. They are blurred and they only start to come into focus as they bypass the queue and are shown through a gate by the side of the turnstile. At the threshold they stand where the light filters in and the man holds forth about the skeleton that had been discovered in a small cavern just to the left of where they are standing. How these are the oldest human remains. He has read leaflets in their holiday cottage. He has looked it up online. The woman wonders whether her husband is aware the skeleton they can see is a plaster cast. She shares a look with the guide who smiles but says nothing and moves them on.

The plaster cast of his bones is confusingly similar though it is not the same as him at all. We remember when he arrived. It was a long time ago. The people who came then never went any further than this point. The point at which shadows start to eat away at the daylight. Well, few of them. He was not dead when he arrived, but he could not stand like the others. He was carried in and placed on the ground and left. He coughed and moaned and slept and dreamt and slipped in and out of consciousness as the night wore on and throughout the next day before he stopped moving. He was not the first to arrive, not by a long way. The living and the dead, brought and left. We remember a mother. She carried her son to the entrance. His head was caved in on one side and before she left, she asked us to help him, as though she thought there was something we could do. Before he died the boy lay on his back and watched the bats as they flitted in and out of the entrance and when it became too dark we showed him more images of bats to comfort him until his breathing became too quiet for even us to hear. And then there were long periods when they did not come. Still air. Creatures that walked quietly. The spring torrents. The movement of the rocks. Wearing away and building back up. Flooding and emptying. Ebb and flow. The slow shifting and rearranging of rooms in the darkness.

The couple move further in, away from the daylight. The man struts and points his camera at everything and talks to the guide with authority. The guide nods in the right places. The man ignores the curtain stalactites that glow softly in the halogen light and the small forest of ferns that have grown up beneath the lamps in niches in the wall. The woman sees them and lingers, taking them in. She likes the lights in the recesses best, the ones that hint at other places just out of reach. We remember the first lights. Burning sticks. Candles. Oil lamps. Lights on strings, like burning thread that runs through the labyrinth. We have heard that story too. They leave the lights on all the time now, even when they are not here. We sometimes make them flicker and watch the shadows dance on the walls.

As they pass them, the couple stare up at the pallets of cheese, unsure what to make of them.

Is this normal then? the man asks. The cheese, down here. It can't be hygienic.

He has read about this too, though he did not believe it, somehow. It does not fit with his image of the cave, nor of what he is doing here. He will edit it out of the picture later. The guide explains the constant temperature in the caves makes them the perfect place to mature the cheese, but they do not linger. Further in, the guide pauses at a small offshoot and points out to them a feature in the rock.

If you part-close your eyes and tilt your head slightly, he says, you can make out the curve of a mammoth's tusk, and here the back, and its hind legs. It follows the curve of the rock.

They both stare at it and the man nods and says yes, he can see it.

I think it's unlikely, the guide continues. The people who found it were looking for this, or for something like it. So, they found it. We see what we want to see, and if someone points something out to us and tells us it is there, we want it to be true, so we convince ourselves that it is. We create the story for ourselves. If there were carvings here, they've been long washed away by the floods.

She was with the university, the woman who discovered the mammoth. She saw herself as much a caver as an academic. She had examined the walls of almost every cave in the country that was known to have been inhabited. We heard the word Altamira as it repeated itself endlessly in her head. She was slow. Methodical. Sometimes she forgot what it was she was looking for and seemed to be feeling for something else in the rock. She cared for each of the tiny scars and nicks on the walls much as the guide cares for the goats. She inched along, sometimes stopping and staring, tilting her head to one side and then the other. She put a hand up to the rock face. Traced a tusk, the dome of a head and the curve of a back with the tip of her finger and we felt her excitement through the rock. She could see the carver, had already started to flesh him out in her mind, his life and habits, his hidden motivations. We had felt this before. It is palpable, this need to understand.

We do not remember anyone having carved this here. But it has been a long time, so, perhaps.

Others stop to inspect the carving, to puzzle at it. It is busy in the caves today. When it is like this, we think about sending cats out. Thousands of them. Especially when the caves are full and the lights seem too bright and the noise builds until they are shouting over themselves. A little further on, the guide lifts a chain and they turn away from the families milling around on the main path. He asks the man and the woman to turn on the lights on their helmets.

They clamber up to the foot of a large boulder, where they clip on to a safety line and make their way up a series of aluminium ladders that are roped to the rocks. We see her thoughts clearly here, away from the well-lit passage where everything is slightly fuzzy. They are just married. It is her first marriage. They were married on a cloudless day that marked the beginning of the hot summer and the day itself had seemed long to her. The photographer had complained that there was too much light and when she looked at the photographs later, she was inclined to agree. They looked washed out, their faces pursed, skin pale. They lacked depth. If someone had told her they were fakes, she might have believed them. The ladder shudders as they cross gaps that the guide tells them have names like Endless Drop and Bottomless Pit. If only he knew.

Isn't it dangerous? the woman asks.

It is the first time she has spoken since they entered the caves. The man laughs.

Here, the guide takes them to where the roof dips and they crouch and then crawl and then lie on their stomachs and pull themselves through, into the diminishing gap between the roof and the floor. They contort themselves through the passage, though the guide knows there is a way a few metres from them where they could walk and their heads would not touch the roof. There is a climb, a scramble through mud. They sweat and flush and their hearts race. When they emerge into the next chamber, they rest for a while as the guide tells them a story about a young man who went caving alone, who kept pushing on as the cave got narrower and narrower, as the passage tipped downwards and he pushed on with his arms out in front of him until there was no way forward and no way to get back. That he was found weeks later, wedged into the rock. He has told this story before.

We have heard a great many stories. Some of them we remember well, cannot dislodge. Others lose their way. They disappear into the crevasses. Most of the stories we have heard were told close to the entrances, pieced together from whatever scraps were lying around, detritus and lies built up until they became as intransigent as the rock walls. Stories told by firelight, tentative explorations and explanations. Stories told by candlelight, when grand feasts have been assembled, tales of awe and of the sublime. Stories told by torchlight as cards were shuffled and bets placed. Stories told in dark places, whispered close in to another's ear. Confessions and stories to enlighten, to comfort, to seduce. And our favourites, the ones in which the teller does not even recognise what they are doing is telling a story at all. Those that took place a long time ago and those that are closer, they blend and converge, overlap and run on into each other. Perhaps it is because they are similar stories. The same ones, told over and again, in different voices. Some of the older stories degrade and grow increasingly vague. This is how we know they are older stories. Some we have forgotten entirely.

They scramble up over the boulders at the far end of the chamber and the guide points them towards a small gap in the rocks above. He will meet them at the top, he says.

Who will go first? The woman. She did not want to be here, although now she is, she feels the blood in her face and the sweat slick between her shoulder blades and she is glad she came. The gap becomes narrower and the way steeper and halfway up the climb she is convinced she will not get through. She holds herself still for a moment, breathes, kicks her feet against a narrow ledge she cannot see behind her and pushes. And she is moving through the space that a moment ago looked impassable. She squeezes herself through the crack and we feel her pulse race, the thrill of it. Below, the man rubs more dust into his eyes and curses. He starts to climb up towards the woman. We are tempted to compress the walls around him, just slightly. He comes to the push and can get no further and he claws at the rocks and kicks against the smooth walls.

You just need to jam one of your feet . . . the woman calls down to him. Do you need a hand? I could pull you through.

The man ignores her and continues to scrabble. His hands cast about, sweating and slipping on the rocks. He pants like a crow.

These stupid caves, he says and he pushes against the rocks again, his elbows out to the sides and his feet now swinging in space. He thinks no one else has heard him say this, though the woman hears it and the guide too. In the end, the guide comes round and pushes him up by his feet.

They come out at the top of the cave, having worked their way up the steep sides, and peer down into the dark. The guide explains to them what will happen next and asks again which of them will go first. The man pushes himself forward and the guide talks him through the abseil and he lets himself down in short jerky movements. Halfway, he hears a crash against the rocks below. The woman, when she comes to it, swings back off the ledge and abseils into thin air into the middle of the cave as though she is falling back onto a bed or into cool water. She lets out cord in long sweeps and her movements are confident, relaxed. The man does not notice when she lands beside him on the floor of the large chamber. He is trying to piece the camera back together and cursing under his breath. While he does this, the woman looks around at the boulders strewn across the floor and at the telephone on a box on the wall. They have both lost all sense of direction now. This always amuses the guide.

This is as far as we go, the guide says. Further on there are more chambers we know about. There are long passages that are permanently flooded. We're always finding new ones, small openings, caves we've not explored yet. It's possible this network is just a small part of a whole system we've not even discovered or that it links to the other networks we know about.

Can we turn the lights out? the woman says. Just for a while? To see the darkness.

The man, who is now holding the broken housing of his camera, does not look keen. The guide asks them to sit on one of the boulders and then walks over to a set of switches on a board on the cave wall and turns the cavern's side lights off.

When you're ready, flick the switch on your head torches, he says.

The man's is the last to go out and when it does, the woman thinks maybe they have left a light on somewhere in the cave. There is a low purple glow, though she realises soon after that it is an illusion of the total darkness.

Hold a hand up in front of your eyes, the guide says. It's impossible to adjust to this.

The man starts to say something but the woman asks him to stop. Just to stop.

Can we sit like this for a while? the woman says. Without the light. Without talking. Just for a minute?

There was a man who came here once and did this. Sat in the dark. The one we called the hermit. He made camp just where the couple are sitting now. Surrounded by boxes of books and candles and food. He sat and read, wrote stories to his daughter, paced the caves, turned the lights off and then on again. Sometimes he cried. Most of all he slept and when he was asleep we looked at him more closely. When he slept, he dreamt of flight. He had a problem with a cough. After a while he had a problem with time too. He started to feel like we do. We showed him images in the dark and he did not like this. And then he was gone. Four months. Blink of an eye, though we felt we had started to get to know him. Before he arrived, a group of men installed a yellow telephone. Bright yellow. Sometimes, in the night, we make it ring. It is one of the many things left behind, along with the strings of lights, tusks and flints, bones and mushroom spores, a wedding ring, a child's toy that was dropped into one of the deeper caverns and that lies on its back looking up into the darkness. And now shattered glass from the lens of the man's camera that he has trodden into the clay.

Most people seem to think they are opaque. In the darkness, though, they become clear. Luminous. Readable. The two men and the woman sit in silence and the woman tries not to listen to the sound of the two men breathing. She tunes into the faint echoes of the cave and thinks about the ones that are flooded. She thinks about swimming in a submerged lake in the perfect darkness. She can feel the silt between her toes as she kicks off the floor, the velvet water on her back and on her legs as she stretches them behind her, as she loses sense of place and time. Shapes dance in front of her and she knows she is projecting them, and it is beautiful. It is so dark she expects that if she looked hard enough she would see stars, constellations, galaxies in the blackness, as if she was not looking out at walls, but onto a firmament. She feels the darkness pouring into her.

It is then we show her. Just a single image. A negative. She blinks and it is gone. We show her the four of them, suspended, mid-solution. They are in one of the chambers we keep permanently flooded now. They do not touch the sides, not ever. We move them sometimes, just slightly, set off currents and eddies, tiny vortices in the still water. Ripple and fade. Two of them, the lovers, we keep close together. It seems right. They are locked in a slow dance in the water, cold cheek to cold cheek, while the other two look on.

It was not due to rain that day, so they weren't looking out for it. They were a mile or so in when the rain began and they had just decided to turn back when it started to flood. The kind of thing where the sky just opens up. They were young. Caving club types. We had seen many like them before, in other wings of this sprawling house. And when the water started to roll in, it rose quickly down there and cut them off where they were. When they realised what was happening, they moved towards each other rather than looking for an exit, as though collectively they were more protected.

None of them said it, but the water trap was clear in their minds as they made their way back towards it. It had been a couple of metres when they made the dive the first time. The rain took the whole tunnel out and it flooded fast, and pushed them back towards the larger chamber. They knew, immediately. They knew. The tunnel was still flooding and there was no telling when it would open out again, so they did the only thing they could and swam. Down into the airless dark, back through the crawl hole through which they had emerged. And the rain continued, the trickle of water at the entrance now a cascade. Two tried to turn back, though by then it was too late for all of them. We watched them fight it, for longer than we would have thought possible, before they were still. Later, there were lights on the hill, flashing and pulsing. And a crowd of people turned up at a clearing by an entrance that was nearby though not the right one. Some went a way in. First one group, then another. We recognised the names they shouted. We recognised their need for an answer. A few days later, another crowd gathered outside the same entrance, and huddled in to hear what the robed man said over the wind. Afterwards they boarded the entrance up and later they replaced the boards with a metal door and secured it with a padlock.

We care for them like we cared for the others. Perhaps that is why we are here. To care for the ones who were left.

The guide asks the man and the woman to close their eyes and to cover the lamps with their hands when they turn them back on. The woman blinks several times. Each time she does, the image of the four cavers flashes onto the red canvas of her eyelids. She has accepted it.

When they are gone, and when the screaming children are

gone and the elderly gentlemen who are on a tour of sorts too, and the students who talk in a language we recognise but cannot understand, we forget about the man and the woman for a while and watch the bats as they emerge from their caves and take back the space for themselves, balletic and swift. Their choreography is strange even to us. Even after all this time. The bats have been here the longest. In the evening, in the between times, they flit and dance, and at day they cluster and rustle, unfold and refold their paper wings. And under the heat of the cave lamps, the ferns continue to grow.

The caves are never empty for long. They cannot stay away from them, as though an itch that started a long time gone has just grown as the centuries have worn on, has built incrementally, as stalagmites grow. We recall being woken by voices at the entrance, dynamite blasts in the deep, the opening out of new chambers. We marvelled at the speed with which they did this. The talk of opening this cave out and extending this passage. Theorising. Mapping and sketching. On paper, the cave's thin fingers stretch out for miles. There is a passage just beyond this point. We can feel it, the ones with picks and dynamite, say, and continue their digging and blasting. Their voices echo in the chambers.

It is like this now, but it will return to the way it was before. A flood or a fall. The filling of the caverns with limestone deposits. To the way it will be after the swift passing of men.

And the slow drawing of a stalactite from a rock.

And the slow violence of water.

And the slower violence of time.

OWEN BOOTH

THE WAR

WE INTERVIEWED THE war. The war was depressed, smoking too much. And we were paying for the drinks. The war polished off three bottles of good red.

We were thinking by the third bottle how can you even tell the difference? The war could tell the difference. The war had been doing this for years. And what did we know about anything anyway? We who weren't the war. We who would never be the war.

The war was a mean drunk. The war said things about us that would have been better left unsaid. But wars, we discovered, do not apologise.

Actually, according to the war, there is only – has only ever been – one war. All wars are the same war. All over the world. The war, so the war told us, contains multitudes.

Consequently, the war contradicts itself, time and again. The war reserves the right to change its mind. The war which is too big to be tied to facts. The war which, when it acts, makes its own reality (war, says the war, being the locomotive of history, and so on).

The war likes to refer to itself in the third person.

The war, says the war, won't stand for this sort of thing.

The war, says the war, is tired of your nonsense.

The war, says the war, thinks you'd better watch out.

And so on.

The war claims to have had a job once, claims to have worked in, of all places, a Viennese coffee house, back in the days when that meant something. Back in the early days of the twentieth century. The war remembers the moustachioed waiters gliding between the tables with glasses of Einspänner and piles of apfelstrudel and punschkrapfen, remembers the slanted pre-war afternoon light - that sort of light *you don't get any more* - the light glancing off the polished marble table tops, the light skidding along the brass rails and the zinc counter, the light spinning off millions of suspended, dancing dust particles.

And it was as if all of Europe was suspended, dancing like that.

The war knew the beautiful, bent neck of every female customer, knew the brave shoulders of every strapping young man.

It was a time of obscene innocence, says the war, back in the days before the war changed everything. The war which was me.

Of course the war has regrets. You have no idea.

I remember every face; every sunrise, says the war. Don't you think I had hopes and dreams of my own?

The war smokes all our cigarettes. The war with its feet on our table. The millions of feet of soldiers and prisoners of war and displaced peoples. And all of them needing shoes.

The war says you try five thousand years of this, ten thousand years of this.

The war doesn't go back further than the end of the last ice age. The first thing the war can remember is the retreat of the great ice sheets. Then the carcases of millions of mammoth and woolly rhinoceros and giant ground sloth strewn across the vast plains of Eurasia and the Americas. And the last of the Neanderthals, cornered in some damp, foggy wood on the Atlantic coast, about to get its head smashed in.

Before that, nothing.

Not knowing is a relief.

The war dreams of forgetting.

The war says, But look at all the things I invented. Smartphones. Superglue. Mass production.

Wasn't that . . . weren't those things more generally the result of capitalism, we ask, rather than war?

Plastics, the war continues. The welfare state. The motorway . . .

The war spilling someone's drink on purpose. The war making dangerous friends at the bar. The war starting a fight and getting us all thrown out of the pub. The liability of the war.

Under an ice-cream moon the war sits on a beach throwing pebbles into the surf. The sea is glowing with the light of millions of phosphorescing bacteria. The war is subdued, thoughtful. How many hundreds of thousands of years, the war wonders, would it take to throw every pebble on this beach into the sea? Will the war even be around that long?

Likely a lot of the pebbles would be washed back up onto the beach anyway . . . we suggest.

High explosives, says the war. That would do it.

We can't argue with that.

And was there also time for romance, we asked, back in those good old days? Was there a special woman in the war's life?

Death was my only mistress, says the war, but, oh, she was a glory to behold. Give me another one of those cigarettes. Death in a black cocktail dress, two hundred feet tall. Death wading through filth and horror and not a hair out of place. Death swatting fighter planes out of the sky. Have you ever been with a two-hundred-foot-tall woman, ladies and gentlemen?

We shake our heads.

You have to lift your thinking, that's the first thing you find out. You have to raise your game. A woman like that – it changes your perspective. Her eyes, iced over in the bomb bay of a Lancaster twenty-eight thousand feet above Germany, as I begged her to run away with me. Her devastating smile as we tumbled through the frozen night sky . . .

Landscapes of the war (not to scale):

A hollowed out factory, the roof gone

A burning jungle (plus terrified locals)

The iron-grey sea at dawn

A row of partially collapsed buildings, leaning into each other like drunk dancers

Endless wheat fields, and you can make out every blade of grass, and the tanks in the distance . . .

The war isn't without a certain attractiveness. A certain worn and melancholy charisma. The war has kept its hair. Those wounded eyes are still clear. The war, then, trying to get off with our wives and girlfriends, our husbands and lovers. The war trying to seduce our seventeen-year-old daughters, turning the heads of our sons. The war with its grief and melancholy and its wounded eyes, at the windows of our husbands and wives and our sons and daughters in the early hours of the morning.

That slick bastard. That sneaky fucker.

Then there was the time the war tried to go on holiday. Soft rain in the mornings, long grey cloud rolling down off the hills. The war, trying to put up a tent. The war flailing around like a dad in an advert, tripping over tent pegs and so on, accidentally flattening whole towns. The war hilariously burning cities and taking the tops off mountains. The low comedy of war . . .

Is war inevitable? we ask the war.

As inevitable as the weather, says the war. As inevitable as childbirth and laughter and famine.

Is war preventable? we ask. Put off-able? Delay-able?

But the war is crying in the forecourt of the all-night garage at four in the morning, wrestling with the wrapper on a cheese and onion slice. Huge, embarrassing sobs. The self-pity of the war.

I can't get the fucking thing . . . it won't . . .

The war as a victim – of history, of the modern world, of its own success. The war haunted by the deaths of children. The endlessly photographed deaths of children. The incomprehensible deaths of children. The war in its gigantic self-indulgence.

A crowd has gathered. At four in the morning, for God's sake, in the forecourt of an all-night garage. Where did all these people come from? Don't they have homes to go to?

The war wants to tell them about the Russian winter, the Indian campaigns, the conquest of Gaul. The war remembers Viking raids and cannibalism and human sacrifice. The war remembers breaking horses in the high desert, remembers rolling across Asia with the Golden Horde, remembers pulling back the tent flap at dawn to see thunderstorms dancing on the horizon, at the edge of the known world. All that important stuff that nobody wants to hear.

We take the war home, tell the war it can sleep on our sofa.

Ceramics! shouts the war as we stumble up the stairs. Clingfilm! The Gatling gun!

We don't know if the war even believes any of this any more.

But the sun is already coming up and the war has fallen asleep at the kitchen table, its huge snores sounding like the end of the world. Probably there are birds singing somewhere. And we have no choice but to start thinking about how we'll all get through the next impossible day.

TANIA HERSHMAN

AND WHAT IF ALL YOUR BLOOD RAN COLD

WE DO IT gradually. Well, you have to, don't you. No replacing all someone's blood in a hurry. We've not done it on a real patient, you have to wait, for the right kind to turn up. Exactly the precise situation where this might work. Which doesn't happen often. The patient who has no other chance, who is going to die. Who *is* going to die. That kind of patient.

There's someone here whose job it is to keep track. Of how many do die. Our mortality rates. She sits at her desk, she has a spreadsheet. She's excellent with those. She loves numbers, lists, moving and shuffling them around. But every now and then she comes down, stands in a corner and watches. I see her there, like a ghost, as we're resuscitating, intubating, all the blood, the noise. She hovers there in her corner and there's a look on her face, I see it as I rush past. I can't place that look.

She's in love. No, not with me. I don't know who with. Not yet. But she sits at her desk, and although she's precise, she has files and folders keeping track of heart attacks, infections, of treatments given, of the names of those who fill the morgue, the cold ones whose hearts we weren't meant to restart, whose infections resisted all our efforts, she's not focussed. Not any more. She used to be. When she first arrived, she was keen as mustard. As the sharpest mustard. She didn't come down to watch then. She was all about figures.

Maybe it's not love, maybe it's death. Or deaths. All of it. But I'm pretty sure. Because being surrounded by the almost-dying is what you get used to here. It's not what begins to slide under your skin; it rolls off. Whatever's eating her, it's something else.

We've only practised it, so far, the new technique, on the newly-dead. With permission, of course. There were no loved ones then, we used homeless people, people that no-one claimed. People that no-one visited. Hospital lawyers gave the go-ahead. After all, it's to save lives, no? And they were already. Unsaveable.

She wasn't there then. No-one watched, because we were clumsy, slow, we bungled. It's a lot of work, the wholesale blood removal. It's a lot of liquid. Hours. It's not like we dry them out – we replace the blood. With salt water. It's cooler, the body temperature drops and then they can stay like that while we try and fix them. That's the theory, anyway.

I think the person she's in love with, our death accountant, isn't someone she works with. She's not got that silly, I've-just-seen-my-beloved look when she watches us.

It's cold. So
cold. They
think I don't
know. They
think I can't. But
I do. I
am. Still.

You know, I'm not the only one, there's one of me in every hospital. Accountants of doom, that's what we call ourselves, our joke, when we get together! It's not like we're doing the killing, we say, and we do laugh about it because if you don't laugh about it, when you do what we do, what else happens but that you go home every night, every night, and sit and look at the moon and drink something to stop yourself from thinking about it but then you dream about it anyway, all the ways. You soak it into yourself when you are the one who knows all the dead, all the dying, it's inside your skin, and you've got no barrier, no anti-morbid raincoat, which is something else we laugh about. What a gap in the market! we say as we pass around the Hobnobs. Someone needs to develop that kind of technology, help the doom accountants! Then we giggle, there does seem to

be a lot of gigglers amongst us, no matter what
age, no matter how long you've been doing what
we do. If you saw me sitting in my office, if you
saw me in front of my computer, you might
think I was so serious, checking my spreadsheets,
with all the different flavours of death in neat
columns, with dates, times, of course. But
inside I'm probably chuckling at something
someone has sent by email, one of those cartoons,
Death doing this, someone cheating Death,
you know the kind of thing. We laugh a lot.
Part of the job gets me out from behind the
desk, I have to go and talk to the staff about what
the situation is, quite often, I do the rounds,
I wander, and I ask quietly, gently, about this
week, about the almost-dying, the almost-died,
the chances of, the attempts to save, and there
isn't much laughing then, of course, we're
usually in the corridors, I don't like to take too
much of their time. They're the ones doing the
saving, the resuscitating, the caring. I just add
it up. I just do the sums. Who's left us this
week, and who gets to stay for a while longer.

We found one! I know, don't sound too excited.
But – the perfect candidate. They tried everything
else on him. Motorbike. Silly bugger. So we
snap into action. Not the best coordinated team,
despite the practice. I mean, all those years of
med school but the minute you come out and
there you are, real world, it's different. There's

no pausing. It's all blood and insides and people crying and, hopefully, patients hugging you and actually leaving the hospital. Properly.

So we did it. Drained him and refilled. It all seemed to work. The saline instead of blood. And now we've got time. Or rather, he's got time. We hope.

It's cold. So
cold. They
think I don't.
They
think I
can't. But
I
do. I
am. Still.

We do talk, when we all get together, about why we ended up in this job, we know it's not something our parents can boast about, My Daughter the Death Statistician! We know that it's a job that's as old as the hills, of course, all throughout history someone was charged with adding them up, the fallen. Or someone took it upon themselves, the Chroniclers. How many died in wars, how many in fires, plagues, pestilence. We humans, we like numbers, we find some kind of comfort, maybe from the fact – we discussed this last time we met – that we're reading the numbers so it means we're not one

of them, we're not on The List, not yet, and we
can pretend we never will be. Or it's some kind
of talisman, you know: talk about it, read about
it, do the sums, but me, never, I'm immortal!
We know better than anyone about immortality.
We know better than anyone the chances.
They're greater now – clean hands, antibiotics,
surgical techniques, robots, nanoparticles, on
and on. But still, the viruses get smarter and
shiftier, who knows what's in the air around
my desk, or what's coming in through that
window? You just don't. You just never know.

And while we're working on him, Bike Boy, she comes down. She stands for a while in the corner of the room, and then she says, to all of us, What's happening exactly? And I see my chance, so I tell her. Replacing his blood? she says. All of it? Yes, I say, and she says, So he's still . . . alive? Without . . . blood? Ah, I say, well, that's sort of tricky. Tricky? she says, and she tilts her head to one side and I swear she's almost grinning. He's in a sort of . . . I say. Suspended animation, I think that's the technical term, and here her eyes light up, honestly. Oh my god, she says, and her hands do this fluttering thing. I don't have a column for that, I don't have . . . Neither do we! I say, and for a moment we're both standing and grinning at each other. Then I'm called back and before I turn around she says, How long . . . ? and I say, Well, it's experimental, you know. We just don't. We really . . .

I want to tell everyone, I want to email round and say, Guess what, I had to create a new category, I've got a new column, do you know about this, suspended, half-way-between? But of course, I can't, it's experimental, it's hush hush, it's more than that, hush hush hush HUSH. My fingers are itching to do it, but instead I choose a new colour for the category, I write his name down, a tick in that column. For now. And then I sit, and I think I'm sitting for ages and ages, wondering about it, wondering if he knows, wondering, for the first time really, you'd think I'd thought more about how dead might feel, but this is someone who might feel it and then come back. Come back. Jesus, Mary, Joseph and all the others, this really does feel like some sort of witchcraft.

They worked on him, Bike Boy, for days. That's the point of all of this: time. The thing we run out of round here, the main element which we wish we could bag and attach like a drip. Slow it all down, as we run and run, we're running to try and outrun it. So this, if it works . . . my god. I mean, last night I sat at home and thought, What if we could do this with everyone who comes in? Slip in a drain, slide out all your blood, salt and cool you, and then we'd be walking, dancing, as we fixed you up, no? We could say, Oh look at that liver, hmm, what should we do? And then we'd hang out, drink tea, weigh up our options. And you'd be oh so chilled. And then I thought, But we don't know anything about what'd be in your head. Would you be having dreams of walking through Antarctica, being trapped inside a freezer, becoming icicles? And then I thought of her, and I remembered how we'd grinned at each other, her and me, at this new thing, this new category. New. New and newness. Isn't always better, though, is it?

When the time came, or rather, when the point arrived after which no-one knew what might happen to Bike Boy in his suspension, I thought she might like to see it, so I went upstairs to find her. She was at her desk and before she saw me I watched her. It's rare to see someone doing what she does looking so damn happy. Even gleeful. I mean, she's a numbers person, she's not reaching into chests to start a heart, she's not inventing things, she's not teaching, and I know that all sounds patronising as hell, but it's true, no? I tapped on the glass. When she turned, first she looked worried, but I smiled, to help. And realised how I'd wanted her to look at me like she'd looked at her screen, her lists. Happy.

We stood around his bed, so many of us, me the only one, I guess, not really a medical person, it was so nice of them to let me, to send someone to come and fetch me for this. I was trying not to seem as excited as I was feeling. My god! Here was this guy, in suspended animation, hovering, hovering in my brand new category, and we – they

– were about to bring him back. And you could feel it, a wave shivering between all of us, I've never known anticipation like that, so thick, like we could pass it round, eat it almost, a rope of it tying us together. It was simple: they'd done all the hooking up, someone nodded at someone, they pressed a button, there was whirring, and we all stared at his face. His face! The blood was coming back into him, I couldn't see where exactly. His blood, that they'd kept. Nudging all the saline out the way, and it made me think of some cartoon, of little blood men arriving and the salt maidens not wanting to leave, and I did have to stop myself giggling because this was serious, this was it, this was the moment. A sort of miracle, perhaps.

She was watching Bike Boy's face, so was everyone, we were all pretending we weren't unbelievably desperate for it, for it to have worked. But I was watching her. That might sound like I'm in love with her or something, but I'm not, I don't have it in me, not for love, not right now. Something about her makes me so curious, about her job, how she goes on when she's staring at it every day. She's staring at it not in the way we do, she can't think, Death, how can I try and avoid it, how can I save this one? She must be thinking, One death, and another one, and another one . . . and on and on. How does she do it?

Nothing happened, and more nothing happened,
and it wasn't like those films, where when they
zoom into a close up of the coma person's face,
you just know that their eyelids are going to do
that twitchetty thing and someone will come
running and shouting, She's awake! Real life
doesn't work on a schedule that suits an audience.
We stood there and then after about 20 minutes
there was some more nodding and someone said,
Well, it might take a while, and we all began to
wander off and I went back upstairs to stare at
my categories. And I put my mouse over his
name, I highlighted it as if I was going to move
it, from its own special hush hush column into
one. Or the other. And I really felt, really truly
and so strongly, that if I moved him, it might . . .
I might be able to. And I swear, I started shaking.
I dropped my mouse and I put my hand over my
own heart and it was like a drum was inside me,
someone was pounding on it, just pounding.

Later, I went and stood by him. Nothing.
Nothing had changed. He was officially,
medically, himself again, I mean, he was all blood,
no salt. But he hadn't moved, no twitching, no
sighing, nothing. He was still on the ventilator,
we were doing all his functions for him. I bent
down. I bent down right by his ear as if I was
going to whisper something. But I didn't know.
I just didn't know what to say and I felt like a

right idiot, so I fiddled, made it look like I was just checking. And when I got up, she was there.

'Nothing?'

'Nothing. Nope.'

'How much longer? I mean . . .'

'No-one knows. We've really got no clue, this is so . . .'

MIKE FOX

THE HOMING INSTINCT

IT STARTED JUST after sunrise one September morning and inexplicably went on happening thereafter. The heron flew down the twisting river, circled a few times enquiringly, then veered off to alight on the small oblong of grass in front of the ornamental arches where they slept. Once settled it stood like a priest in a moulting cassock, erect and vigilant, while gradually their heads emerged from beneath the sleeping bags, old blankets and cardboard that formed their bedding.

The arches, really an ornamental terrace, were no more than fifty feet from the river, damp but sheltered, quiet at night. It wasn't an ideal sleeping place – all of those were indoors – but it had things going for it. It was near a public lavatory, they were not under anyone's feet, and in the warmest nights of summer it could almost feel like camping. In fact last May a passing nomad had done just that, setting up a small tent across the path, where a broader sweep of grass sloped down to the river.

Jessie and Orlando were comrades by default. She probably in her forties, but with heroin's parting gift of taut, youthful features; he a large, affable boy who, if asked, replied simply that it all suddenly went pear-shaped.

They had met at morning breakfast in the Crypt, eyeing

each other suspiciously during the short mandatory prayer that preceded the food queue. Both were wondering why the other was there. Jessie, Orlando thought, looked tough and capable: someone who should be able to work the system, even in its current state. Orlando, Jessie thought, was an overgrown cherub who must surely have a home somewhere.

She came over to sit beside him when they'd collected their food.

'Rice Krispies and a banana?' she said.

Orlando eyed her sideways, his face low as he spooned the cereal. He'd known fights break out when food and warmth had thawed the numbness of a freezing night.

'I'm only fucking asking,' Jessie said.

'It's what I like,' he said defensively, and the way he said it made her want to smile.

The conversation didn't really progress, but they found themselves walking up the stone steps together when the final part of the morning session, a more formal prayer followed by a short homily from the verger, was over. This they tolerated: food mostly came with God attached. Outside the church basement they found brilliant early autumn sunshine. Both carried a can and an apple: lunch and supper in entirety, barring providence.

Having the gift of time but nothing specific to do with it, they continued walking together. Each had been outside long enough to know that people could fall into your life then out again at any time.

'How about the library?' Jessie asked, after they'd strolled a few hundred yards.

'I don't mind,' Orlando said. It was quiet, warm, and only a handful of older people used it now. And providing you stuck to a few basics no-one threw you out.

They made their way there, picked some reading matter, and settled into the armchairs in the corner.

'Do you like bikes?' Jessie asked, seeing the magazine he chose.

'I used to have a mountain bike,' Orlando said.

Jessie nodded as though this was significant. She was reading *The Grapes of Wrath*.

'We did that for GCSE,' Orlando said. 'It was seriously depressing.'

'It's meant to be,' Jessie said. 'It's about real life.'

Throughout the day Orlando caught Jessie looking at him, and his rucksack, appraisingly. He was used to this and said nothing. As evening fell she said, 'Where are you kipping?'

'Probably outside the bookies in the high street.' He had noticed immediately that she wasn't carrying any gear, which meant she had settled somewhere.

'I've got a better place if you want,' she said. 'There's always space. Been there nine months and never got hassled.'

So he went with her to the arches, a small folly which faced the river and was built into the lowest part of a steep hill. At the front a series of brick pillars supported a substantial flat roof, from which grew clematis and ivy. A concrete plinth, raised a foot above the grass, carried the whole structure. Set well back, four inscribed benches rested within alcoves. Behind the benches were stacked tight black bin bags, bedding and utensils, spare clothing, and what looked like a brazier, improvised from an old park waste bin. An elderly golfing umbrella peeked out next to the head of a teddy bear. Each corner was tucked in carefully with cardboard.

Jessie saw Orlando taking this in. 'We make sure it's all

neat,' she said. 'And there's nothing there that rats or foxes will go for.'

'Brilliant,' he said. The benches were long enough to lie on, and raised slatted timber was a lot warmer than stone paving.

'Alright, George?' Jessie enquired of an older man who sat fiddling with some oversized trainers in the corner. He had a long, heavy tweed coat that might once have been very expensive.

'Yes,' he said.

Orlando soon realised that George's breathing wasn't great, so he mainly spoke in monosyllables. Jessie explained later that he came from an artistic family, and was known to have directed a film about Hieronymus Bosch. The trainers, two sizes too large, had been plucked from a jumble sale as a remedy for feet that, after several months without shoes, wouldn't tolerate anything tighter.

Orlando had slept on his bench for about ten nights when the heron arrived. Along the river path geese, gulls, pigeons, ducks and even moorhens could vie for human attention when food was around, but herons were more aloof. It was unusual for one to come so close. Orlando saw it one morning when he was first to wake. It was standing no more than six feet from where they lay. It seemed detached, as if in reverie. Coming out of troubled dreams, he found the bird's stillness calming.

Gradually the others woke and stretched inside their bedding. The heron craned its neck forward in response to each movement but stayed where it was, seeming to look at some oblique point to the left of the shelter. They sat watching it for a while, as though sharing in its presence. No-one tried to stroke or even approach it: it was obviously not that sort of animal.

'I think it's someone's spirit,' Jessie said eventually. 'Do you know anyone who's died?'

'Loads of people,' Orlando murmured quietly, and Jessie bowed her head as though regretting the question.

The bird returned daily from that point on, standing silently for two or three hours before flying off down the river like a small pterodactyl. Positioned between the arches and the footpath, it brought them attention, but also deflected it. Police occasionally strolled past. They should, of course, move these people on. But the situation, as they viewed it, caused them not to. If a wild bird felt safe, how could humans come to any harm? It was almost like a sentinel: statuesque except for the occasional minute twitch of its neck. It fled when George was taken off to hospital in an ambulance, but came again the next day to resume its vigil. Jessie and Orlando began taking turns to bring a tin of sardines from the morning session at the Crypt, placing one carefully a couple of feet from where it stood. The first time they did this it inclined its head in apparent surprise, then with a sudden abrupt movement stepped forward and darted down with its beak. They watched as the small fish made its way down the elastic gizzard. It stood slightly closer from then on.

The autumn nights grew colder. When a frost began to settle they drew two benches alongside to share body warmth, opening their sleeping bags, doubling their blankets, grateful to absorb each other's heat. On one particularly raw morning a young woman in a thick quilted jacket came to see Jessie, sitting close on the bench and passing her coffee and a packet of mints.

Jessie introduced her. 'This is Maggie, my keyworker,' she said to Orlando. Then putting her arm round Maggie's shoulder, 'You're going to find me a nice little gaff in Putney, aren't you, darling?'

'Not aiming quite as high as that,' Maggie said, rubbing her palm between Jessie's shoulder blades, 'but we're getting closer to some shared accommodation in Hounslow.'

'That's my girl,' Jessie said.

'Can you do anything for me?' Orlando asked.

'Sorry – I'm in assertive outreach,' Maggie said, suddenly looking embarrassed.

It was then that he knew Jessie must have had mind problems. It should have been obvious really – every morning he had watched her shake a tablet from a little phial she kept in her breast pocket. She never missed.

'Keep hoping, sunshine,' she said now, patting his knee.

'Hope's like a drug to stay away from,' he thought, but he said nothing.

As the days drew up to Christmas they found themselves alone together beneath the arches. George had never returned, and most of the people they met at the Crypt had taken to sleeping in shop doorways, where light gave the illusion of warmth. It was worthwhile sitting yourself down on the pavement with a cap in the week before Christmas, though everybody did it, and you had to compete with chuggers and the *Big Issue* as well. So they sat two hundred feet apart on the high street, and pooled whatever came in.

They were there one Tuesday afternoon when it all kicked off. Orlando heard Jessie's raised voice, even over the traffic, and jumped up to run towards her patch. As he got near he saw her chasing a group of lads, and when one of them tripped, she hit him with a bottle. The boy had run off bleeding from his head by the time Orlando reached her.

'Little sod said I look like a fucking lesbian. He needed sorting out,' she said, panting.

'You've cut your hand,' Orlando said. 'We need to go to A&E.'

It took some persuading, but she went with him. To stop the bleeding he wrapped the wound with his scarf, tying it tightly around her wrist. When they arrived the small reception area was busy and they sat together in a queue, feeling exposed under the strip lighting. They were nearing the front when two police officers came through the automatic doors and looked round.

'That's got to be her,' the female officer said.

Before Jessie rose to go with them she kissed Orlando on the cheek. It surprised him almost as much as how gently she allowed herself to be led away. He never saw her again.

Two days later the basement at the Crypt flooded, and was closed for emergency repairs. There was no food now, only a notice of apology.

Orlando reconciled himself to Christmas on his own under the arches. Late on Christmas Eve he rummaged through some refuse sacks outside one of the fast-food chains, and found four baguettes still in their wrapping. Just past their sell-by date, he reckoned he could make them last three days.

But each morning the heron still joined him, though now there was nothing he could spare to give it.

The day after Boxing Day Maggie came by, bringing him a coffee and a slice of cake with icing.

'I just wanted to tell you about Jessie,' she said. 'She's been charged and she's in The Orchard. Whatever happens she'll be there for a while, but this time I'll make sure she isn't discharged with nowhere to go.'

Orlando looked at his feet. 'Is she okay?' he asked.

'She's safe and she's well,' Maggie said, 'and she's not confined to her room, so she can exercise.'

'She's an amazing person,' Orlando said, as if to himself.

'I'd say so,' Maggie said. 'Not many people manage to clean themselves up while they're still on the street. I need to get along now – you take care of yourself.'

He watched her walk away and wondered who the next person he might meet would be.

After that he checked the Crypt every morning. One day a notice on the door said it would re-open on the third of January. Jessie had called the time between Christmas and the New Year 'the charity vacuum', and now he could see why, but he thought he could hold on for these few days. 'You can get used to anything,' he said to himself.

And then it happened. One morning the heron was late to arrive. He was sitting up, but still shrouded in his sleeping bag when he saw it beginning to circle. It looked different, its neck stooping, and he realised it was carrying something. He watched it land awkwardly, balancing the weight in its beak. It stood impassively for a moment, then drew closer with its stilted walk. The bird always brought its own silence and he looked on, sitting very still, as it leaned to drop a fish before him on the grass.

BRIAN HOWELL

MASK

'There's no art to find the mind's construction in the face.'

Macbeth

THERE HAD BEEN no other experience like it for Yuki. Perhaps it was a kind of drug, an addiction, but a subtle one, to be sure.

It started with a simple recommendation to try out a new dentist. He had been grinding his teeth for some time and had felt that his regular dentist no longer cared about his welfare. This dentist wasn't even interested in making money out of Yuki, it seemed. He was just indifferent. Where his regular dentist had been local, the new one was located in Tokyo, in an area between Ueno and Akihabara, also known as Electric Town. He had been to these places before, of course, but seldom to the area in between.

His new dentist, a man in his mid-fifties, was polite and friendly and wrote him a letter to take to a university hospital, but Yuki never went. In a sense, he lost his way. He could not describe it in any other manner. He became distracted by what turned out to be an endless round of teeth polishing and cleanings which started with him, a man of forty, being shown how to brush his teeth. Not once, but on several occasions.

However, this series of tutorials was not administered by the dentist who ran the clinic, but rather by a female hygienist with a nice manner; as far as he could see, she was attractive.

'As far as he could see' was to be taken literally: he simply never saw her face as she was always wearing a mask. But that was OK. He could see her eyes and ninety-five per cent of her body, and the main thing was that she was doing a very good job.

What he remembered from that first cleaning session, then, was not so much his attraction to her as the fact that he accepted so calmly the idea of being pampered and the accompanying enticement of buying their range of inexpensive accessories, which included their simple, cheap toothbrushes (one a month) and their interdental brushes (a pack of four per month). The latter were a novelty for him and by far and away more tactile, invasive, and pleasurable than he could have imagined, as he stood in front of the mirror at home in the evening and in the morning inserting them into the gaps in his front and back teeth. He was wary of overusing them and forcing them where they surely could not go, though when he asked about overuse on his return he was gently disabused.

On his second visit he began to notice the local area more, the antiquarian shops, the secondhand junk shops, the lively market on the edges of Ueno, the ramen shops of the kind you found anywhere in the country, steak houses, 'family' restaurants, and in fact the innumerable restaurants, generally. He began to wonder why so many businesses were concentrated around what was after all a very mundane overground train station. The more famous Akihabara and Ueno had a greater reason for existing, to his mind, and yet this place had been here just as long, probably, waiting for him. He knew it was an irrational feeling, but it was real.

And alongside the usual shops and specialists such as a whole shop devoted to the paraphernalia of the idiotic sport of golf, he started to notice the occasional doorway or sign, usually advertising massage.

It became clear as early as his second, maybe his third, visit to the dentist's, however, that something else would keep him coming to the area for some time: the matter of cleaning the 'pockets' around his teeth. They called it deep pocket cleaning, and the expression had an appeal for him he could not quite explain. This was despite the fact that however many X-rays they showed him, he felt he would not ever quite understand what or where these pockets resided, exactly. He knew only that they were back there somewhere, minute, but significant enough to let his imagination picture small grooves that were being chipped away at to remove the tartar that was accumulating there and endangering the stability of his teeth. Occasionally, his mind conjured a castle whose walls were slowly being undermined by soldiers working away at its foundations underground.

So on that second visit he became aware as one becomes aware of something that one has taken for granted for a length of time, that the hygienist, Mariko, was still wearing her mask. He was not even afforded the opportunity of seeing her face for even the brief few minutes when dentists and their assistants sometimes lowered their masks when they were not doing close work or when they appeared in the reception area. Consequently, he felt licensed to observe her eyes more attentively than might otherwise have been the case. Pleasingly, her eyes were the type that he preferred and many of his countrymen and women felt embarrassed by: single-lidded, with a pronounced epicanthic fold. He had lost count of the number of past girlfriends who had pouted with displeasure at such an unlucky throw of the evolutionary die, usually when he had complimented them.

Naturally, he wondered if he would ever get the chance to do exactly that with Mariko. It was a long hill to climb, though, to go from being ministered to impersonally to going on a date, which would almost definitely result in his having to switch clinics afterwards. He had to put it from his mind, and for the time being that was fairly easy, given his propensity to drift off in the chair, a guilty pleasure, though he did not know why.

'I'm just going to lower your chair now,' she said, not for the first time. He never really tired of these accommodating punctuations to a procedure he would soon become very used to. In fact, he found it rather winning of her.

Then, 'I'm just going to do a little mouth irrigation now.'

And so it would go. If it was a simple cleaning, he would feel that chiselling sensation to remove the tartar around and between his teeth, a sensation which he actually found pleasant, unless a nerve was touched. He would have been the first, however, to make it clear that he was no masochist. And he felt genuinely discomfited not being able to swallow with ease, but there was a sense of comfort in being entirely at the mercy of another person under such a regime, to be sure, not least when the hygienist's small chest occasionally pressed up against the back of his head when she had to stand behind him.

Most sessions proceeded in this way, with him making only the barest small talk with Mariko. Part of him resented the number of trips he would have to make to see this deep pocket cleaning through, yet another part was happy to see the process extended like this, for both the opportunity to see Mariko and to be lightly pinioned by the triangle made by her slim arms and hands.

Added to all this, he was becoming more curious about the area around the station. A few times, as he walked from the station, he had seen the same young man, who had shoulder-length brown hair and a permanently startled look, standing by one of the exits in the lee of the raised train platform. Perhaps he had seen the same young women, too, hurrying determinedly into buildings where they worked.

On perhaps his fifth visit now, he wondered about the furtive businesses being run in the area. In his mind, sometimes, he saw a narrow staircase with uninviting metal doors and cryptic signs and had the sensation of both being drawn in and repelled. Perhaps he would enquire nevertheless.

'That's you done for today, then.' Mariko's words dug him out of his reverie.

When he exited the surgery, it was already dark and raining, but he did not feel like going home. There was something missing, something he hadn't thought of that he felt to be on the edges of awareness. On the corner of the street the surgery was located in there was a handy shop that sold cheap cans of some of his favourite drinks and chocolates, so he headed there. Feeling vaguely satisfied at this little find, he started to walk to the station, but as it was a Friday evening and he hadn't lined up anything, he walked across a busy main street into the very lively market that sheltered under the raised train tracks. It was a muddle of side streets, stalls, nooks, and cross-paths that reminded him of scenes from films set in North Africa. After some while trudging around and from his knowledge of previous forays, he knew that one edge of this market was bounded by clubs and what were probably hostess bars, in which he had never had any interest. Just a big scam for salary men. Plastic bag in hand, then, he stood there on the corner of one of the streets he had just come down, and for the first time he wondered if he was doing this in the absurd hope that he might bump into Mariko by chance. He surely would if he did it often enough, of course, but the odds could just as easily be that he could walk though a wall, which he had read could happen, except that it would probably take longer than the eventual history of the universe to come about. Or it could happen with his next step.

In the meantime, he spotted what he had probably not wanted to admit to himself all along: an advertisement on the ground floor for a relaxing massage on the third floor of a nearby building. It showed a woman lying on a tropical beach, and he thought it was rather ironic for such a business to be showing the sort of client that was probably the last person to come to them for a massage. He was drawn to the idea, but at the same time, part of him did not want anything inappropriate to take place. Inappropriate to whom? a voice inside him said.

He went up the ill-lit staircase, which was surprisingly quiet, to his mind. Not sure of himself, he knocked on a door on the second floor and a young woman in a Bo-Peep outfit came up to him. Thinking this was the same business as advertised outside, he asked for a price list, but as soon as he was given it, he realised this was a different place, out of his financial league.

He made his apologies and went on up to the top of the stairs, where a dowdily dressed middle-aged Chinese woman was speaking to a man of about his own age and looking through a brochure of photos of young women, all Chinese. When his turn came, he determined that he could not exactly know what he was going to get for his money, let alone know what the rooms were like, so he made his excuses, saying he would come back some time. He half-meant it. The woman had been friendly, and the whole experience had not been totally dispiriting. He had dipped his toe in, without taking the plunge.

On his next visit, on the train journey into town, he was touched by the sight of an attractive woman practising a dance routine. Supporting herself lightly on a vertical handrail, she seemed to be running through a very limited part of a flamenco routine. There was nothing flamboyant about what she was doing; on the contrary, she was concentrating so much that she must have been almost oblivious to the few people on the carriage who noticed her. He admired such single-mindedness. That someone could almost disappear within themself like this, almost hide in plain sight, comforted him. He would like to have asked her if it indeed was flamenco she was rehearsing, but it would have been uncool, and he did not want to disturb her.

This fortunate event almost succeeded in taking his mind off a familiar habit of his but ended up reinforcing it: counting the number of people wearing masks on the train. In contrast to the woman, their way of hiding was crass – and antisocial. Opposite him were two young, probably attractive (though you could not exactly be sure) women in their thirties chatting away quite contentedly, as if half the features of their faces weren't indecipherable. He spotted two middle-aged men with masks, one sitting, one standing, as well as a teenager. He could not explain exactly what annoyed him so much about this practice, but it was something to do with the way the masks made one focus on the wearers' eyes, and especially how they made those eyes seem as if they were targeting him, in contrast to the way Mariko's eyes seemed totally welcoming.

At the surgery, he was told he would need an injection, as the deep pocket cleaning might be particularly hard on his gums this time, so, as Mariko went off to one of the many partitioned spaces, he surrendered himself to the least pleasant aspect by far of any session, barring having a tooth extracted, something which he had not experienced since childhood and was determined never to let happen again. He could still hear the dentist from long, long ago shouting at him how he was a coward. So ingrained was the memory that he could remember her thick black-framed glasses and over-sized fake gold earrings.

In this case, the injections were done by what must have been a young trainee dentist, as Yuki felt a certain unsteadiness in the man's hand. It was not that Yuki was hurt in any way, rather that the trainee seemed to be taking extra-special care to steady himself. And it was not just one injection, but several.

In such instances, Yuki found it calming to think of his Jimi Hendrix collection, of the many different CDs he had, official and non-official, studio and live performances, not to mention the various versions he had downloaded from the Internet. Trying to remember what he had learned about the various live versions of Jimi's famous standards and how they had been messed with and corrected and updated over the years was enough to make him forget his nervousness for a while. The different masterings on CD of a handful of the posthumous compilations was a mind-bogglingly complicated area on its own. At the same time, in his head, he was listening to a favourite solo, and, strangely, he thought, if he were to experience a sharp pain from the needle and it were to coincide with one of the high notes on Jimi's guitar, it would somehow mitigate that pain, if not dissipate it. But luckily, there was no sharp pain on this occasion.

When Mariko reappeared, her face bound by her mask as usual, his bottom lip was already feeling numb. He managed to exchange a few pleasantries with her, but he was feeling a little sleepy even before she started cleaning. He could not be sure, but he thought, before his eyes closed and his mind started wandering again, that he heard himself invite her to have a coffee with him.

He was walking along a dark, narrow corridor, being led by a woman. The hand was soft to the touch. The décor was brownish-orange, and there was a strong smell of incense. He noticed drab nylon sheets at intervals on either side, covering what were probably small cubicles. He heard a knocking against one wall and stopped to listen, but the hand pulled him on. She gave him a towel and told him to step into the shower. She insisted on him putting his phone in a waterproof bag and taking it with him into the shower, where he hung it on a hook. After checking the flow and temperature, she directed the shower head on him.

❧

He woke with a start as he realised that he had fallen asleep in the middle of cleaning.

'So,' she said when she was finished. 'Which date is good for you?'

'Date?'

'For coffee.'

'But . . .'

I don't even know what you look like.

He could hardly say that, though.

'Oh, oh, yes, I think any day is fine,' he said, pulling himself together.

'*Any* day?'

They set a date for the following week, the day after his next appointment, as it turned out. It was a busy surgery, and she had only the one day off.

'I'll meet you downstairs' were her last words and, as she said them, she pulled down on her mask, almost dramatically, as if she were demonstrating a mundane but necessary procedure, revealing thin lips, a small jaw, and very slightly prominent teeth, before, just as suddenly, letting it snap back into place. He decided in the end that she had performed the action absent-mindedly, as someone does at home when no one else is around.

The woman was about thirty, her hair reaching down to her shoulder blades; her breasts were soft and puffy, yielding to pressure like small, slightly deflated balloons, a sensation he adored. She showed him a picture of a village in China on her iPhone. He felt it could have been on another planet, it looked so unfamiliar.

With a start, he suddenly wondered where his own phone

was. If they got hold of that, who knows what they could do with his data. But then he remembered that they had insisted on him putting it in a waterproof bag and taking it with him into the shower.

She pushed him gently onto the narrow futon so that he lay flat on his back. Before he had expected it, her head was already at his crotch, working on him. Whilst he took pleasure from what was happening, he found his mind wandering. He liked her cleanliness, the strangely dry texture of her hair, and what was almost a non-smell on her. He feared the raw smell of women more than anything. Almost any bad smell could put him off a partner whilst in the act. But perhaps it was all blanketed by the intensity of the incense in the place.

He thought of the picture on her mobile phone. Why did she make such a connection with him? Why did she even want to make such a connection? He stroked her back, moving his hand down that shallow defile to her buttocks.

She hadn't looked up at him since she had started. That was good, he thought, though it would be nice to remember her face.

Still, he found himself thinking now of her village, particularly of whether she had a child. He could just imagine that she had a mother looking after her young son or daughter right now, while she did this to him. Then, he started asking himself where the money was going, how much she kept of it in the end. There must be a trail. How much of it trickled back to her family in the village in China? How long would she have to go on doing this?

As he stood in the alcove adjusting his umbrella, about to step out into the dark and the warm rain, a figure blocked him. It was the man with shoulder-length, slightly scary hair and drab clothes. They made eye contact. Did this man guess or know something about him? More pertinently, was he judging Yuki? Maybe he even worked there in some capacity, because he went up the stairs in the direction Yuki had come from.

He realised he was back in the market; he had hardly registered it before going up to the place, having walked around so long. He didn't like the look of some of the vendors, many of whom appeared foreign, quite a few being Chinese. The market wasn't really crowded enough for him to need to push against anyone, but he felt as if he were pushing into soft currents of flesh and clammy air. Then he realised he was a little dizzy, and stumbled. Something told him he had to get off the street into the station or he would drown in people, faces, objects.

On the way home he realised he wanted to go back to the woman even if it meant before his date with Mariko, as hypocritical as that made him feel. He found himself trying in his mind to reconstruct her features, her bony, angular cheeks, her thin arms, and doll-like frame, a frame that could be adjusted almost like that of a marionette. By contrast, the masseuse was fuller-bodied, more womanly, in a sense. And then he thought of all of the things he could have done with her in the room which he had not dared although he had licence to do so, for a price. He wished he had a photo of Mariko, or at least some contact on social media but he didn't even have her email address yet!

On that first date, his heart dipped a little when she turned up wearing a mask, but as they were going for a coffee, he knew he was guaranteed some time without that particular barrier. As it turned out, they had cake and her mask came off for longer than he had expected.

But an unexpected preoccupation came over him. As she neatly cut up the cake and ate, he found himself observing the fork as she slid the sections into her mouth, the cream topping occasionally catching on her top row, soon removed by her tongue. As the fork was divested of its load, he noticed the hook-like end of the shortest tine, and it sent a shiver through him. Then it was obliterated as it caught the light and she put it down for a while. She was talking about her interest in modern art and what she liked to see in museums, and he was encouraged by that. Maybe she would relate to his own interest in freer forms of music.

'Actually, I'm also in a band,' she then said.

'Oh, really? What do you play?'

'I sing!'

'What?'

'A kind of jazz, sometimes soul, sometimes even hip-hop.'

'That's quite a mix. Let me know when you play next. I'd love to come.'

There was a pause.

'Ah . . . yes. But an exhibition would be nicer, first.'

'I'll look out for something.'

As their dialogue continued, he thought about his concentration on her fork. They were an unfair match. She could dig away at his tartar with sharp objects and he got pleasure from it, but he could not do that in the same way with her mouth, and he was not about to train to be a dentist. He would have to content himself for now with his regular treatment.

He went back to the Chinese masseuse; she seemed happy to see him again. After the cursory oiling, he wanted to play a bit more, so he asked her if she would put on a mask. He had bought a pack of new masks just in case. She agreed, and there she was sitting in seiza, naked, wearing only the mask. He asked her to slowly pull down her mask and started to examine her teeth, running his index finger along the ridge of her upper row. She looked at him curiously but did not seem put out. She started to pull on him slowly and in turn he explored her teeth even more until he got release. Even after he had come, he started thinking of buying some implements, the kind that had a handle and a short crook. Of course, he would never use it directly, but maybe one day Mariko could teach him . . .

The next time he saw her was at the surgery; she said the cleaning was almost done for half a year. He was almost depressed by this news, and tried to think of some way of prolonging their sessions, but he consoled himself with the thought that he could meet her somewhere on another date.

Eventually, months on, they met at an exhibition of modern art that had come to the National Museum of Western Art in Ueno. The exhibition was a stunning compendium of the best examples of modern art that had come to Tokyo in decades and the show united the two of them to an amazing degree. It did not matter what kind of art they saw. They liked everything, but after a while they did seem to have a mutual preference, and that was for the more angular works, especially for the installations that consisted of objects with sharp points or ridges. And most especially one that was of a splayed, skeletal, rusty figure on its back with its mouth open. Possibly, it represented a person who had been tortured or burned in a fire, or simply some decayed sculptural form that had rusted in the depths of the ocean for many years. It was almost impossible to say if it was a found object or a truly sculpted piece.

It was as Mariko bent over this installation and he moved to follow her inquisitiveness that she did the most startling thing, surreptitiously grabbing his crotch. He had to make a huge effort not to cry out, not really believing she had done this in a public place. But her look confirmed everything.

They left soon after, tightly holding hands. Her grip was almost hurting him.

They sat outside a restaurant in the park for a while waiting for a table, barely saying a word until they got inside. It soon came out.

'I have a boyfriend. He scares me. But I want you. I do.'

'I want you, too.'

'It's deeper than that. He knows about you. He's been following you when you come to the surgery.'

'I don't care.'

Fuck!

'What are we going to do, then?' Yuki blurted.

'Be honest with each other?'

'You mean say what we want to do with each other?'

'Yes, and *to* each other.'

'I've . . . I've been going to a . . . place around here.'

She smiled slightly. Not the reaction he expected. Or was it a smirk?

'I know.'

'You know?'

'He told me.'

'And?'

'It's OK. If you stop now.'

'I was only thinking of . . .'

She placed a finger on his lips to stop him. It excited him beyond what he had a reasonable right to expect.

'Let's go,' she said.

'Where?'

'To your place.'

Then she added, 'By the way.'

'Yes?'

'Do you have a computer?'

Once in his flat, he felt both a thrill and a strong sense of matter-of-factness, almost as if he were arriving home with his girlfriend or wife of many years. But he had never been married and had not had a girlfriend for a long time. Where to start now? He went for something mundane, offering her tea whilst sitting on the floor.

He would turn on the television soon, if for no other reason than to deflect from the erotic reproductions around the room, all quite tastefully done, some from films such as Robbe-Grillet's *Trans-Europ-Express*, some by established artists such as Makoto Aida with his vision of young naked girls all mixed up in a blender. Inwardly, he had sighed. There had simply been no time to tidy up or re-arrange his place, given the rapidity of events. At least, there was nothing truly perverted on the walls.

'I . . . I'll miss you, you know.'

'No, you won't.'

'I will!'

She burst out laughing.

'No, you won't miss me - because I won't go away!'

'You mean you'll leave him?'

'Yes, and I'll show you what you'll miss till your next appointment.'

While he took this puzzling information in, she reminded him to fetch his computer. By the time he had brought it and set it up on the table, she had produced from her bag a huge camera and several pieces of rubberised plastic or perhaps silicon that looked almost like geometrical experiments in shape. Then he realised that the folds on the plastic parts were actually handles, and everything fell in to place.

Taking off her sweater and deliberately unbuttoning her blouse so that he could see just enough of her cleavage to get him hard, she said,

'Do what I say. You'll like this.'

After motioning him to lean back on the sofa, she asked him to hold the plastic handles so that they hooked into his lips, spreading them so that he made a grimace, not of pain but one that he was sure hardly presented an image of how he truly looked. Standing, she undid her blouse completely and took off her skirt so that she was only in her tights and bra. She pulled gently on him, then left it to pick up the camera. Placing a small mirror inside his mouth, balanced between the plastic sections, she aimed the camera right into it, oblivious of his distorted features, her crotch a gimbal that anchored her whole body and the camera above him. Eventually, she stopped to take off her tights and took his hand, letting him slide it in just enough to harden him more. When she had finished taking the photos, she took out the SD card and put it in the computer.

He was half-expecting that it had all been an elaborate ploy to take pictures of his nakedness and put them on the Internet, but actually she indeed showed him photos of his teeth, going into extreme detail about each one's designation and characteristics – and how best to keep them clean. He did notice perhaps one unintended photo that showed his distorted features, but it was so extreme that he doubted anyone would recognise him from that. But as she showed him the others, she could see that he was getting even more excited, so she pulled on him, eventually taking him in her mouth. With his penis poised over her, then forcing the tip into the narrow spaces between her teeth and the insides of her mouth, the red wall that on the other side was her face, he finally realised that she had a beautiful smile.

'Now,' she proposed. 'What do *you* want to do?'

CD ROSE

SISTER

IN APRIL 1992, shortly before I started taking photographs, my sister went missing. I have never seen her since.

We were twins, me and Marie, though identical only in our solitude. She was as blonde as I am dark, her skin as dark as mine is pale. As if we'd been half-swapped, bits of us crossed over in the womb. Chalk and cheese they'd say, refusing to believe we were even related, not trusting our common surname, our strange silent language. We never invented any code or secret babble to protect our world but always knew what the other had done, was doing or would do. Even though I haven't seen her for so long now or know anything of her whereabouts, I still feel her close sometimes, a part of myself missing.

I couldn't say when I started to realise she was different. All of us are mysteries in our way, and her way was close enough to mine as to make it hard for me to see. We walked the same pathway, though looked in different directions. People asked if I worried about her or if she was OK and I'd just nod and say *Sure it's nothing*, not seeing what others could. There was nothing strange about her to me, but I often make the mistake of thinking I'm normal.

Her disappearances were little ones at first, tiny moments

when she was, then wasn't, there. All children do it some way or another, those instants when they make themselves invisible, testing a distracted parent's anxiety a little longer every time. But Marie was different, she had a way of slipping into and out of being, reappearing at your shoulder the moment you started to notice. At the foot of a shady garden, in a supermarket, on a beach in the summer: the places where children often go for minutes at a time, and Marie would do no different, but then she'd begin to do it at home as well, absent herself just long enough so it was realised and then, the moment people began to worry, reappear.

Until one day she didn't. But that would happen much later.

We never spoke about growing up. I just thought it would happen, but my sister didn't. She existed in her own space and her own time, letting the world move around her while she stayed fixed, exactly where she was, choosing whether or not to be there.

Age didn't touch her. She never did the things I did, go through phases, get spots or boyfriends. When we were teenagers she started not turning up to things or arriving hours too early. She never really found the knack of telling the time, never wore a watch. It got her detentions but she didn't mind, indifferent to whatever time she had to stay. Recently, looking through some old pictures, I tried to find us but there is no image in which her face isn't blurred, slightly out of focus or only half in the frame. She was too slow or too fast for the shutter, resistant to chemicals.

It was later, after I'd gone to university and she'd stayed with our parents, drifting and circling, that I started to get phone calls at strange times of night, the ring in the hallway at 3am ignored by flatmates knowing it would be my crazy sister. Her voice would be slow, as slurred (I thought) by sleep as I was, emerging from the murky night and the dirty receiver, or delayed as if she was calling from the other side of the world. Other times I'd hear a hyperactive babble, impossible to follow, the words piling up on themselves. I thought it was drugs, but it wasn't.

She came to visit once, turning up unannounced early one morning, the sun hardly risen. I had no idea how she'd arrived or where she'd come from, but by then such behaviour was normal. She walked into my room as though she knew the place already and built a nest from a pile of books in the middle of the floor. I can't remember how long she stayed, a week, maybe more, but I do remember she never went out, nor spoke to anyone else. I don't even remember her eating. She passed the days opening all of my books, sometimes poring over a page or a word for hours, other times flicking through as if she could read them in seconds.

'How do you know,' she asked, 'when these things are happening?'

'I don't know what you mean.'

'I mean, that these books are full of stories, yes . . . ?'

'Some of them are . . .'

'. . . which happen in the past . . .'

'Well . . .'

'But when you read them, they're happening now . . .'

'That's the effect they can cause . . .'

'So how do we know when anything's really happening?'

I was baffled at the time, put it down to her oddness, tried to explain something I'd read about a *remote* tense, the one we use to talk about something that happened time ago, or that is hypothetical, or even when we just want to be polite, but she'd gone before I could finish.

I didn't see her for years after that. Mother told me she went travelling, that she'd disappear, sometimes for days, sometimes for weeks, then reappear again with no word, as if nothing. Marie was always vague about where she'd been, but seeing as she was healthy and clean and not apparently troubled my parents never worried.

Until the day they found her staring at the clock on the kitchen wall, in tears. 'It's just . . . *not right*.' All she could say, panic rising in her voice. She couldn't tell the time any more; I wasn't sure she'd ever been able to. They took her for a brain scan, fearing some kind of stroke, but it showed nothing. Doctors sighed, gave her antidepressants and telephone counselling. Meanwhile, Marie gave up on the idea of time altogether. She seemed much happier, mother told me.

It was '92, late March, the year finally starting to turn, when I got another call. 'She's not well.' She never is, I thought, but listened patiently to my mother's descriptions of Marie's ever more frequent absences alternating with long periods locked in her room then accepted her request to go the old house they kept in the country, the one which had been my grandfather's and where we'd spent summers as children.

I hadn't been back there for years, always too cold even in summer, shot through with the smell of damp and rot, miles from anywhere, useless for a hurriedly arranged rendezvous or weekend escape.

Marie was already there when I finally arrived, sitting on the massive broken-springed sofa we'd jumped on as kids. There was a large stain on one end of it, the result of a bottle of red wine and a row between my parents. She didn't look up when I walked in. I went to put the kettle on but there was no electricity.

'There's gas,' she said. 'I've fixed the gas. I usually put a pan on the hob.' The water took an age to boil and we sat there in silence. My mother had told me the doctors had looked at her again but found nothing wrong with her, so they couldn't put her away. 'But best for her not to be on her own,' they'd advised her. I handed my sister some tea and searched through her things: the shambling clothes she'd had for years, a worn-out toothbrush, a packet of fluoxetine, unopened. Also, a stack of books, dog-eared and stained, lay on the floor of the tiny upstairs room she always chose. I recognised some of them – ones I remembered reading as a kid. She must have brought them from my parents' house where they were still shelved on the landing or stacked in cardboard boxes in the attic.

She seemed no different, so I settled myself in for a long stretch. Little of the looking-after my mother had requested needed doing. I didn't resent the intrusion, was doing little myself at the time and had enough money to last me a couple of months. Marie could take care of herself, I had no worry about that, food always a minor but annoying essential for her, a piece of toast or some old fruit enough to keep her skinny body from vanishing completely, though I'd often find her having breakfast at midnight, then asleep at noon.

When asked, which I did with decreasing frequency, she'd tell me she was fine, but as the days wore on I realised she wasn't. That's why I stopped asking, the words made no sense to her. It was a twin thing, I suppose, knowing the desperate sadness in her, touching it myself, but having no idea where to go with it. Other times she would move so slowly, be sitting so still, she would take hours to drink a cup of the tea which had become the only thing she'd eat or drink, the liquid so cold when it got to its dregs. Hours became seconds, and seconds could shift into hours.

I went out most days with the excuse of needing to get milk or cigarettes or a newspaper, but mostly just for my sanity, rambling the long way round to avoid the narrow roadside, cutting through long-forgotten footpaths and the edges of muddy fields. After a week, maybe ten days, I returned to the smell of burning. The kitchen was filled with smoke and an acrid stink, but no flames. Marie had put her pan on the hob and forgotten about it. This was what I'd worried about having to do with mother one day, not my sister.

She was on the sofa, cross-legged, a book open on the space in her lap.

'I only just put it on,' she said when I confronted her with the burnt pan, 'a second ago, just as you were going out.' I'd been gone two hours, at least.

Many of the books she'd brought with her had now shifted down the stairs and into the main room. I was sure there were more there than a week ago, as if they were breeding. A couple sat, smoke-smelling now, on the kitchen table. Reading was the only thing she could manage to do. Sometimes she would stare at one page or even a single word for hours, other times flick through the pages as though she could read an entire book in seconds, like I remembered her doing all that time ago.

'All these books,' she said, 'their pages are empty, perfect blanks until you begin to read.' Madness is as madness does, I thought: who could say she wasn't right? 'When we were children,' she went on, 'I read a book full of smoke and fire, shadow and flame. I only remember a boy coming through a doorway, fearing what he'd find in the room. That's all. I tried to find it again later, looking at pages and pictures and jackets, picking books up and flicking through them, trying to find an illustration or a turn of phrase I recognised, something which brought the story back to me, but even though I came close, often, I never found that book again, never could recall what happened in it, what the story was, or worse than the story, recapture the atmosphere it filled me with. I read every book there, but it wasn't. It wasn't there any more. And always, since then, I've been going back and looking.'

I got on with scrubbing the pan, it was the only one we had, and resolved not to let her alone so much. It was in the days which followed that she began to disappear. Only slightly at first, those tiny things she had always done, slipping out of view even though she was in the same room, reappearing just as you'd noticed her missing, nothing but a voice at my shoulder at first, then materialising, and vanishing again as I acknowledged her presence.

Every madness is logical to its owner. Marie had got lost, gone mad, call it what you will, when time had ceased to mean anything to her. Even if she never moved, she would never know where she was.

Sometimes, if I remained completely still, holding my breath and slowing even my pulse as far as I could, I could see her perfectly. She'd slide into view and then out of phase again as I drew breath, let my heart beat and blood flow. She moved not at twenty-four frames per second, but just one.

It wasn't all slow stillness. There were times when the film sped. I kept a close watch but she vanished anyway, and these were the times I wondered, I worried, if she had moved into another slipstream, time now passing for her so quickly she vanished from view.

How else could it have happened?

The time I was out in the garden, minutes at most, then came in to find the house had moved on years. The mould had grown, the season outside the window had changed, and all the clocks had been smashed.

There had only been a few in the house, all wound down or batteries exhausted. One on the kitchen wall, one in the hallway, another on the mantel in the living room. Their insides mixed on the floor as I walked in: the different ages of chronometry scrambled. The shards of a small black plastic battery pack, springs and cogs, shattered glass, twisted hands and, so sad, the broken faces.

'Watch,' she said. 'They were all watching me.' I couldn't tell if her tears were of happiness or relief or distress. 'On your wrist.' She pointed. 'It's watching you.'

Time was her enemy, stretching out for ever or forcing its entire weight into tiny moments of her life. For Marie every second was an eternity, every eternity a second. She was there from the big bang until the eventual heat death of the universe, sitting on the sofa in that room, looking for a story whose ending she would never know.

The next morning she'd gone. Or perhaps it had been the one before that, or the day after. I can't remember any more. There was no car abandoned near a bridge, no pile of clothes neatly folded on a beach or a riverbank. There was no bag ever found in a left-luggage locker at an international station.

CHLOE TURNER

WAITING FOR THE RUNNERS

WHEN I REACHED the bottom of the hill path, there was a pumpkin on the corner, rammed onto the sawn-off lamp-post like a head on a stake. A rotting, putrid thing, weeks old. It wasn't even upright – it sagged towards the road, so the tea light inside was a silvery pool of rainwater. The stalk was furring like a baby rabbit's pelt, and the smirking mouth was starting to pucker down at the edges, but I still felt it was laughing at me.

I'd known she'd be there, up at the top, so I'd wanted to be prepared. To get up there before her, so there could be no surprises. Not like that other time: me stood there in an old vest and my painting jeans, watching them leave, not having to wonder too hard why he might want her over me. This time would be different. I'd find a vantage point. Pull a group round me. She wouldn't have the upper hand.

I was later than I'd have liked starting out, though. One of the chickens had woken sickly, stalking the pen like a drunk in search of hooch, and I'd had to wait for the vet to visit at the end of her rounds. Danny always said I was far too soft – he'd have wrung its neck before breakfast – but it's the rest of the flock you have to worry for. Anyhow, it was a false alarm in the end: just a sore on the wing; thanks to that old bully Mabel, no doubt, who takes issue with any challenge to the pecking order.

Climbing the path to the top, at last, my heart was thundering. Arial was bounding up the slope as if he'd just been let out of a box: snapping at leaves; taking great gasps of air, and sniffing at the ivy berries, green and black starbursts like the fireworks last weekend.

When we passed the little allotment at the back of the cottages, the sunflower grove I'd admired there just weeks back now stood sunken-headed and brown. Hunched seed-heads of shame, unharvested and spoilt by the rain. And further up, that stubby-legged pony the children used to call to was standing in a sticky mire around the rusted trough. The ground was greasy there, and I had to grab at the hand rail to heave myself up the steep bit. I felt my boots slide under me, and tried not to yank on Arial's lead. Bright yellow maple leaves fanned across the slick mud, lurid toddler handprints amongst the gritty rust of the beech masts.

She was there first.

Alone, but first. She had her back to me as I rounded the summit, sweat pricking the hair follicles around my face. I paused a moment to get my breath. Right beside the hole Annie used to call the fossil pit, where the cavity left by a fallen tree spills tiny clams and crinoids, and the occasional sea urchin, from its crumbling limestone. There was no time to pore over it today. I lifted the shirt from the small of my back, let the breeze flash cold against my skin. A blackbird flew down from the half-dead oak on the curve of the path, picked at something amongst the leaves, then stopped to stare at me with its unblinking yellow-rimmed eye.

She might turn any moment. I had to walk the final thirty paces, and join her at the finish line.

Normally I'd have been delighted for my Benet to have made a new friend. My mother's always saying that he's a strange boy, but he's only different from the splashy men she's drawn to: jazzy trousers and clown specs, comedy turns once they've had a drink. Wouldn't know they'd been slighted, their skin's that rhino-thick. Benet's not like that. He's strong and healthy, never happier than when he's out running, but he's always been delicate when it comes to people. The first to cry after a playgroup scuffle; I don't mean a tantrum – not just some toddler injustice – but a genuine sorrow that he'd been knocked back by another child. He couldn't stand to be told off, was inconsolable if I lost it over the state of the playroom or something broken at home. His sister Annie used to tease him sometimes, but she knew when to stop. She could sense his fragile heart.

And then, well . . . it wasn't surprising really, given how things fell apart. Somewhere along the line, he stopped listening to people, in case they said something he didn't like the sound of. Drove his teachers mad. And though he made one friend in junior school – Rob Cowbridge, scrawny little shrimp of a thing – Rob ended up going to the Grammar in town, and Ben had been bobbing about like a lost balloon ever since.

It would have to have been that Will, though, wouldn't it? Not that it was the boy's fault. He seemed a nice enough lad. But *Julie's boy*. Of all the kids to make friends with, to pick the son of your Dad's . . . well, I hardly knew what to call her now. He'd moved on from her too, I knew that much. She'd lost him just like I had, and with him had gone the smug grin she'd been wearing that day, sitting in the passenger seat while he threw a bagful of threads together and then walked out of our lives for good.

Down in the valley, I could see bonfire smoke coming up from the new-builds where the old factory used to be, though they'd only been lived in a couple of months, so who knew what they'd grown so soon that they might be burning. I wondered which one was hers. Handy being so near her mum, who still lived in the 60s estate the other side of the stream. But they were tiny houses, those new ones. Close built. Poky, I dare say, if you were used to something much bigger.

He'd been building the place in Stroud for the four of us: Danny, me, Annie and Benet. Julie hadn't been working long as the receptionist in his builder's yard, but time enough to make a connection, it seemed. Then came the day when Annie was hit by a car on her way back from ballet, thrown in the ditch like something fly-tipped. Everything went dark that day, for all of us, and things between Danny and me were never the same after. I dare say Julie was a consoling shoulder, where mine was somehow found wanting.

I was getting close now – couldn't avoid it – but I'd only covered half of the distance between the two of us when there was a great shout from the gorse hedge at the top of the field. Mrs Harris's Lycra thighs emerged from the shrubbery like purple hams. Her neon rash vest and visor followed after, slipping through the gap in the hedge where the stile is.

'Alright, ladies?'

Mrs Harris could out-honk a ship's horn. She was marching down the slope towards us, and that's when Julie

– realising she was no longer alone – turned round and saw me.

'They're about five minutes off. You'll not thank me for the state of them, mind, with this mud. Your Benet looks like he's been surfing in the stuff.'

Neither of us replied. If Mrs Harris thought we were rude for ignoring her, she didn't show it. She just kept on talking: about the state of the ground, about some stray dog, and about how she'd caught a couple of them – naming no names – having a crafty fag round the back of the scout hut half way round. All the while Julie and I were looking at each other but not looking at each other, like a couple of feral cats.

Mrs Harris was still gabbing on, now about a deer heading off into the old hill fort, when I noticed that Julie hadn't come alone, after all. There was a little girl in a yellow headband hiding round the back of her knees, tracing lines down her mum's skinnies like she was drawing a helter-skelter. I'd forgotten she'd got another one. The girl looked about two years old, with blond curls like wood shavings. I wondered if she was his.

'I'm off back up the track to check them in. You'd better be prepared to make some noise, if you're the whole of the welcome party.'

Mrs Harris stamped back up towards the break in the hedge. First time I'd felt like smiling all day, watching that socking great arse trying to hoick itself over the stile. Like a Thelwell pony in Spandex.

'You look happy. Can't say I enjoy this much, waiting around knee deep in it.' Julie was pulling at a tab on her quilted jacket while she spoke. *I dare say you don't*, I thought. *I bet you never used to have to do it, either*. This would have been his job, supporting the boy that he swapped for mine.

I could look at her properly now she'd spoken to me. I'd seen her from a distance in the playground, of course. They'd all swarmed round her that first day, like they do, when anyone new appears on the scene. She'd brought her mum along for moral support, and the PTA head was in ecstasies at the scent of new blood. That was before they all knew who she was. They might think me hippie and odd and not-their-sort, but the ranks close quickly when an outsider threatens one of their own. Everyone took my side, but even so I'd kept my distance, and we'd never been this close before.

You'll forgive my first reaction, I hope: noticing that time had not been kind to Julie. It gave me a flutter of pleasure to see that those cheekbones had sagged like the melting rim of a church candle. I wasn't unhappy to note that that pretty scattering of freckles across her forehead had now merged into a tea stain of brown. From the way she was thrusting out her chin, it struck me she was trying to hide a fold or two, though God knows we've all got them. But then, and I could have kicked myself for feeling it, there's that sadness in seeing a beautiful woman who's faded, even if you wished all kinds of bad things on them once. I found myself wondering why she wore her hair like that, so that the bare patches at her temples were on show, and why no-one had told her about the tidemark of foundation that ran along her jaw.

'They shouldn't be long, now.' My mouth was all wobbly while I was saying it. Malleable, like I couldn't rely on it to do what it was supposed to do. 'I expect we'll hear them coming.'

The little girl was pulling on Julie's coat, and I noticed she had a big plastic ring on her finger. See-through and candy pink, like the one Danny gave me when we had our first wedding: the one in the Juniors' playground at St Peter & St

Paul's. So sodding long ago. It must have been springtime, because I remember the girls throwing cherry blossom over us before we'd even got started. And Phil Simmons acting the vicar, though he had to go in for his sandwiches before he'd got to the 'man and wife' bit, so perhaps the marriage was on shaky ground from the start.

The little girl had started to come towards me now, and Julie cried out as if she was walking towards a fire.

'Hannah!'

Danny's mother's name. So that answered that one.

'It's okay. I expect she's interested in the dog.' Arial was sitting on the toes of my boots, his tail thumping the wet grass. His eyes were on a rook sitting in one of the pine trees. 'He's friendly, if you want to say hello. He's just watching that bird.'

A great big sigh shuddered up through me. I felt like lying down and rolling away over the turf towards home. What would Julie think of that? Danny's mad wife tumbling face first in the mud like an out-of-control toddler. I expect they used to laugh at me often enough. What was Julie thinking that day, drumming painted fingernails on the steering wheel of her Golf, waiting to take my husband away?

A few more parents were drifting up the path now, some hovering close to us, some hanging back by the fossil pit. The woman with the triplets in Year Three, who never smiles. Mrs Palmer, Benet's class teacher, with her red setter, Raggie. Mike Hows – such an angry man – was stamping down the remains of a thistle stand as if it'd done him some wrong. And Jackie Fell and Lorna Vaughan were fiddling with their phones while they chatted, never lifting their eyes to each other. There were plenty of glances directed at me and Julie, though. Kay Wellon gave me an *Are you okay?* look, but I just nodded and turned back to the little girl.

There was nothing of Danny in her face, but there was no mistaking those curls, and when Hannah smiled at Arial, I saw something there. A memory. Of Annie, strangely enough, which was harder to take. Annie's big lopsided grin when she knew she'd done something right. Lighting the cake candles with a match, like a big girl. Blowing them out for nine, ten, eleven . . . and then no more.

'He's called Arial, but my son calls him Biscuit. Because he's always trying to eat them. I expect you like biscuits too.'

She didn't answer, but she knelt down next to him. Arial let his long black ears be patted, never taking his eyes off the distant bird. I could feel Julie's eyes on me, but I wasn't ready for that yet. I looked at the girl and I looked at Arial. Then I looked over and down the valley, just as a green woodpecker burst from the shaggy depths of a box tree, trailing its rough laugh as it disappeared out of sight down the hillside.

'Tally ho!' Mrs Harris again, from the far side of the hedge. Then a shout, further away. Laughing, and the crunch of trainers on the rotting maize stalks in the field. Flashes of blue and white where the hedge was thinning. They were on their way.

Mrs Palmer had told me that they did everything together, so it shouldn't have been a surprise that our boys vaulted the stile in quick succession and then ran down the slope towards us arm in arm. Will was kicking something ahead of him: a browning maize cob, trailing what remained of its husk. As they got near, he hoofed it over our heads, and I brushed a strand of rotting silk from my hair.

'We were first. We won!' Benet's navy cotton shorts were

lifting above his mud-slicked thighs on each side in turn, baring a white triangle of flesh. His hair was crumpled and damp. His face was flushed, smudged. He still looked like a boy. Julie's Will was taller, his hair shorter, the armband with his race number tight across his biceps. His lower legs were covered with hair, not the fine down that still dusted Benet's calves. 'Can Will come back to ours?' he said, skidding to stop.

'Willy,' the little girl interrupted, saving me from answering as she ran towards her brother. He straightened up, as if treading water, trying to break his momentum so that she wouldn't be tangled in his long legs.

'Hannah, wait!' Julie snatched her up. And then: 'He could, if you wanted . . .'

There was a pause, and I thought about that first night after Danny left, when I'd pulled the clothes from every drawer. Buried my face in the rough cable of his Aran sweater until the loose fibres caught the back of my throat. Tipped the chicken pie I'd made for tea - his favourite, for his birthday - into the back pen for the pig.

'Thanks. We have something to do.'

'Fine, just a thought.'

She looked at me then. Her eyes were pink all round the lower lids, and there were two short furrows between her brows. I could see her jaw working under the slack skin of her cheek. I thought about my Ben, and how he'd cope if he was on his own again.

'Another time, perhaps,' I said. And she smiled at me, so that deltas of lines fanned from the corners of her eyes.

The boys bumped and punched each other as they separated, and then Julie left with her half-grown man and her little girl. The other parents drifted away. Mrs Harris raised her hand as she left with an armful of marker flags. Benet was jumpy and high, but I made him wait, hang back, until they were all far down the hill. To distract him, I pointed out the tree where I'd seen the woodpecker. As we stood there, it came back across the hillside – arrow straight between wing-beats, a bolt of green across the valley.

Eventually, I couldn't hold them back any longer, and we set off, Arial sniffing at every stile post, and barking at the poor pony with its sodden coat. I looked at the sloes and reminded myself to return when the first frost had been. Where the path meets the road at the bottom, Benet helped me lift the pumpkin's rotten carcass from the post. We carried it, with its smirking face, to the paddock below the house, and Benet stood on the wall and drop-kicked it across the field. When that thing splintered into a hundred coppery pieces across the plough-carved mud, we got free of something. From that day, we started to move forward.

ELEY WILLIAMS

SWATCH

PETER NOTICED THE unspeakable colour during Stuart's twelfth birthday party. The house was erupting with all the usual paroxysms that accompany excellent games of Hide and Seek. There was shrieking, stomping, hissed invectives and sharply slammed doors. Peter and Stuart had happened upon the same bolt-hole at the very same moment and they eyed each other warily on its threshold, but within the moment there was no point wasting time negotiating terms or rights of way – they bundled into the airing cupboard on the upstairs landing in one movement and pushed the door shut by falling against it in a shushing, adrenalised heap.

In the airing cupboard Peter and Stuart could hear bellows of triumph and dismay through the door for the first few minutes, and partygoers' footsteps came as occasional thunder in the corridor. Each time this happened both boys covered their own mouths as if aware that some involuntary primal mechanism might prompt them to give an answering call and reveal their whereabouts. All returned to quiet soon, however. A triumph! They celebrated their success with hushed giggles and congratulatory dips of the elbows into each other's ribs.

These nudges gradually changed and became tangled, bored tussles for space when it became more obvious that their spot had been chosen perhaps rather too well. It occurred to Peter that they had unwittingly committed to a whole new way life. They had already endured sharing this airing cupboard for at least thirty years or possibly a whole half an hour and the initial giddy fear of possible discovery was transforming into horrified suspicion that they might never be found again.

Stuart was not like Peter and the birthday boy decided that he must put their cloistered time to good use. He produced a bag from his corduroy dungarees and with a solemn expression began demonstrating the best way to fit handfuls of marshmallows into Peter's mouth without causing suffocation.

'Five – six—' Stuart counted in whispered tones.

Peter crouched a little tighter with his back against the water-heater and his legs were beginning to go to sleep, but the twinge of incoming pins and needles and the discomfort of the heater's scald-creep-bloom across his back did not feel entirely bad. Peter was wearing his very favourite jumper – *Hawaiian Blue 4* cotton that featured a *Volcanic Red* alien vinyl decal giving a thumbs-up – and the water-heater made the airing cupboard smell like tinned peaches. Stuart had been hitting the jelly and ice-cream table pretty hard since breakfast and his pupils were larger than usual. As he let marshmallow upon marshmallow push past his teeth, Peter was aware that he was looking at his friend's eyes rather than looking into them, and that realising this meant that he had to look away at once. He concentrated on a knot in the wooden shelf above him for a second then felt his gaze slip back down.

Peter knew that his own eyes were an odd mix of colours. When asked for their colour he would say, 'Brown!' but not only were there odd squiggles, quirks and dots within the colours there, soft twisted braids and paisley patterns in the meat of his iris, but the actual shades of Peter's eyes changed minutely, but crucially, according to both the season and time of day. He saw *Cocoa Latte* in his eyes some days, *Truffle Leather 3* during others. There was even a greenish contour of *Enchanted Eden 2* to be found if he examined his eye in strong morning light. Some years ago Peter really, *really* leaned in against the bathroom mirror to work out what was going on there, straining on tiptoe over the sink and making sure that he did not knock over his dad's shaving cream or contact lens fluid. In this position if Peter stared himself down in bright summer sun he could see a notch of *Tangiers Flame* in one of his eyes and the shadow of a shadow of *Amethyst Falls* right beside it. At this discovery Peter had not been at all sure that he liked the fact that infinite variety was playing out in his face – in a way that was so plain for all to see! He burst into tears and his eyes grew hot and the blue and orange there became more vibrant: *Cerulean* shot through with *Scorched Topaz*. He had to stay in the bathroom with his head to the cool tiling for a good while before he felt brave enough to unlock the door and leave.

He had mentioned the colours in his eye to his dad at bedtime that evening and made sure not to let fear edge into his voice.

'You have hazel eyes,' said his father. He was still wearing overalls and had speckles of dried paint above his eyebrow.

'But the orange and the blue,' Peter pressed and his father turned on the bedside lamp to examine Peter's eyes very carefully, tutting and tsking, then gave a professional's nod.

'Mud and milfoil,' Peter's father said finally. 'Pondweed and a fast, peaty, strong-flowing river – that's what I see.

But, you know, would you believe it? There are occasional kingfishers along the bank.' He let Peter sit up a touch in bed. He smelt of calico dustsheets and turpentine, Peter's favourite smell in the whole world. 'Do you know what a kingfisher is?'

Peter had nodded but his father was already tapping on his phone and bringing up pictures. Peter leaned in.

'I knew that,' he said.

'Have you heard the word *glaiks* before?' asked his dad. He let Peter look it up on the phone.

'"Chiefly Scots",' Peter read there.

'Go on.'

Peter hesitated, his eyes close to the phone's screen. '"*Deri* – no – der-i-sive deception, or mockery",' Peter read. The paint on his father's eyebrow had lowered at this, and Peter let him take the phone back and scrolled a little.

'This,' he pointed, 'is the one I meant. This is the meaning I meant, I mean.'

'Under the number 2?'

'That's it.'

'"Chiefly Scottish",' Peter said.

'Go on.'

'"Quick flashes of light",' Peter read and then he pulled his blanket up and asked if he could look once more at the pictures of kingfishers, and that night he went to sleep knowing that what was really important about the secret colours in one's eye is the fact that somebody would have to be very-very-very close in every way before they could know about anything about them.

'You have to really shove them along the sides,' Stuart was saying, sternly, as he pressed another marshmallow into Peter's mouth with his thumb. Stuart was training all his attention on the task at hand. Efficiency was not the only consideration with the current procedure and as Stuart drew each marshmallow from the bag, he insisted on inspecting it with a specialist's courtesy before putting it in place alongside Peter's teeth.

Peter tried not to breathe because he had a sense that not-breathing in this circumstance might be important. He shifted against the water-heater and studied his friend's irises a little more carefully.

French Vermouth? Was that a colour name? He thought about his dad's pyramid pots of sample paint in the shop window and the magic names printed on their labels that you could say aloud and cast like spells. *Atmosphere 1? Jade White?*

'Ryan managed fourteen,' Stuart said in a low but conversational voice, his hand dipping once again into the marshmallow bag. 'Fourteen and he could still sing the whole of the school song and you could hear every word really clearly. Even the—' and Peter watched Stuart's eyelids narrow as he sought the right word '—the letters with the lines in them. The—the sharp ones – *ts* and things.'

Peter's throat creaked or rumbled a taut appreciative yes.

'*Lift! Up! Your! Hearts!*' Stuart sang quietly. As he emphasized the final glassy sibilant his wide eyes drew even wider with wonder at the memory or the imagined memory of Ryan's performance.

Peter squared his shoulders against the water-heater and gave a trial run. '*Lift! Up! Your! Hearts!*'

'*Lift!*' Stuart urged. Peter thought about the machine at the back of his father's shop. Customers could bring in an object or a picture or a fabric or a fleck of paint that they liked and Peter's dad would pass it beneath a special lens so that the computer could run its programme and mix a combination of all its millions of potential colours. You could reproduce the exact shade you wanted and take it home with you that day sealed in a little tin. *If the surface area is half a centimetre in diameter, we can match it!* promised the poster that was fixed next to the machine. Peter's dad had allowed him to Blu Tack this poster right onto the wall and in the summer holidays, when the kingfishers in Peter's eyes were at their most obvious, the Blu Tack would swell an infinitesimal amount and the poster would sometimes slip to the floor.

'*Lift!*' Stuart repeated.

'*Lift,*' Peter said, forcefully, but the word came out all disappointing and claggy, chewy somehow and too muffled to be much use. He saw that Stuart frowned a little as he selected another marshmallow. Peter had always hated the school song. *Above the swamps of subterfuge and shame*, all the pupils around him would shout on the first day of every term to the tune of a thudding piano, not needing to refer to their hymnals because they were so familiar with the lyrics, *The deeds, the thoughts, that honor may not name.* The whole school would swallow cubic fathoms of dusty air and announce with one voice the lines to the Assembly Hall's Polycell textured ceiling. *The halting tongue that dares not tell the whole!* For whatever reason Peter always imagined the other boys sitting next to him in their arranged ranks were all thinking about turning around to him as they sang, and that the secret skirmishing colours in their eyes would all be suddenly brighter. *Lift! Up! Your!* They would begin to pull at his blazer buttons and at his shirt. Peter could not sing this song without seeing in his mind's eye all these phantom bright-eyed boys closing in and tugging a *Brick Red* weight free from his chest. They would sing and he would fall to the parquet floor and they would raise the messy thing way above their heads in their newly *Brick Red* and glossy hands.

Stuart was reaching once more for the bag. 'Thirteen—'

Both boys heard the hand fall upon the cupboard's door handle at the same time and Peter, mouth glazing over, watched his friend's extraordinary and unnameable eyes dart to the door, appalled and thrilled in equal measure.

LISA TUTTLE

THE LAST DARE

'I'LL BUY YOU a Halloween treat,' said the grandmother.

The little girl backed away from the display of walking zombies and howling ghosts, rubber spiders and blood-shot eyeballs, shaking her head: she didn't like scary things.

'Let's keep looking,' the woman coaxed, and, taking her granddaughter by the hand, walked further down the aisle of the store.

They came to a shelf of stuffed toys, featuring ghosts and grinning pumpkins, teddy bear zombies, vampires and witches. The little girl stared, then swooped on a sweet-looking black kitten with green eyes, a conical orange hat rakishly cocked over one ear.

'You like that one?'

Anxiously, the little girl nodded, even as she pulled away.

'Sweetheart, of course you can have it. Or whatever you like. We'll go buy it now. I love Halloween; it's my favourite holiday. How about you, Madison? Do you love Halloween?'

Madison shrugged her skinny shoulders and raised the stuffed cat to her face, rubbing it against her cheek. She whispered, 'Love *her*.'

'Has she got a name?'

'Holly.'

'Holly? That sounds more like Christmas to me.'

'Holly – for Hallo*ween*.'

They had reached the line for check-out, and at the grandmother's characteristic short, sharp bark of a laugh, another woman turned, looking startled.

The grandmother apologised. 'I was just laughing at myself for being silly.'

The other woman, a well-maintained platinum blonde of indeterminate age, widened her eyes. 'I know you. Elaine Alverson? Is that you?'

'Yes, but how – Bobbi? Bobbi Marshall?'

With exclamations of surprise and delight, the two women embraced.

'Gamma, who is it?'

The girl who spoke was dressed like a tiny Goth in a black T-shirt and ripped leggings, her hair teased and gelled into spikes.

'Ruby, my youngest granddaughter,' said Bobbi. 'She doesn't *always* look like this.'

'Just for Halloween,' said Ruby. 'Tonight, I get to wear eyeliner and black lipstick, too. I never met you before, did I?'

'No, you didn't,' said Bobbi. 'This is Laney . . . Elaine . . . Ms Alverson?'

'Call me Lane.'

'Lane and I were best friends when we were little, since second grade.'

'I'm in second grade,' said Ruby.

'Me, too.' Lane was startled by Madison's voice, no longer a whisper, but piping and clear, the way it had been before she left New York. Her daughter had told her that Madison was finding it hard to settle at her new school, having arrived late in a class where friendships and pecking order were already firmly established. Someone had made fun of her accent, and the child's response had been to clam up. Lane was even more surprised to hear Madison address the other little girl: 'Your hair looks so cool. How do you get it like that?'

'Actually, my mom did it. With a ton of hair gel. She's going to do my make-up, too. Black,' she added, with relish.

'Mine won't let me wear make-up.'

'Not even for Halloween?'

Madison cocked her head. 'Well – maybe. I'll ask.'

As the girls chatted, Lane's attention was claimed by her old friend. 'This is so amazing! When did you move back?'

'I didn't.' She barely repressed a shudder. 'I would never move back to Texas. But Kate – my daughter – came here for her husband's new job. They wanted me for Thanksgiving, but I'd made other plans.'

'You must miss them. Your only grandchild?'

Lane nodded, glancing at the girls who had progressed to exchanging secrets, hunched close together, whispering and giggling.

The two women traded personal details as Bobbi's purchases were scanned, and with the impulsive warmth Lane remembered so well, her old friend invited them to lunch. 'We have so much to talk about – and I do believe our babies feel the same – look at them! Best friends already. You don't really have to rush off.'

'I was just going to look for somewhere nice for lunch.'

'My house! I've got a heap of fresh shrimp.'

'Where do you live? Is it far? I don't know my way around anymore, the city has grown so much.'

Bobbi grinned, a familiar, mischievous gleam in her

dark brown eyes. 'Oh, you'll find my house all right. It's on Cranberry Street.'

Cranberry was one street over from Blueberry, where Lane had spent the first twelve years of her life. She remembered well enough how to get there, but since the girls wanted to stay together, Ruby came along to direct: 'When you get to Cranberry Street, she'll show you Grandma's house.'

The entrance to the old neighbourhood was a wide, quiet boulevard that wound like a slow, concrete river through the heart of the residential area, divided by a central esplanade.

Lane had not thought the children were paying attention – she never did, at their age – but when she put on her turn signal, Ruby cried out: 'No, not this street! Cranberry is the next one.'

'I know, Ruby, but this is Blueberry – where I lived when I was your age. Wouldn't you like to see my old house?'

'I would,' said Madison.

The pink brick house on the corner was as she remembered, but Lane stared in bafflement at the house next door. Her old home had disappeared. A chain-link fence enclosed the property, which boasted a mini-mansion so new it was still under construction. The tree she used to climb, the bushes she played under, the flowerbeds and lawn were all gone, churned up in mud in front of a house that was patently too big for the lot, dominated by a huge garage.

'Which one?' Madison asked. 'Did you live in that pink house, Nanny?'

'No. That was the house next-door. My house is gone.' She felt hollowed out, and did not understand why.

'How can your house be gone?'

'Somebody bought it, and tore it down to build a new house.'

'Why?'

'Well, probably the people that bought it wanted to live in this neighbourhood, but they needed a bigger house.' Glancing along the street, she saw this was not the only new, much bigger house to replace a modest, single-storey home from the 1950s.

'Why?'

Putting the car back into drive, she moved on. 'Can you think of reasons somebody might want a bigger house?'

'If they have lots of children.'

'Or lots of pets.'

'So they could have a home movie theatre, and a gym, and a game room.'

While the girls competed to come up with reasons for a bigger house, Lane drove to the end of the street, then took a left and went on six blocks to cross the boulevard. Ruby noticed as the car turned right into Azalea Court.

'Hey, where are we?'

'Haven't you been here before?'

'Don't think so.'

Blueberry, Cranberry, Blackberry, Bayberry, Gooseberry – and she could not remember how many other -berries – had been part of a brand-new subdivision in 1950, streets filled with affordable starter homes built to an identical plan. On the other side of the esplanade the streets were named after flowering plants, and the houses were larger and more expensive. It had been unknown territory to her when she was seven, like the girls in the backseat, but once she was a little older, she went exploring.

'Spiders,' gasped Madison. They all stared at the oak tree, draped in white gossamer strands. A spider the size of a large dog clung to its trunk; two others, puppy-sized, dangled from the branches.

Ruby laughed gleefully. 'Cool! And look next door – zombies! A zombie invasion!'

Lane checked her mirror, tilting it to see her granddaughter's face. The little girl was pale, but her eyes were wide, absorbing the sights that delighted her new friend. She was reminded of her own long-ago relationship with bold Bobbi who never worried, the way Lane did, about dangers or getting into trouble.

The residents of Azalea Court had really gone to town with their seasonal decorations, she thought, turning her attention back to the street. Ghosts, witches, a multitude of jack-o-lanterns, flapping bats, black cats, and gravestones decorated the well-tended lawns. One red-brick walkway hosted a parade of brightly painted skeletons – more *Dia de los Muertes* than Halloween.

There were no construction sites, no tear-downs here: the handsome old houses, designed by architects to appeal to their well-heeled clients, had retained their value into the twenty-first century.

She stopped the car in front of one she named after its most striking feature, a rounded, tower-like end construction topped by a roof peaked like a witch's hat. She stared up at it, trying to remember why it made her feel uneasy, but the memory would not be caught.

Ruby breathed heavily on the back of her neck. 'What are you looking at, Mrs Madison's Nanny?'

Madison chimed in: 'What do you see? I just see a house.'

'The tower house. Sit back, please.' She drove on.

'What's the tower house?'

'That's what I called it. It used to fascinate me. That tower appealed to my imagination, I guess. It didn't seem to belong to the world I live in; it was more like something from an old book, a fairy tale or a fantasy. I wondered what might be inside, and what sort of people lived there.'

'Did you go there for trick-or-treat?'

Her stomach gave a queasy lurch. 'Of course not.'

'Why not?'

'I would,' said Ruby.

'It was across the boulevard, and we weren't allowed to walk that far. We didn't know the people who lived over here,' she explained, as she reached the intersection.

'I'll ask Gamma to take me there tonight. She will. I'll find out who lives there – maybe a witch!' Gasping with excitement, Ruby clutched at Madison. 'You too! Madison's Nanny, can she *please* come trick-or-treating with us?'

'Please, Nanny!'

Lane had not yet crossed the boulevard, although there was no reason to wait, with no other vehicle in sight. 'Sweetheart, you're going to a party—'

'I don't want to. I want to go trick-or-treating with Ruby.'

'You'll have to ask your mom. And Ruby will have to ask her grandmother.'

'She'll say yes, I know she will! You can meet my brother and my cousins,' Ruby said.

Lane spotted Bobbi's silver Lexus and pulled into the driveway behind it. Bobbi was waiting at the door. 'What took y'all so long?'

Ruby clutched at her grandmother. 'She showed us the

tower house. Can we go there tonight? Can Madison come trick-or-treating with us?'

Startled, Bobbi met Lane's eyes. 'The tower house? You told them that story?'

'Gamma, *can* she? What story? Can we go trick-or-treating at the tower house?'

'No story,' said Lane quickly. 'I just wanted to see if it was still there.'

'Of course it's still there.'

'My old house isn't.'

Bobbi winced. 'I should have warned you.'

'Gamma, Gamma, please? Please can she come?'

Bobbi looked at Lane, who shrugged. 'I told Madison she'll have to ask her mother.'

'Phone,' said Madison, with an imperious thrust of her hand towards her grandmother.

Lane handed over her cell. 'Do you know your number?'

She frowned. 'Don't you have us in your contacts?'

'Of course – your mom's cell is under "Kate" but your landline—'

She'd already found what she wanted. 'Mommy? It's me. Can I – *may* I please go trick-or-treating with Ruby tonight? Her granny says it's okay. R*uby*. What? Yes, she's here. – but can I? Okay, okay.' She handed the phone to Lane.

'Where are you? What on earth is going on? Who's Ruby?'

Slowly, carefully, but as succinctly as she could, Lane explained.

'She's *talking?*' Kate's voice was hushed, reverential.

Lane couldn't help smiling, as smug as if it was her own doing. 'She and Ruby hit it off right away – like best pals already.' She watched Madison put her arm around Ruby's waist, saw the other girl reciprocate with a friendly squeeze. 'Wait till you see.'

'I didn't know you still knew anybody here. Where do they live?'

'Not far. Actually, it's the same neighbourhood I lived in when I was Madison's age.'

There were a few more questions, Kate needing to be reassured, but the outcome was never in doubt. Madison did not want to go to the school Halloween party, and this alternative, the appearance of a new friend, was a godsend.

Lane stowed her phone away and followed the others inside. It was a strange experience, to be inside a house with the very same design and floor-plan as her childhood home; it struck her like a weird sort of *déjà vu*. Even the furniture was familiar – maybe Bobbi had inherited it from her parents. In the kitchen, there was a lunchtime feast of cold, succulent Gulf shrimp to be eaten with either red sauce or Thousand Islands dressing, a mound of fresh salad, saltine crackers, grapes and apples.

'Tell us the story about the tower house,' Ruby commanded once the ice tea had been poured and they were sitting around the table.

'What story? I don't know any stories.'

'Oh, you liar,' Bobbi drawled, and cackled before addressing the children: 'This lady used to tell stories all the time – scared me half to death, some of them. The one about the tower house was really weird. And she swore it was true. Most of the time I didn't believe it, when she said that, but that story I believed. I kind of had to.'

The girls stared at Lane, open-mouthed, eyes gleaming. 'Tell us!'

Not since her own daughter had grown out of make-believe had Lane known such an eager audience. She shook her head. 'Sorry. I don't remember.'

'I do.' Bobbi's look was a challenge. 'Go on – you can tell it much better than me.'

Lane mimed helplessness.

'Well, okay then.' Bobbi cleared her throat and began. 'As I recall, an old, old lady lived in that house, all by herself. One summer, all her grandkids came to stay. There were seven of them. She was too old to keep up with them, so she told the older ones to watch the little ones. The house was big, and she said they could play anywhere, outside or inside, with one exception. They were not allowed to go into the tower room, and never, ever go near the big wooden chest in that room.'

Smiling slyly, Bobbi glanced at the girls. 'Well, you know what kids are like, don't you? Do they ever do what they're told?'

'I do,' murmured Madison, but Ruby grinned proudly, shaking her head. 'I don't.'

'That's what these children were like. Too curious for their own good. At first, the older ones kept the younger ones in line, but one day, one of the little boys was bored and he decided to go into that tower and see what was there. The only thing in a big empty room was this big old carved wooden chest.'

'Carved how?'

'With designs and things. Pictures of animals and people. The little boy traced these pretty carvings with his finger and made up stories about them until he got bored again and decided to see if there was anything to play with in the chest. So he lifted up the lid and looked in, but it was too dark and the chest was too big, and finally he just had to get inside and feel around and then, while he was sitting there, the lid came down, slowly and quietly. And nobody ever saw that little boy again.'

'Did he yell? Did he scream? Couldn't he push it up again and get out?'

Bobbi shook her head.

'Why didn't they look for him?'

'Oh, they did. They did at first. And his favourite sister went on looking even when the others had given up. And one day she went into the tower room – for about the tenth time – all by herself, and she lifted up the lid of the chest that none of them were supposed to touch, and she could see that it was empty, but just to make sure, she climbed inside, to check that there wasn't a secret compartment, or another way to get out, and slowly and quietly, the lid closed down.'

'No!'

'She had been such a quiet girl that they hardly noticed she was gone, and, after a while, they forgot about her.'

'No!'

'And one day, they were all playing hide and seek, and one little kid went to hide in the chest in the tower room, thinking that nobody would ever find her there – and she was right. And another time, two of them went into it together, thinking, you know, they would protect each other, but again the same thing happened. Finally there was just one girl left, and she meant to be good and mind her grandmother, but one night she was dreaming about her missing cousins, and she got out of bed and went walking in her sleep to the tower, and opened the chest and climbed inside.'

She stopped speaking. The girls stared at her 'But the

parents? Why didn't the grandmother call the police? What happened?'

Bobbi speared a large shrimp, dunked it in the red sauce and ate it. 'Lane made it up. Ask her.'

'I didn't make it up,' said Lane. It had come back to her while she listened. 'I used to tell you stories I'd read – I never made them up myself. That one was written by Walter de la Mare. Back then I thought it was a ghost story, but now I realise . . . He called it "The Riddle", which gives you a clue – really, it was more of an allegory. About memory and the passage of time. The old lady's thoughts were drifting, she remembered the child she had been, her friends, maybe her own children, even grandchildren, now all grown up and lost, the way time takes everyone.'

They all stared at her blankly.

'Ruby, don't play with your food; eat that shrimp, or leave the table.'

'Can we go trick-or-treating at the tower house?' asked Ruby.

Bobbi shook her head. 'Forget it.'

'Why?'

'It's too far, for one thing—'

'It's *not*.'

'And I don't know who lives there.'

'*Please*.'

'It's nicer to go to the neighbours who know you – or know me, anyway.'

'Please, Gamma, please, pretty please can we go to the tower house?'

'No. I said no, and I mean it. Now stop nagging and finish your lunch.'

Lane thought that was the end of it, but after the children had left the room Bobbi suddenly asked, 'So what did happen in the tower house?'

'What?'

'Were you just pretending, to scare me? After you came out. Why wouldn't you talk about it?'

A sense of unreality swept over her, the opposite of *déjà vu*. 'I never went inside that house.'

Bobbi laughed scornfully. 'This is me you're talking to, remember. I saw you with my own eyes.' Reading the bafflement on Lane's face, she slowly shook her head. 'Really? How could you forget?'

'Why would I go into a stranger's house?'

'Because I dared you.'

Suddenly it made sense. They'd played the 'dare' game for a year or more, and some of Bobbi's challenges would make any parent quail. 'Honestly, I don't remember anything about it.'

'I could never forget,' Bobbi said emphatically. 'I can practically see the look on your face now. And the way you told the story—'

'How?'

'You went into the house, and you met a girl – older than us – who told it to you. All her brothers and sisters and cousins had disappeared into the tower room, and she was afraid to go in to look for them by herself, so you agreed to help. She led you up a winding staircase into the tower room, which was empty except for this big old chest, and while you watched, she opened it and climbed inside, and the lid came down.

'You rushed right over and opened it *immediately* but she was gone! You were leaning in, looking, trying to figure it out but afraid to lean in too far in case you fell inside yourself. It looked completely empty. Then you heard a soft voice speaking behind you, a high old lady voice saying, "Go in, go in" and you looked around and saw this little old lady – she was only little and frail looking, but you were sure she meant to try to push you in, so you ran out past her, down the stairs and outside.

'Laney, you were scared. You were as white as a sheet. It was obvious *something* had happened to you. You really don't remember?'

'When is this supposed to have happened?'

'I don't remember the exact date. We were eleven. It was the last time we ever played dares. You told me that was the last dare, and you'd won, and I couldn't argue. You'd never talked to me like that before. And afterwards, you were . . . different.' She turned her head sharply. 'What was that?'

'Sounded like a door slam.'

'Ah, that will be Ruby giving Madison the grand tour of the backyard. Coffee?'

'Sure.'

Lane wanted to ask her more about that long-ago dare, but was wary of showing too much interest in something that might be a hoax. If she had gone into a stranger's house and seen something that frightened her, surely she would remember it? She didn't quite trust Bobbi, and thought her story might be a Halloween trick to pay her back for all the times Lane had scared her with ghost stories when they were children. And yet, there must be some reason for the hold the tower house had on her imagination. Maybe it would come back to her.

They talked about their children and jobs as the coffee

brewed, and then Bobbi remembered she had made chocolate chip cookies. 'I'll call the girls.'

There was no response from the house, or the backyard.

The front yard was a small, bare, open patch of grass and flower beds, with nowhere to hide. Before the echoes of her own voice calling could die away, Bobbi was walking briskly down the street. Fearful and sick at heart, Lane hurried after.

There was no need for discussion; they had the same idea of where the girls had gone. The only question was what route they had taken, and how far ahead they were.

'Maybe we should take the car?'

But turning back, the search for keys, seemed a promise of more delay. Bobbi was power-walking; Lane had to break into a run to catch up to her.

At every corner they paused just long enough to peer down each street, hoping to spot two small figures, but they saw no one except a boy doing lonely wheelies on his bicycle, who shrugged when asked about two little girls, and a man raking leaves, until at last they reached the boulevard.

At the corner of Azalea, Bobbi gasped, 'Ruby!' and Lane squinted against the sun and made out the solitary, diminutive figure dressed in black.

'Where's Madison?' Despite her pounding heart, Lane sprinted forward, intent on grabbing the little girl and shaking the answer out of her, but Bobbi was in her way.

'Don't you ever, ever go off like that without telling me! You are in trouble, young lady, big trouble – no treats for you tonight.'

'Where's Madison?'

Looking scared, the little Goth pointed at the tower house.

'She went inside? When? How long—' Then she saw

Madison stumbling down the walk, a wobble in her course suggesting she'd been forcibly ejected from the house. Lane rushed and caught hold of the child. She was shivering. Freckles stood out boldly on cheeks otherwise drained of color, her eyes were wide and staring.

'Sweetheart, I'm here, it's all right, you're safe now - oh, what happened? What happened, what did you think you were doing, you silly girl?' She jabbered, a mixture of fear and relief driving her questions and not allowing her to pause and wait for answers. 'Come on, let's go, you can tell us all about it later.' It seemed imperative to get away from this house as far and as fast as possible. Bobbi must have felt the same, for she was already nearly at the end of the street, hustling Ruby along.

Madison moved slowly, leaning on her grandmother and dragging her feet as if the force of gravity were too much. Lane felt wildly impatient, but the child was too big to lift and carry. Then, just as they made it across the boulevard, Madison swooned, and Lane only just managed to catch her dead weight before she hit the ground.

'No! Oh, Madison, wake up,' she groaned, but it was no good, she had fainted.

They sat, the woman supporting the child, like a living pieta on a stranger's front lawn for perhaps as long as a minute before Madison stirred and sat up.

'Sweetie, what happened? Are you all right? What happened? Can you remember?'

Too many questions, but Lane couldn't help herself. 'Honey, tell me, please.'

The little girl opened and closed her mouth a few times before she whispered, 'Save her.'

'What?' She bent closer to catch the faint, breathy little voice.

'She's in the box. Save her.'

'Who?'

But Madison only struggled to her feet and together they walked back to the house on Cranberry Street, where they found Bobbi waiting anxiously, half-in, half-out of the front door. 'Is she okay?'

'I don't know. She fainted.'

'Come in; what shall we do? Water? Juice?'

'She's cold; could you get a blanket?' Esconced on the couch, cocooned in a fluffy blue blanket, Madison shut her eyes and relaxed. She fell asleep at once, her breathing shallow but steady.

'Probably best we let her rest,' said Bobbi, looking down with a worried frown before trailing Lane back to the kitchen. Lane picked up her purse. 'You're not going?'

'If I can leave her with you; she needs rest. I won't be long.'

'You're going back there?'

'I need to know what happened. I'll talk to whoever lives there, get their story.'

Bobbi stopped her at the door. 'Wayne will be back at five, he'll go with you.'

'I can't wait.'

'Call the police.'

'And say what, my granddaughter entered a stranger's house and when she came out said . . .' Lane shut her mouth and turned away. 'No. I need to find out if there is a *reason* to call the police, or if it's just . . . kids fooling around.'

'What did she say?'

'A girl in a box.' Lane shook her head, scowling. 'That *story*.'

'Call me,' said Bobbi, following her out the door. 'Call me when you get there.'

Lane got into her car without answering.

'Call me,' Bobbi repeated. 'I mean it. Leave your phone on.'

Too late, as she watched the car leaving, Bobbi remembered they did not have each other's phone numbers.

It had been half an hour. Madison woke as Bobbi was carrying her out to the car.

'What's wrong?'

'Nothing. Go back to sleep.' As she started the car, she heard the girls whispering to each other in the backseat. She glanced in the rear view mirror and saw Madison sitting up. Her colour was better and she looked more alert.

'Oh, no,' said Ruby as they turned onto Azalea, and when Bobbi stopped the car in front of a driveway, 'Gamma, no!'

There was no sign of Lane's car. Bobbi opened her door.

'Don't go in there!'

'Ruby, settle down. I am just going to knock on the door. You kids wait right here.'

Ruby moaned as her grandmother got out of the car, and Madison whispered, 'It's okay, it's okay now, she's not there.'

No one answered the knock on the door, and the bell made no sound. Tentatively, she tried turning the knob, but the door was locked. A scattering of dusty advertising flyers littered the doormat. The longer she stood there, the more Bobbi felt that no one was home, and the more frightened she became.

The police broke down the door. The house was empty and appeared to have been unoccupied for many months. There were a few pieces of furniture, but nothing in the tower room, and nothing anywhere remotely like the carved wooden chest Bobbi insisted they had to find.

The police were polite, and as patient as they could be, but they must have thought she was a crazy old bat. Ms. Alverson was a competent adult. There was no reason to believe any harm had come to her, and certainly no reason to put out an alert, especially as her own daughter was of the opinion that her mother, who had been a reluctant and difficult guest, had probably made a spur-of-the-moment decision to go home early.

Bobbi never saw or heard from Lane Alverson again. Only in her dreams, she sometimes heard her old friend calling, but when she went to look, the room was empty, except for the presence, inexplicably sinister, of a carved wooden chest.

No matter how many times she had the dream (and it would haunt her the rest of her life), Bobbi never dared to open it.

IAIN ROBINSON

DAZZLE

IT SEEMED TO Lucian that there was almost nothing between him and the horizon. The sea had peeled back and the wet sands shimmered and calmed in the cool afternoon light. The waves were breaking nearly a mile out, on the first sandbar, and the wind ruffled the surface of the lagoon that had formed with the falling tide. Sometimes he would dare to wade into the shallows. He knew though that when the waters turned and began to run in, it was wise not be too far out.

He walked where the wet sands were firm and pocked with the holes and curling initials left by lug worms. The sun was low but he had the sense it was all around him, a glaring sheen on the flats and shallows. He had his field glasses around his neck and his camera bag slung over his shoulder, although this was strictly a casual walk, a way of giving Judith a bit of time on her own. He didn't expect to see anything special, just the usual coastal birds, but this was enough for him. In the distance, where the river ran out its diminutive estuary, he could just discern a cloud of oystercatchers, a dazzle of black and white plumage almost melting into the haze. This simple display left him breathless. Holding the glasses steady, he felt the shifting flock as though he were a part of it.

They had two more days in the cottage. It had been a

mistake, he realised that now. Judith would want this again and he would have to call a halt to things. He would wait until the evening. There was a spare room made up with a single bed; he could sleep out the remaining nights there, or else leave, make up some excuse to tell Sally when he arrived home early.

As he pulled the binoculars away he became aware of two dogs bearing down on him, full of the rush of the wind and sea. He crouched to fuss them as they sniffed around his legs. A man, the owner, strode towards him and called them to heel. Lucian hadn't noticed them approach, he'd been too engrossed with the birds, or perhaps the light had tricked him, the glare of it off the sands. Lucian raised a hand in greeting, but the dogs were already pounding up the beach and the man shrugged apologetically and carried on after them.

Lucian felt a little relieved. He didn't want to talk. The landscape was enough. The wind was blowing dry sand off the dunes and across the wet flats. It blew like a snaking mist at ankle height, or perhaps, it struck him, more like a river, a wide river of dry sand, and its sinuous currents alive and alert around him. He'd met Judith the previous autumn in one of the hides on the marshes. She was younger than him, a little nervous, but they'd hit it off, and when he suggested a pub meal together that evening, she'd accepted. It wasn't the right thing to do, he knew that, but it had felt right, the way the estuary and the marshes felt right. The attention was flattering; he'd long ago given up on himself. Things had been tough for him and Sally.

He glanced over at the dunes and realised that he was straying further from the high tide mark. His route had taken him across the salt marshes and into the dunes before he'd struck out along the beach toward the estuary. The cottage overlooked the marshes. From the bedroom you could see right over to the sandbars. It meant that they could set up a camera with a tripod and telephoto and watch the birds from there. He wondered whether Judith would have seen him, and if she had followed his progress along the raised footpaths to the beach. The circular route would take him as far as the estuary and then along the back of the dunes to the village again. With luck by the time he reached the head of the estuary the waters would be on the rise, pushing the wading birds off the mud and back to their roosting places. She would only lose sight of him when he reached the estuary and the path went behind a line of trees. Of course, he realised, there was no reason to think she would be looking out for him.

He squinted into the wet sheen of the sands. He was well along the beach now and to his right, off the shore, he could see the rusted hulk of a freighter on the sandbank, broken in three. At high tide nothing of it showed except for the warning mast. There was a deep water channel into the estuary on the other side of the bank. A further channel ran between the bank and the beach, though it was shallow enough to wade out to the wreck at low tide. He could hear the cries, the distant yelps and shrieks, of black-headed gulls, the wind carrying the sound. He walked on, cutting across the sands towards the head of the estuary. The cries came back, keening and pleading. He looked out towards the sandbank. The water was moving in along the channel, the sun dancing white light off its surface. He shielded his eyes, wishing he'd brought his sunglasses. There was something. He couldn't be sure. The light seemed to move, the air thick with it, distorting. He told himself it was the head of a seal; they came up the channel sometimes. He screwed up his eyes. The head was gone, something else. It looked for a moment like an arm, a flash of red. He pulled his field glasses up to his eyes and scanned. Nothing. He felt his heart pumping. The wind dropped a little, and the cries returned. He knew that people got caught out, spent too much time with the wreck and found themselves cut off. The sand bank was already sinking below the waters. He dropped the binoculars from his eyes and squinted into the dazzle. For a moment he saw the outline of a man, chest deep in water, then nothing again. He could have stumbled, gone under. Lucian waited for him to appear. He did not. Lucian looked back at the shore, wondering if anyone else on the beach had seen the man, but there was nobody else. He realised how far out he was. He had wandered off course, carried by the drifting sands, fixated on reaching the head of the estuary. It would be a short dash to the edge of the channel and then a longer run back to the safety of the beach. He could do it though. He had to be sure. He had to do what was right.

He set out at a jog, his boots slopping in the soft sand, the glasses banging against his chest. He wasn't a runner. Coming to the estuary was all the exercise he got, the walks around sands and marshes a break from the sedentary day-to-day of suburban commuting. Sally was content with the semi in Aldershot, and all the clubs and societies she kept herself busy with, the women's institute and the girl guides, the sports centre for gym, but it was nothing he'd ever felt able to share with her. Perhaps if the fertility treatment had worked out – but neither of them could face that again, all the anticipation and grief. At the weekends he had found himself walking the reservoirs and gravel pits where birds would stop off on their exhausting migrations. He felt an affinity. Every long journey needed a rest point, a break, and his was to be found by the water, with the birds, and he soon learned their names and calls, their distinct movements, losing himself in the migratory masses. Sally didn't mind the trips to the estuary. She almost seemed to welcome them. Three times a year he would drive up the M11 and grow lighter with every mile.

He slowed to a walk, his sides aching. It didn't help that the sand was sinking beneath him, the water rising up over his feet as the tide came in. He was wading like a sandpiper. The light glistered off the waves. He was in the channel, the sea already around him. As he looked over at the bulk of the old freighter, he thought of how in the First World War the ships were painted black and white, like the oystercatcher, to trick the eye. He waded deeper into the channel, felt the tug of the water coursing in around his calves. He thought he saw it again, something rolling in the currents and then gone. He splashed towards it.

Everything went black for a moment, and then he surfaced with a gasp. Saltwater slapped against his face. He'd have to swim for it now, get back to shore and call the coastguard. His camera bag was lost. His phone too then. He thought of how he'd tell it to Judith. It felt like the sort of thing that might bring them closer though, they'd laugh about it, and then it would make things all the more difficult. He would mend things with Sally, explain how all the years of hope and loss were a journey for him, and that he couldn't go back now to the way things were without a change, a sense of arrival.

He was treading water, trying to lose his welly boots with each kick. He thought he must have slipped off the edge of a bank into a deeper channel, the shallower water would be nearby. He had never been a strong swimmer, but he could hold his own in a pool for a few lengths. If there was anyone else in the sea they'd have to make it on their own. It was a cold jolt. It was him in the sea. It was only ever him. The same way he found himself, felt himself, in the wheeling flocks, he'd sensed himself in the channel and had followed the mirage like a fool. Judith would be looking out for him. Judith would see. She would be waiting for him with a towel and a cup of cocoa when he got back to the cottage.

He managed to free his feet and writhe out of his jacket. The binoculars still hung uselessly around his neck. He pulled them off and let them go, nearly going under as he did, then he took a few strokes towards the point where he thought he'd slipped and a few more to be sure. He let his feet sink, feeling for the bottom, but they met nothing but the rocking, coursing waters. The sunlight flared off every wavelet. A swell broke over the now submerged sandbar and the water grabbed at him. The tide was pulling him, he realised, away from the sands and towards the head of the estuary. He kicked against it, trying to crawl back towards the beach. If he could get back he could explain things, put it right. Sally would have so many questions, and Judith wouldn't know the right answers to give. That girl hardly knew him.

The sea clutched his wet clothes, constraining him, as if in a fevered tangle of sheets. The muscles in his shoulders began to ache. He came gasping out of the crawl and trod water again, seeing the beach further away this time. There was a man on the shore, walking. Lucian tried to raise a hand, called out. The water swelled and he went under and up again, coughing water, struggling to locate the figure on the sands. He called out again, louder. He thought he saw a figure stop, break into a run, hit the water and wade in towards him, and then the vision faded, undid itself in the slap and dazzle of the sea. Lucian felt the current lock his legs and drag him, it flexed and flowed around him, muscular and swift. He was dissolving into the sea, into its skittering jabs of light.

He kicked again towards the shore, but he felt his legs fading. It didn't matter. Sally would understand. Sally would forgive him, with all they'd been through. Judith would be calling the coastguard. She'd be watching. He'd be pulled towards the mouth of the estuary and then pushed out again to sea. His hands grew numb. He could only tread water, struggle to keep his head up. He gasped, kicked, gasped, kicked. He could sense them, the redshanks and curlews, sandpipers and turnstones, as they took to the wing. He was losing himself in the great cloud of gathering oystercatchers, soaring and turning in their musical clamour, skirling in the last of the daylight. His body loosened. His legs were gone and so were his arms, and then his body and face as well, until there was nothing left but the sound and sight of rising birds.

CONTRIBUTORS' BIOGRAPHIES

OWEN BOOTH is the author of *What We're Teaching Our Sons* (4th Estate). He was the winner the 2015 White Review Short Story Prize, and won third prize in the 2017 Moth International Short Story Competition.

KELLY CREIGHTON was born in Belfast in 1979. She teaches creative writing to community groups and has curated *The Incubator*, an online short story showcase, since 2014. She is the author of *Bank Holiday Hurricane* (Doire Press), a short story collection shortlisted for a Saboteur Award and long-listed for the Edge Hill Prize. Her debut novel *The Bones of It* is on the Political Violence degree reading list in the USA, and was the *San Diego Book Review* 2015 Novel of the Year.

COLETTE DE CURZON was born in 1927. The daughter of the then French Consul General, she wrote 'Paymon's Trio' in 1949 in Portsmouth, at the age of 22. Having no knowledge of available routes to publication, she tucked it away in a folder of her work, where it remained until 2016. Mother of four grown-up daughters and three grandchildren, she died in March 2018.

MIKE FOX is married and lives in Richmond. His stories have appeared in, or been accepted for publication by, *The*

London Journal of Fiction, Popshot, Confingo, Into the Void, Fictive Dream, The Nottingham Review, Structo, Prole, Riggwelter, Communion and *Footnote*. Four other stories have been published in paperback by the Bedford International Writing Competition. His story 'The Violet Eye' is forthcoming from Nightjar Press as a limited-edition chapbook. Contact via www.polyscribe.co.uk.

M JOHN HARRISON is the author of eleven novels (including *In Viriconium, The Course of the Heart* and *Light*), five short story collections (most recently *You Should Come With Me Now*, longlisted for the Edge Hill Prize), two graphic novels, and collaborations with Jane Johnson, writing as Gabriel King. He won the Boardman Tasker Award for *Climbers* (1989), the James Tiptree Jr Award for *Light* (2002) and the Arthur C Clarke Award for *Nova Swing* (2007). He reviews fiction for the *Guardian* and the *Times Literary Supplement* and lives in Shropshire.

TANIA HERSHMAN's third short story collection, *Some Of Us Glow More Than Others*, was published by Unthank Books in May 2017, and her debut poetry collection, *Terms & Conditions*, by Nine Arches Press in July. She is also the author of a poetry chapbook, *Nothing Here Is Wild, Everything Is Open*, and two short story collections, *My Mother Was an Upright Piano*, and *The White Road and Other Stories*, and co-author of *Writing Short Stories: A Writers' & Artists' Companion* (Bloomsbury, 2014). She is curator of short story hub ShortStops (www.shortstops.info), celebrating short story activity across the UK & Ireland, and has a PhD in creative writing inspired by particle physics. Hear her read her work at https://soundcloud.com/taniahershman and find out more here: www.taniahershman.com.

BRIAN HOWELL lives and teaches in Japan. He has been publishing stories since 1990. His first collection, *The Sound of White Ants*, was published in the UK by Elastic Press in 2004. His novel based on the life of Jan Vermeer, *The Dance of Geometry*, was published in March 2002 by The Toby Press. His second novel, *The Curious Case of Jan Torrentius*, about the notoriously libertine Dutch painter, was published in 2017 by Zagava. He likes film, cycling, Japan, the Low Countries and listening to podcasts.

JANE MCLAUGHLIN's fiction and poetry has appeared in many magazines and anthologies. She was longlisted in the National Poetry Competition 2012, shortlisted in the Bridport Prize 2013, and has been commended and listed in other competitions. She was selected for the Cinnamon Press mentoring programme in 2013. Her e-book, *The Abbot's Cat*, a crossover novella for adults and older children, was published by Cinnamon Press in 2014 and some of her stories appeared in the anthology *Quartet* in 2015. Her debut poetry collection, *Lockdown*, was published by Cinnamon Press in 2016. She lives in London, where she belongs to several writers' groups and works as a consultant in adult and further education.

ALISON MACLEOD's latest story collection, *all the beloved ghosts* (Bloomsbury), was shortlisted for Canada's Governor General's Award for Fiction and chosen as one of the *Guardian*'s 'Best Books of 2017'. Her stories are often broadcast on BBC Radio 4. Her most recent novel,

Unexploded, was long-listed for the 2013 Man Booker Prize and, in 2016, she was a joint recipient of the Eccles British Library Writer's Award. Alongside her writing, MacLeod has appeared at numerous international literary festivals and has served as a judge for a variety of literary awards. She is Professor of Contemporary Fiction at the University of Chichester. www.alison-macleod.com

JO MAZELIS is a prize-winning novelist, short story writer, poet, photographer and essayist from Wales. Her first collection of stories, *Diving Girl*, was shortlisted for Commonwealth Best First Book and her debut novel, *Significance*, won the Jerwood Fiction Uncovered Prize in 2015, while her third collection of stories, *Ritual, 1969*, was longlisted for the 2017 Edge Hill Short Story Prize.

WYL MENMUIR is a novelist and editor based in Cornwall. His bestselling debut novel, *The Many* (Salt), was longlisted for the 2016 Man Booker Prize. In November 2016, Nightjar Press published a limited-edition chapbook of his story *Rounds* and in 2017, the National Trust published his story, *In Dark Places*. He has written for Radio 4's *Open Book* and the *Observer*, and is a regular contributor to the journal *Elementum*. He teaches creative writing at Falmouth University and Manchester Metropolitan University and is co-creator of Cornish writing centre The Writers' Block.

ADAM O'RIORDAN was born in Manchester. In 2008 he became the youngest Writer in Residence at The Wordsworth Trust, the Centre for British Romanticism. His first collection of poetry, *In the Flesh*, won a Somerset Maugham Award in

2011. He is Academic Director of the Manchester Writing School at Manchester Metropolitan University. His first collection of short stories, *The Burning Ground*, was longlisted for the Edge Hill Prize.

IAIN ROBINSON's short stories have appeared in the journals *Litro*, *The Missing Slate*, *Wales Arts Review*, and *The Lonely Crowd*, as well as in the anthologies *Hearing Voices* and *Being Dad*. His novel, *The Buyer*, was published in 2014. He was formerly an editor at *Lighthouse Journal*. He teaches at the UEA and lives in Norwich.

CD ROSE is the author of *Who's Who When Everyone is Someone Else* and the editor of *The Biographical Dictionary of Literary Failure*. His short fiction has appeared in 3:AM, *Gorse*, *Lighthouse* and *The Lonely Crowd*.

ADRIAN SLATCHER was a COBOL programmer for nine years, and currently works on digital innovation projects in Manchester. He has an MA in novel writing from the University of Manchester and his stories and poems have been published in *Unthology*, VLAK, *The Rialto*, *Confingo*, *Verse Kraken* and elsewhere. He blogs about literature at artoffiction.blogspot.com.

WILLIAM THIRSK-GASKILL was born in Leeds in 1967. He performs at spoken-word events throughout the north of England. His poetry collection, *Throwing Mother in the Skip*, and his short fiction collection, *Something I Need To Tell You*, are both published by Stairwell Books.

CHLOE TURNER's stories have appeared in *The Nottingham Review*, *MIR Online*, *Kindred* and *Halo*. She won the 2017 Fresher Prize and the Local Prize in the 2017 Bath Short Story Award.

LISA TUTTLE has been writing strange, weird and fantastic fiction nearly all her life. Her first short story collection was *A Nest of Nightmares* (1986); her first novel, a collaboration with George R R Martin, *Windhaven*, first published in 1981, has been widely translated and is still in print. She is a past winner of the John W Campbell Award, the British Science Fiction Award and the International Horror Guild Award. Most recently she has written the first two volumes of a supernaturally tinged detective series: *The Curious Affair of the Somnambulist and the Psychic Thief* and *The Curious Affair of the Witch at Wayside Cross*.

CONRAD WILLIAMS is the author of nine novels: *Head Injuries*, *London Revenant*, *The Unblemished*, *One*, *Decay Inevitable*, *Loss of Separation*, *Dust and Desire*, *Sonata of the Dead* and *Hell is Empty*. His short fiction is collected in *Use Once Then Destroy*, *Born With Teeth* and *I Will Surround You*. He has won the British Fantasy award, the International Guild award and the Littlewood Arc prize. He lives in Manchester with his wife and three sons.

ELEY WILLIAMS is currently writer-in-residence at the University of Greenwich. Her collection of prose, *Attrib. and other stories* (Influx Press), was listed among 'Best Books of 2017' by the *Guardian*, the *Telegraph* and the *New Statesman* and chosen by Ali Smith as one of the year's best debut works of fiction at the Cambridge Literary Festival. It was also awarded the Republic of Consciousness Prize 2018 and longlisted for the Dylan Thomas Prize 2018.

ACKNOWLEDGEMENTS

The editor wishes to thank Jez Noond.

'The War', copyright © Owen Booth 2017, was first published in *Hotel* issue 3, and is reprinted by permission of the author.

'And Three Things Bumped', copyright © Kelly Creighton 2017, was first published in *The Lonely Crowd* issue 6, and is reprinted by permission of the author.

'Paymon's Trio', copyright © Colette de Curzon 2017, was first published as *Paymon's Trio* (Nightjar Press) and is reprinted by permission of the author.

'The Homing Instinct', copyright © Mike Fox 2017, was first published in *Confingo* issue 8, Autumn 2017, and is reprinted by permission of the author.

'Dog People', copyright © M John Harrison 2017, was first published in *You Should Come With Me Now* (Comma Press) and is reprinted by permission of the author.

'And What If All Your Blood Ran Cold', copyright © Tania Hershman 2017, was first published in *Some of Us Glow More Than Others* (Unthank Books) and is reprinted by permission of the author.

'Mask', copyright © Brian Howell 2017, was first published in *Milk: An Anthology of Eroticism* (Salo Press) edited by Sophie Essex and is reprinted by permission of the author.

'Trio For Four Voices', copyright © Jane McLaughlin 2017, was first published in *Ruins & Other Stories* (Cinnamon Press) edited by Adam Craig and is reprinted by permission of the author.

'We Are Methodists', copyright © Alison MacLeod 2017, was first published in *all the beloved ghosts* (Bloomsbury) and is reprinted by permission of the author.

'Skin', copyright © Jo Mazelis 2017, was first published in *The Lonely Crowd* issue 8, and is reprinted by permission of the author.

'In Dark Places', copyright © Wyl Menmuir 2017, was first published as *In Dark Places* (National Trust) and is reprinted by permission of the author.

'A Thunderstorm in Santa Monica', copyright © Adam O'Riordan 2017, was first published in *The Burning Ground* (Bloomsbury) and is reprinted by permission of the author.

'Dazzle', copyright © Iain Robinson 2017, was first published in *The Lonely Crowd* issue 6, and is reprinted by permission of the author.

BEST BRITISH SHORT STORIES

Best British Short Stories 2011
(978-1-907773-12-9)

Best British Short Stories 2012
(978-1-907773-18-1)

Best British Short Stories 2013
(978-1-907773-47-1)

Best British Short Stories 2014
(978-1-907773-67-9)

Best British Short Stories 2015
(978-1-78463-027-0)

Best British Short Stories 2016
(978-1-78463-063-8)

Best British Short Stories 2017
(978-1-78463-112-3)

NEW BOOKS FROM SALT

NEIL CAMPBELL
Zero Hours (978-1-78463-148-2)

SAMUEL FISHER
The Chameleon (978-1-78463-124-6)

VESNA MAIN
Temptation: A User's Guide (978-1-78463-128-4)

STEFAN MOHAMED
Falling Leaves (978-1-78463-118-5)

ALISON MOORE
Missing (978-1-78463-140-6)

S. J. NAUDÉ
The Third Reel (978-1-78463-150-5)

HANNAH VINCENT
The Weaning (978-1-78463-120-8)

PHIL WHITAKER
You (978-1-78463-144-4)

This book has been typeset by
SALT PUBLISHING LIMITED
using Neacademia, a font designed by Sergei Egorov
for the Rosetta Type Foundry in the Czech Republic.
It is manufactured using Creamy 70gsm, a Forest
Stewardship Council™ certified paper from Stora Enso's
Anjala Mill in Finland. It was printed and bound by
Clays Limited in Bungay, Suffolk, Great Britain.

LONDON
GREAT BRITAIN
MMXVIII